a love worth forever

BRIANN DANAE

BLACK
ODYSSEY
MEDIA

WWW.BLACKODYSSEY.NET

Published by
BLACK ODYSSEY MEDIA
www.blackodyssey.net
Email: info@blackodyssey.net

A LOVE WORTH FOREVER. Copyright © 2026 by BRIANN DANAE

Library of Congress Control Number: 2025916803

First Trade Paperback Printing: March 2026
ISBN: 978-1-957950-93-8
ISBN: 978-1-957950-94-5 (e-book)

Cover Design by Qamber Design

10 9 8 7 6 5 4 3 2 1

Manufactured in the United States of America

Distributed by Kensington Publishing Corp.

The authorized representative in the EU for product safety and compliance is eucomply OU, Parnu mnt 139b-14, Apt 123
Tallinn, Berline 11317, hello@eucomplianceprtner.com

Dear Reader,

I want to thank you immensely for supporting Black Odyssey Media and our ongoing efforts to spotlight the diverse narratives of blossoming and seasoned storytellers. With every manuscript we acquire, we believe that it took talent, discipline, and remarkable courage to construct that story, flesh out those characters, and prepare it for the world. Debut or seasoned, our authors are the real heroes and heroines in OUR story. For them, we are eternally grateful.

Whether you are new to BriAnn Danae or Black Odyssey Media, we hope that you are here to stay. Our goal is to make a lasting impact in the publishing landscape, one step at a time and one book at a time. As always, we welcome your feedback and kindly ask that you leave a review. For upcoming releases, announcements, submission guidelines, etc., please be sure to visit our website at www.blackodyssey.net or scan the QR code below. And remember, no matter where you are in your journey, the best of both worlds begins now!

Joyfully,

Shawanda Williams

Shawanda "N'Tyse" Williams
Founder & CEO, Black Odyssey Media

This book is dedicated to Deborah Michelle Nero.
May you continue to live through me, Mommy.

ONE

RECOGNITION OF WHAT *this* really was hit her the moment they crossed the threshold. Almost every person in attendance, including Shyriq, had their phones out, recording their entrance. It wasn't a regular date night like Cane told his girlfriend. It was their engagement party. One he had been planning for months, and by the stunned expression on her face, it was all worth it. *She* was worth it.

"Watch him start crying with her," Rush, Shyriq's younger brother, teased, making him smirk.

The smooth sounds of Case's "Happily Ever After" crooned through the speaker system before lowering to a faint volume. On trembling legs that mimicked her hands, Autumn gripped Cane's hand tightly as he led her to the middle of the sparkling white marble floor. Tears dripped from her cheeks as Cane was handed a mic.

"Are you for real right now?" Autumn gasped, in desperate need of an answer.

It was evident, but Cane still reassured her. "Yeah, baby. All of our family is here. You ruining your makeup," he chuckled as she fell into him.

"I can't believe this," she blubbered, squeezing him tightly.

Overwhelmed, excited, and damn near on the verge of a panic attack, Autumn told herself to calm down, but that didn't seem to work. Cane's comforting stroke to her back did the trick, especially once he whispered exactly what she wanted to hear in her ear.

"I know you wanna see this ring," he said, making her laugh.

Lifting her head, Autumn gave him a quick kiss and patted her face with the back of her hand. Despite there being well over a hundred guests in attendance, all they saw was each other.

Cane cleared his throat before speaking into the mic. "We almost didn't make it up here, y'all," he said, and everyone laughed. "Baby had to be all dramatic and ask me a million-and-one questions, but we're good now."

Autumn swatted his arm before he took her hand in his. She could feel his heartbeat through his palm, not out of nervousness but eagerness. He'd been waiting what seemed all his life for this moment and had to make sure it was perfect. Lovingly, he stared into her eyes and gave a speech that had Autumn ready to walk down the aisle that moment. It was so him and that was why she loved him as much as she did.

"You know I've wanted to change your last name since I met you. Make you really live the life of two seasons in one. Everything about you was made for me. I can't even begin to tell you how grateful to God I am for you. He sent you specifically to me for a reason, baby. On your worst days, I want you to know that I'ma be there to cheer you up. Even when I piss you off, I know it's still all love because you cook for a nigga."

Autumn grinned and shook her head. She sometimes let him starve, but Cane wasn't going to let everyone know that.

"You make life worth living, Autumn. I can't see myself without you. You're my reflection through and through. The reason everything in our world makes sense is because you're in it, baby. I know we said for life, but that doesn't really mean shit unless some action is behind those words."

When he reached inside his pocket for the velvet box, lowered to one knee, and opened it, the hired photographer captured Autumn's wide eyes and jaw-dropping look in 4K. The diamond solitaire ring was one she'd been gushing over for months. It cost a pretty penny but was nothing to Cane. For her, she could have whatever, and that included his last name. Baby girl already had the codes to the safe, insurance policy information, and his only son.

"Autumn Gaines, will you marry me and become Mrs. Winters?" Cane asked.

She nodded as tears continued to fall. So choked up, Autumn forgot to use her words.

"We can't hear you!" a family member in the crowd yelled out.

"Yes. Yes! I'll marry you!" she shouted into the mic he held out to her.

With her hand still trembling, Cane slid it on and stood to his feet. They embraced in a hug and kiss that made you think they'd just gotten married.

"Congratulations to Autumn and Cane!" the deejay said from his table. "Let's give it up for the newly engaged couple."

Shyriq took in the scene as rounds of applause, whistles, and chatter filled the 3,000-square-foot layout, and a pinch of regret settled in his chest. He wasn't a jealous man, but seeing the love his best friend and fiancée shared reminded him of one he thought he'd had. Putting his ill feelings to the back of his mind, he walked over with a grin to greet the couple.

"Of course, you knew!" Autumn greeted with a squeal and slap to his chest.

Gingerly, Shyriq rubbed his pecs as if she'd done damage. "Abuse the best man, why don't you? Congratulations, sis. Let me see how that ring looks on you."

Happily, Autumn popped her hand in the air and wiggled her fingers. Pursed lips and a look that showed true love danced in her eyes as she showed off her new bling. It was perfect for her dainty hand, yet still a statement piece that let you know Cane hadn't or would never half step when it came to her.

Shyriq and Cane embraced in a brotherly hug, letting Cane know his boy was proud of him.

"You deserve this happiness, bro. Congratulations. Now, you can stop blowing my line down," Shyriq jested.

"My man, uh hunnid grand, I appreciate you for everything," Cane told him sincerely.

"Had it not been for you introducing us, this moment wouldn't have happened," Autumn said.

Cane cocked his head to the side. "Not in this manner, probably, but I was cuffing you for sure, Mrs. Winters," he said, calling her by his last name.

"I know that's right!" Autumn's sister yelled out, overhearing him.

Grinning, Autumn smooched his cheek. "Right, because you just couldn't leave me alone. I'm glad you didn't."

"I don't know if I'll ever look at a woman the way you're looking at her," Rush said with a shake of his head. He sported a grin, but he meant those words.

"Yeah, until you are on a bent knee like I was," Cane told him.

"Never. Congrats, though. Long as Autumn is happy, that's what matters," Rush said as he gave her a quick hug and dapped up Cane.

Shyriq could remember thinking the same thing, then found himself in the exact position Cane had just been in. Bended knee, professing his love for a woman he just knew he would spend the rest of his life with. It was funny how life worked out . . . or, in his case, didn't.

As the couple made their rounds around the room, Shyriq made himself useful by engaging in conversation that he was fluent in. No matter the occasion, talks of future business endeavors, ways to make more money, and giving back to his community were always discussions Shyriq found himself in. Usually, he didn't mind it. Tonight was different, though.

"I'm going to grab a drink from the bar. We can continue this conversation sometime next week," he told the owner of Sip, a local coffee shop that Autumn loved and visited frequently.

Ever observant, Cane made it his duty to invite everyone he knew his woman would want to experience this moment. He'd picked her up so many cups of coffee from the place that over the years, Cane decided to become a silent partner in the company. Now, Autumn sipped for free and got paid to do so.

Making his way to one of the three bars stationed, Shyriq waited behind two other guests. On most evenings, especially recently, his nights ended with a strong drink on the rocks—preferably something dark. The duo ahead of him placed money in the tip jar before moving along.

"Hi. What can I get for you this evening? We have two signature drinks, or would you prefer something else?"

The woman's chipper voice isn't what caught Shyriq by surprise. She was at work and had to be polite. At least fake like she was. What had him not giving her an answer was her beauty. He'd come across many beautiful women in his thirty-five years, but the one standing before him was rare, and he was intrigued.

His brooding eyes drank in her mocha-brown skin, tight, slanted-hooded eyes, and round button nose. Her resting bitch face as she waited for his order made him wonder what she was thinking about. Shyriq's gaze was so intense that she was sure he already knew her thoughts. They were as loud as the music playing over the speakers.

Her lips, ones that he could stare at forever, moved, but he had no idea what she'd said. They were plump and perfect, as if she'd gone to the best dermatologist, but she never had. Her top lip was slightly bigger than the bottom and shades darker. They fit her triangular-shaped face to perfection and had Shyriq wondering what her favorite lipstick to buy was. Shit he never before cared to ask a woman about suddenly had become relevant, and he didn't even know her name.

He'd assessed her features from the chest up in ten seconds flat. Her silk-pressed hair was pulled back into a low ponytail, showcasing a face he knew he'd store to memory for later use if need be. As gorgeous as she was, Shyriq noticed the fatigue in her posture and eyes. Though her eyes were naturally slanted, he knew what it looked like when someone hadn't had any rest and needed it badly.

When his eyes did land on the embroidery on her crisp white button-down, Rush bumped into his arm. Shyriq slowly turned his head his brother's way, snapping him out of the brown sugar haze he'd fallen into.

"Damn, what you order?" Rush questioned.

"He hasn't ordered yet. Are you sure you need this drink?"

Shyriq's right cheek lifted slightly as he captured her name. "I do, *Nhuri*. What do you suggest? I prefer dark and strong. Something that'll make me feel the burn but goes down smooth."

Her name falling from his lips almost sidetracked Nhuri. Had it not been for how sinfully fine he was, she would've forgotten about him gawking at her like she was a special drink on the menu. His voice was powerful yet soothing as well. Just the perfect pitch to lull you to sleep or to an orgasm and through it before delivering another. Nhuri shook away her lewd thoughts. She was on the clock and getting paid a more-than-excellent hourly wage to serve drinks, so that's what she did. She jumped right back into her role as a sweet bartender who was dead tired and asked him a question.

"Long day?"

"Try long week," Shyriq told her.

Nhuri's eyes scanned the numerous bottles of brown liquor in search of one of her favorites. Thanks to her late father, she too loved a dark drink on the rocks. Preferably whiskey—the Nine Oak brand. Grabbing the round bottle, Nhuri held it up for him to see.

"This is one of my favorites. It's strong enough to make you reconsider but smooth and slightly sweet, so you'll finish the glass and be glad you did."

Shyriq's head nodded forward, encouraging her to pour him a glass. No plastic cups were given at such an event. The glass tumblers had Autumn and Cane's names across them in a fancy white cursive font and were gifts to their guests. Nhuri could only imagine what the wedding would look like.

Handing him the glass and a napkin, Nhuri waited to see what he thought. It was her turn to stare, and she did so without shame. Her dark brown eyes trekked every inch of him—and there was a lot. His large, manicured hands and feet were a true reflection of his height. Shyriq was tall as hell, at least compared to most people. Not Nhuri, though. She guessed that he stood about six feet four to her five foot ten stature.

Shyriq's height wasn't what made him stand out, nor was it his inviting walnut-colored eyes and smooth cinnamon-hued complexion. It was his precisely lined mustache that led to a thickly shaped beard that stretched outward from his face instead of down. It was a good three inches, and Nhuri knew it was soft to touch just from her eye examination. It looked as soft as his lips, which pressed firmly into the rim of the tumbler.

Nhuri unknowingly held her breath as he almost consumed every drop of the amber liquor. She never wanted to be a glass so bad in her life. Homed in on every move he made, she swallowed hard at the thick veins aligning his hand as it cupped the glass. Ice clinked gently as Shyriq whirled the remainder and nodded his head. He approved, and Nhuri exhaled.

"Great taste. Thank you for choosing for me," he told her.

"No problem. Glad you enjoyed it," Nhuri replied. "I'll be here all night if you need another."

Shyriq kept that in mind as he fetched his wallet. Pulling out a crisp hundred-dollar bill, he placed it in her jar. Nhuri watched the transaction with a tight chest before her eyes connected with his. She was silently asking him why he'd tipped her that much, but dared not utter the question. She didn't have to because, again, Shyriq could hear her thoughts.

"For holding up your line. Have a good night," he told her and walked off, finally letting other guests into her space.

Surprisingly, Shyriq wanted to tell her she was off the clock for the rest of the night so he could pick her brain. Not about business, but to find out who she was. How she became a bartender and what she knew about whiskey . . . his brand to be exact. Nhuri had no idea who the man was she'd just encountered, but Shyriq was sure she'd never forget him.

Running a family-owned business wasn't for the weak. Shyriq's schedule for the week was unusually busy, but he knew why. It was peak season, and their company was in high demand. Rarely did he have a day where his mind wasn't on the business, and today was one of those days. Inside his office at the Great Hendrix Co. headquarters building, Shyriq sat towering over his desk with squinted eyes focused on his desktop screen.

Stop squinting and put those glasses on, Shy.

He heard his mother's voice without her being physically present. Reaching inside his fifty-inch natural oak desk, Shyriq grabbed the blue lens frames and slid them onto his face. They'd been there since the last time he wore them, which was weeks ago, and the reason a headache was making an appearance. Shyriq exhaled, feeling the strain ease up immediately. Hours spent looking at reports, emails, business proposals, sales, and a plethora of other information was how Shyriq kept their million-dollar business afloat, becoming the first millionaire in their family. The duties didn't belong solely to him but his family and employees as well. Everyone contributed to GHC's success.

The Hendrix family was the first Black family in Missouri to own a whiskey distillery. Shyriq's great-grandfather, Richard, had come into a nice amount of money in the mid-nineteen-forties and knew he wanted a business to pass down to his children's children. Richard Hendrix had kept his word and did just that.

He passed away when Shyriq was thirteen. By then, he had lived a life that was pleasing not only to himself but also to God as well. Richard enjoyed the fruits of his labor, along with his wife. Long after, generations would eat off of what he built, and Shyriq would ensure it. He'd been attached to his great-grandfather's hip when he learned to walk at nine months. By age seven, Shyriq knew every step it took to produce whiskey, down to the names of the ingredients he studied as if they'd be on a spelling test.

Many assumed the business was handed to him, and in a sense, it was. Shyriq had been the one to take Great Hendrix Co.

from a successful moneymaking company to a million-dollar one in less than four years. When he became the owner at twenty-seven, he gave himself three years to expand to the next level and hit that million-dollar mark. Beyond the connections it took to get there, Shyriq was disciplined. There wasn't anything he wanted that he couldn't get, no matter how long it took. Once he had his mind set on a goal, he didn't stop working toward it until he achieved it, and that's how he'd been his entire life.

So, even though it wasn't likely for him to be at the office on a Wednesday evening, here he was, reading over a contract that needed minor corrections before he signed his name. Minor mistakes led to major problems, and Shyriq wasn't a fan of those, even though he had the money to solve them. He preferred for things to go accordingly the first time. Meticulously, his eyes scanned the document before he sent over the email. It gave precise instructions on what needed to be changed, and he hoped, for their sake, that they would follow them.

Just as he shut down his computer for the day and exhaled, the phone on his desk gave a low double beep, indicating that the front desk was trying to reach him. Shyriq glanced at the stainless gold watch on his wrist. The hands displayed five thirty-five. He hit the speaker button and spoke.

"Yes?"

"Cara is on line two, sir," Lamont, one of the male interns, told him.

Shyriq couldn't help but wonder what Cara wanted and how she knew he was at the office. Timing was everything because had she called a minute later, she would've missed him.

"Thank you. Put her through," Shyriq told him before picking up the phone. "Cara, how are you?"

"Mr. Hendrix, hi," she rushed out. "How are you?"

"Great. Wrapping up my day. What can I do for you? Did something go wrong during the meeting?"

As the marketing director for GHC, Cara was out of town on a three-day business trip that was vital to the next step Shyriq wanted to take for the company. She'd been with them for over a decade, having witnessed many of the ups and downs. Yet, they were still striving and at their best right now.

"No, no," she rushed out as she exited the elevator, heading toward her hotel room. "The meeting went amazing, actually. I'll be emailing my minutes over within the hour."

Shyriq was happy to hear that. "That's what I like to hear."

Cara got to her reason for calling. "I know you're a busy man."

"I am," he agreed.

"And I apologize in advance, but I need a favor."

Shyriq almost chuckled. He wasn't new to doing favors, but it was a rarity for someone to come right out and ask for one. They'd typically beat around the bush, so for Cara to be asking, he knew it was something personal.

"Is this favor business related?" he asked.

"Yes, and somewhat personal. Something is wrong with Natalia. I'm not sure what, but I can sense it. I would check on her myself, but I'm out of town."

"Isn't she with you?"

Cara hesitated with her reply. "No. I didn't want to bother you with something I thought I could handle. She canceled at the last minute, so I'm here alone."

Shyriq leaned back in his chair and extended his legs. Natalia was right under Cara as the research marketing manager. She'd been in the position for five years now and was damn good at her job. She was better than good and had been a key component to certain deals being offered and closed on over the last few years.

Even though Shyriq was the owner and employed hundreds
of people, he didn't move how most people expected someone of
his caliber to. Nor were his work ethics those of other million-
dollar companies. Working for a family-operated business could
be tricky, especially with the rumors Shyriq has heard about his
family over the years. Yet, many of the employees were long-
tenured, received the best benefits, got paid holidays off, and
bonuses that were raved about for months.

While Richard's mission was to secure his family's legacy,
Shyriq wanted the same for those who worked for them.
Comfortability and making an honest living was a priority to
him. In doing so, GHC operated like one big family. So he could
understand Cara's concern. What she expected him to do was the
question.

"Can't you give her a phone call?" he questioned.

"I have. We talked before I left, and I could tell she was
holding something back. Until I can lay eyes on her, it will bother
me."

Shyriq could tell by Cara's slightly cracked voice that it
would. To someone else, doing a wellness check on one of his
employees may have been beneath him. Not to Shyriq. He didn't
know Natalia personally but was very fond of what she'd brought
to the company. To ease Cara's worries, he added the reminder to
his note's app on his phone.

"I'll stop by to check on her. Is she married?"

Shyriq didn't want to walk in on something that may have been
a domestic situation. Sometimes, people wanted to keep things to
themselves. Checking on another man's wife was something he
promised never to do, and he prayed it wasn't a situation where
he'd have to lay hands on a man for disrespecting a woman. Shyriq
would gladly do so.

"No, but she does have a boyfriend and a daughter. Please don't tell her I called you."

"I won't. Don't forget to send the minutes over from the meeting," he told her, removing his glasses and tucking them in his desk before standing.

"I'm pulling them up now. Thank you, Mr. Hendrix. I really appreciate this favor."

"No problem," he said. "See you when you return."

He sent a text message to his assistant requesting Natalia's home address. Shyriq hoped this one favor he did wasn't a mistake. Before he could make it to the elevator after closing his office door, which automatically locked, his personal cell phone rang. Seeing his lawyer's name gave him an instant headache. One he'd successfully dodged until now.

"King, I hope you're calling me with good news," Shyriq answered.

"I wish I was. Xena is requesting spousal support."

Shyriq's nostrils flared. Nothing in this world could ruffle his feathers more than someone who fucked with his money *and* intelligence. Xena had to be out of her rabid-ass mind to think he was paying her when *she* cheated on *him*.

"Absolutely not. Her lawyer is as delusional as she is for even moving forward with that notion. It's not happening," he stated calmly.

"Unless you can prove she committed adultery, it will happen."

Shyriq gritted his teeth before relaxing his jaws. He knew Xena was trying him by requesting spousal support because she knew he didn't have proof of her cheating. Not yet, at least. He never wanted to use his money as a weapon, but she left him no choice. The price he was willing to pay to get her out of his life for good was one she'd never be able to pocket.

"What do I need to do on my end?" Shyriq asked.

Dennis King was a beast at his job, and Shyriq knew he would do everything possible to win this case. Xena was in way over her head, and although he was over the ordeal, Shyriq wouldn't give her the satisfaction of fucking him over again. He'd given her the world, and she tried to tour it with another man. If he had it his way, Xena wouldn't be doing it on his dime anymore.

TWO

"**T**HANK YOU FOR taking me to get ice cream, TT Nhuri," Raniya said as they turned down the block toward Natalia's home, her older sister.

She smiled at her through the rearview mirror. "You're more than welcome, Niy. I told you I would if you had a good week at school."

A good week meant not getting in trouble and smart-mouthing her teacher. At six years old and an only child, Raniya tended to think everything was supposed to go her way. She'd boss around the other kids in her class and then try to explain to her teacher why they should listen to her. Nhuri and Natalia thought it was cute at first, but Natalia quickly nipped it in the bud when she came home with yellow and red stars because of her behavior. Since she'd kept her promise for the week, it was only fitting that Nhuri did the same.

"It was tough," Raniya pouted, making Nhuri chuckle. "No one wanted to listen to me."

"And they don't have to unless they're doing something that bothers you or gets you in trouble."

Nhuri heard her hum, considering her words. Raniya didn't quite agree with her statement, but she always wanted to keep her promises.

"If you say so. Do you have a boyfriend?"

Her question caught Nhuri entirely off guard. Chuckling, she glanced at her pretty, chunky face through the rearview before pulling into Natalia's driveway.

"What made you ask me that?" Nhuri asked.

Raniya shrugged. "I was just wondering. My teacher's husband brought her flowers today, and he told us that he bought them as her boyfriend too."

That was sweet of her husband, but Nhuri wanted to ask her niece what that had to do with her relationship status. She already contributed enough to her smart mouth, so, instead, she mused over her question before giving her an honest answer.

"That's nice of him, but to answer your question . . . No, I don't have a boyfriend."

"Hmm. I guess that's okay for now," Raniya said.

Nhuri laughed. "I guess it is. Was that the only reason you asked?"

Something in Nhuri's gut told her that it was an underlying curiosity that had nothing to do with her, and she was right.

"Kinda. I like Mommy's boyfriend, and he's nice, but sometimes, I wish my daddy still lived with us."

Her confession shocked Nhuri, and she couldn't wait to talk to her sister. There was a reason why Raheem no longer lived in the same house and was no longer dating Natalia. That wasn't information Nhuri felt Raniya should know at her age, but she was sure that the older she got, the more questions she would ask. She was smart too, so piecing information together wouldn't be difficult.

Raheem's decision to move out and end things with Natalia three years ago angered Nhuri. She'd never bad-mouthed him to her niece, but she had a few choice words for him back then. He suggested coparenting and promised to always be in Raniya's life, but he couldn't be with Natalia. Raheem had kept his promise and was the best father to his baby girl and a great friend to Natalia in some capacity.

"Sometimes, when relationships end, people move out. Living together isn't always the best," Nhuri said gently.

"Yeah." Raniya sighed. "I know. Mommy said the same thing. Can we go inside now?"

Shaking her head with a smirk, Nhuri shut off the car. "You're something else, Niy. Come on."

They climbed out of the car and walked to the front door. Using her key to unlock it, Nhuri entered the home behind Niy, who took off searching for her mama. Nhuri found them both in the kitchen.

"Hey, sis," Natalia greeted.

Smiling, Nhuri hugged her and kissed her cheek. "Hey, to you too. You feeling better?"

Natalia nodded. "Yeah. Still a bit tired, but I'm used to it."

"Does that mean we can't have movie night?" Raniya asked. Her eyes were hopeful that they still could.

Nhuri's heart broke a little more every day, seeing her sister fight through her chronic autoimmune disease with a smile on her face. For her child, Natalia would push herself to the limit. The rest she did get while Nhuri picked up Raniya from school, took her to the jump house, and then for ice cream after work still wasn't enough. But every third Friday of the month was their movie night day, so there was no going back to bed.

"Yes, movie night is still happening, baby," Natalia reassured her. "You want to go take a bath and put on your PJs before we put some cookies in the oven?"

Raniya's face lit up. "Yes! I'll be fast, I promise." She ran out of the kitchen, then double-backed to hug Natalia and say, "You're the best, Mommy."

Natalia didn't have time to hug her back or tell her thank you before she took off again to her bedroom. A smile was present on her face, and she glanced her sister's way to see if she was sporting the same expression. She was greeted with wet eyes.

"Don't do it," Natalia chastised. "I swear, you better not."

Nhuri sniffled. "Fine. Whatever. That was just too sweet, though."

"It was. I'll never get enough of hearing her say that," Natalia said.

Neither would Nhuri, but she didn't voice her sentiments, afraid of getting choked up. Instead, she took in her sister's appearance. From the outside looking in, it wasn't noticeable that she had an illness. She had a rough week of being glued to her bed, fatigued and in pain, but today had been better. Natalia's smooth brown skin was well moisturized, her pixie-cut curls swirled neatly, and she even wore lip gloss.

"You look cute. You went out before we got here?" Nhuri asked.

Natalia chuckled. "Thank you. Sometimes, I question whether *I'm* the big sister."

"I bet you do," Nhuri chuckled.

They were five years apart, but you couldn't tell Nhuri that. She acted as if she were the one born first.

"You know, some days aren't the best, but I don't let them beat me. So, yes. I got up and got myself decent just to sit in the crib. Is that okay with you?"

Nhuri smirked. "Mm. It is. Is that bottle of wine for me?"

Natalia glanced across the kitchen at the black bottle. "Um, for us."

"I don't think you should be drinking with how you've been feeling these last few days," Nhuri suggested.

Waving her off, Natalia pivoted toward the sink and placed the knife in it that she'd used to smear Miracle Whip on their bread.

"A little red wine isn't going to hurt me. Who said I was opening it tonight, anyway?"

"Oh, girl, please. It wouldn't be sitting there if opening it wasn't the plan. Don't play," Nhuri laughed.

That was the truth. Natalia's pristine kitchen was thoroughly cleaned weekly by the cleaning company she hired. Nothing was ever left on the counters, so the bottle of wine sitting atop it had been her doing. She just wanted to sip wine and eat cookies with two of her favorite girls without thinking about the side effects that may come with doing so.

"When you come to someone's home, a gift is usually brought with them," Natalia joked.

"*I* am the gift!" Nhuri exclaimed, making them laugh. "Plus, with the way that niece of mine had me running all over that bounce house, I need the largest wineglass in the cabinet."

As if it were her home, Nhuri opened the cabinet containing the glasses and grabbed the biggest one.

"You swear Ny be doing the most. She's the calmest child," Natalia defended.

Nhuri pursed her lips outward in somewhat of a disagreement. "Calm sometimes . . . I'll give her that. Inquisitive too, but I love it. Do you know she asked me if I had a boyfriend?"

A laugh escaped Natalia as she grabbed the container of cookie dough out of the fridge.

"I'm not surprised. Wonder what made her ask that?"

"She said her teacher's husband brought her flowers and told the class that he'd been doing that since he was her boyfriend," Nhuri explained.

Natalia smiled. Mrs. Miller was the sweetest teacher and one of the best at Raniya's school.

"My girl wanted to know who's bringing her TT flowers too," Natalia snickered.

Nhuri rolled her eyes. "No one. She didn't have to put me on blast like that, though."

"Maybe, maybe not. She got you thinking, doesn't she?"

"About a man?" Nhuri questioned with hiked brows. Natalia nodded. "Not necessarily. She did bring up wishing Raheem still lived with y'all, though."

Sighing, Natalia leaned against the counter. This wasn't the first time Raniya had brought up her dad's absence in their once-shared home. It more than likely wouldn't be the last, either.

"We've talked about this a few times, but—"

"Mommy! I'm done!" Raniya called out, cutting her sentence short.

Nhuri smirked. "Saved by the bell. You want me to get her?"

"You can. Thank you."

"Stop thanking me. That's what big-little sisters are for," Nhuri grinned.

She headed out of the kitchen and was going down the hall when the doorbell rang. With squinted eyes, she sauntered to it, wondering who was stopping by to visit. Knowing her sister, it was probably one of Natalia's best friends.

"Who is it?" she called out.

To her surprise, a deep man's voice answered.

"Mr. Hendrix."

Natalia entered the foyer. "What'd they say?"

"It's someone named Mr. Hendrix. Do you know who that is?"

By her widened eyes, Nhuri was almost positive she did. She stepped out of the way as Natalia unlocked and opened the door.

"Mr. Hendrix, hi! What a pleasant surprise. Come in," Natalia said, stepping to the side so he could enter.

The man entering the home was just as fine, if not finer, than Nhuri remembered him to be. During her bartending shift, she couldn't take her eyes off him all night. On a few occasions, she also caught him staring in her direction. So, to see him pop up at her sister's home on a Friday evening wearing a suit perfectly tailored to his stocky frame had Nhuri wanting to ask more than a few questions.

"Good evening," Shyriq spoke in an even, pleasant tone. "How are you feeling?"

"Me?" Natalia asked and lightly chuckled.

Shyriq glanced toward Nhuri, whose face was stern but still beautiful. He had no idea the woman he'd been admiring the past weekend was related to one of his employees. But he was grateful that she was. Seeing Nhuri's face was the perfect ending to a hectic week.

"Yes, you, unless she isn't feeling well also," Shyriq answered.

Natalia chuckled nervously, and Nhuri shot her a quizzical look. *Who is this man?* she thought.

"I'm feeling much better. There's no need to do a wellness check. I'm assuming that's what this is," Natalia said.

Shyriq nodded. "It is. I understand you were supposed to be out of town with Cara but fell ill."

"Yes, that's correct."

"Will your illness affect your work capabilities moving forward?"

Natalia gulped. She couldn't give him an honest answer because she knew it would. Nhuri stood idly, keeping her comments to herself, but she had enough.

"I don't mean to interrupt, but who are you, and what does my sister's work capabilities have to do with anything? From my understanding, whatever deadlines and work she has been given were completed and on time," Nhuri said with a bite in her tone.

His eyes drifted inches upward to her face. Natalia was an average height at five foot eight, leading people to believe she wasn't the oldest of the sisters. Nhuri may have been taller, but she was the baby—a protective baby sister who was ready to light into Shyriq's ass behind the lack of empathy she felt he was showing.

Shyriq cleared his throat. "My name is Shyriq, and you are?"

"She's my overprotective sister. My illness won't be an issue moving forward," Natalia said, intervening.

"If it does become one—"

"If it becomes one, *what*?" Nhuri sassed.

Natalia sighed. "Sis, please. I got this."

"And so do I. We appreciate the wellness check, but as you can see, Natalia is fine. Her personal life doesn't reflect the excellent work she does or will continue to do, so there's no need to threaten her. Plus, I'm certain there's a policy in place for sick leave, and she has enough PTO to miss a few days."

During their call, Cara failed to mention that Natalia's FMLA covered her time away from work. Of course, that's not something he was privy to, but it would've been nice to know.

"I was never threatening her," Shyriq deadpanned. "That's not who I am or what my company is about."

Nhuri lifted a brow. "I'm sorry . . . your company?"

"Yes. I own Great Hendrix Distillery, and Natalia isn't just some employee who gets overlooked because we can hire someone else. I value and appreciate everything she has done for us, and checking on her takes no sweat off my back."

He quickly made Nhuri aware of the man she was dealing with and the man her sister worked for.

"Natalia," Shyriq faced her, "if your illness becomes too much to bear, let me know personally. Cara and I will figure something out."

Going into his pocket, Shyriq pulled out his wallet and removed a business card to hand her. Natalia took hold of it and appreciatively nodded.

"Thank you. I'll be sure to do that," she said.

"Were there any other questions you had for me?" Shyriq asked, now addressing Nhuri.

Annoyed with how direct and poised he was, her nostrils flared. "No. I'm *not* an employee of yours."

Shyriq smirked, and Nhuri could've fallen out. "You could be. Have a great night, ladies. Tell lil mama who was peeking around the corner that I come in peace."

Shyriq's parting words left Nhuri stunned as he pulled open the door. She stepped up to the door, watching him descend the driveway. Parked on the curb was a heavily tinted black Suburban. A man with long locs wearing jeans and a plain black shirt stood outside of the passenger door and opened the back door for Shyriq to climb inside.

Nhuri squinted. "That fine-ass man is the owner of my favorite whiskey and my sister's big boss. What are the odds?"

"The odds are that I could've gotten fired for your smart mouth," Natalia said, pulling her away from the door and shutting it.

"You're so dramatic. I wasn't about to stand here and let him patronize you for something you can't control. If he has an issue, you can just quit," Nhuri fussed.

"No. That's not how things work. You heard what you wanted to hear. He wasn't patronizing me. Do you truly think the owner of a million-dollar company would take the time out of his Friday evening to check on an employee if he had ill intentions?"

Nhuri cocked her head to the side. "If he had a hidden agenda, yes."

Natalia waved her off. "I'm not fooling with your crazy behind. He was popping up over here to check on me, and that's one of the reasons why I love working for GHC."

"Yeah, I do too," Nhuri chuckled.

Had it not been for Nhuri completing most of Natalia's workload, her position would've been in someone else's hands long before now. Having lupus wasn't for the faint of heart, nor did it stop Natalia from knocking out her goals, pursuing her dreams, and showing up for herself and the people she loved daily.

Yes, some days, the disease crippled her, forcing her unable to type, walk, or even speak, but she didn't let it keep her down. On those days when she couldn't work, Nhuri covered for her. With an MBA in international business, Nhuri quickly became Natalia's fill-in research marketing manager. The work Natalia did early on in her position was just the groundwork. Every critical component, presentation, business strategy, etcetera, was a joint effort between the sisters. As quiet as kept, Nhuri *could* be an employee of Shyriq's. His words couldn't have been any more accurate.

"Girl, whatever. And I saw how you were looking at him," Natalia said, walking down the hall to check on Raniya.

"He's fine as hell," Nhuri shouted, smiling.

"And going through a divorce, so leave it alone."

Fake pouting, Nhuri plopped onto the couch. That tidbit of information wasn't needed. It wasn't like she'd cross paths with Shyriq again.

THREE

GETTING CHEATED ON by a woman he professed his love to before God, his family, and friends was one of the most humiliating things Shyriq could've endured.

He wasn't sure back then what may have caused Xena to stray, but as of right now, he didn't care. She made it her weekly duty to get on his nerves now that they weren't together. Shyriq would somewhat understand her need to piss him off had he been the one to ruin their marriage, but that wasn't the case. He figured since she cheated that she wanted nothing to do with him, yet she showed him more attention now than she had when they were a couple.

"Xena, I'm giving you another minute of my time on this phone and then hanging up," Shyriq said.

She huffed into the receiver. "Well, look at that. An extra minute of your precious time. That's more than I could've ever gotten when you still treated me like I was your wife."

That was a lie, but Shyriq didn't call her out. If he had, it would only turn into an argument. That's all Xena wanted to do now, and he couldn't help but wonder if her argumentative nature had always been hidden.

"Yeah, well, you forfeited that title. Now, get to the point of your call. Should my lawyer be on the line as well?"

He was pushing her buttons. Calling Dennis would've been doing too much, but he wasn't above it.

"It's not that serious. Had you agreed to give me spousal support from the jump, Dennis wouldn't have had to get involved more than he has," Xena explained.

"I should be the one asking for spousal support. *You* cheated on *me*, remember?"

Xena sighed as if she were annoyed with him stating facts. For the life of him, Shyriq couldn't understand how her brain worked. Before they separated seven months ago, Xena wanted for nothing. Shyriq had been raised to be a provider, and that's exactly what he was during their five years of marriage and two years of dating.

She'd been with him before he reached millionaire status and long enough that Shyriq thought he knew her. But she had become someone else and he didn't want to believe it until it was right in his face. A man of his caliber knew women wanted to be in his world. They flocked to him because of his name and wealth, even with a woman carrying his last name.

When conversations about Xena supposedly being out of town with another man were brought to Shyriq through his assistant from a female employee, he didn't feed into the gossip. Office talk and being in people's business were beneath him. Yet, the whispers never stopped.

Xena was bold with her adultery, never once thinking Shyriq would find out and file for a divorce. She was wrong. She immediately became defensive when he approached her about the spontaneous trips she claimed to be taking with her girls. Shyriq understood why, giving her the benefit of the doubt because she *was* his wife.

His decision to leave her wasn't set in stone . . . until he went through her phone. Shyriq had never been an insecure man, nor would there be a day when he'd be a dumb one. He felt that going through a woman's phone, especially his wife's, was an invasion of privacy, but he had to know. Xena hadn't even been discreet about her affair. She left evidence in plain sight for Shyriq to see, and to this day, her excuse for stepping out on him didn't make sense.

"You don't have to keep reminding me, Riq," she groaned.

Hearing the pet name she used to lovingly call him made his neck hot and his nostrils flare.

"I do because you somehow still believe that what you used to mean to me holds weight. It doesn't," he said uncaringly.

Xena dramatically gasped. "You've turned colder than you were during our marriage. And you have the nerve to wonder why *I* stepped out? Did it ever cross your mind that maybe *you* were the problem?"

Shyriq almost laughed. "It hadn't, but maybe I was. Does me taking accountability for your whorish ways make you feel any better?"

"Fuck you, Shyriq!"

"You weren't, and that's how we got here. Have a better day, Xena," he replied and chuckled before hearing three beeps in his ear.

Sighing heavily, Shyriq rested his head against the driver's seat headrest. He'd been parked outside his parents' home long enough, and he knew his mama would be coming out to check on him any moment. Getting into an argument with Xena always dampened his mood so much that he couldn't quite shake it yet. Then she had the nerve to accuse *him* of being the problem. Shyriq shook his head at that and climbed out.

Entering his parents' home, he navigated toward the sunroom where he knew they'd be. Immediately, Shyriq smelled the alluring aroma of ribs on the grill. He'd come over just in time.

"What's going on, Mama? You out here keeping your man company?" Shyriq teased her.

Joyce smirked and tilted her head back to receive a kiss on the cheek. "Hey, baby. You know it. Where are you coming from?"

"A few meetings. Making sure production is running smoothly."

"You know that's what you have managers for, right?" Joyce asked.

Shyriq chuckled. He knew what she was getting at before she said it.

Glancing her way, he admired his mother's beauty. She'd aged gracefully over the years, and her clear mahogany skin was a sure sign of no stress. Retirement came early for Joyce and her husband, who were now enjoying the fruits of their labor.

"Yes, I know, but I'm always going to be hands-on with production," Shyriq explained.

"Just like your father."

It was the truth. Had Kenny not injured himself right before handing part ownership over to Shyriq, he'd just be getting out of meetings as well. There was always work to be done, and staying in the know kept the business thriving. Kenny entered the screen door with an aluminum tray filled with barbecued ribs, brats, and turkey burgers. He placed the food under the warmer.

"What's going on, son?" Kenny asked as they embraced.

"Not much. Came to see what y'all were up to."

Kenny washed his hands at the sink and poured them two fingers of their signature whiskey.

"That's all? You look stressed out," he said as their heads dipped before guzzling the amber liquid.

Shyriq licked his lips. "It's that obvious?"

"I didn't want to say anything," Joyce said, standing up. "Let me guess . . . It's that wife of yours."

"Soon-to-be *ex-wife*," Shyriq said sternly. "She's a crippling pain in my side."

Kenny chuckled. "Would've been cheaper to keep her, huh?"

"Absolutely not," Joyce voiced before her son could answer the question.

He ran a hand over his thickly waved hair and sighed. "She wants spousal support, and at this rate, I'm just going to give it to her or call this entire divorce thing off."

"Oh no, you're not," Joyce fussed as she made her plate. "You're willing to give up your sanity and money rather than fight this thing out? Is *that* what you're telling me?"

"I'm tired of dealing with her, Mama. I'd understand if we had kids together, but we don't, and she's on me like I owe her."

"And yet, you're about to give in because you can't take a little pressure," she said, shaking her head.

Shyriq heard what she was saying but didn't have a rebuttal. Although Xena cheated, Shyriq didn't lash out at her, threaten to hurt her, or any of the callous behavior one would expect from a wounded man. His ego was bruised, of course. Outside of his slick remarks, Shyriq was still the perfect gentleman when he didn't have to be. Joyce was glad to know she and Kenny raised a great man, but he needed to put his foot down.

"Do y'all think I was a good husband?" Shyriq asked.

Somewhere between the time he got off the phone with Xena and making it inside their home, he found himself needing validation. Joyce didn't want to be the one to speak first, feeling as though she'd spoken her mind enough, so she gave the floor to Kenny.

He cleared his throat. "Every marriage has room for improvement, son. I believe you were a damn good husband and a provider, but only you two know what went on in your home."

"You're making it sound like I did something to make Xena cheat," Shyriq said.

Kenny shook his head. "I'm not saying that at all. I am saying that whatever Xena did was because she wanted to do it. You didn't force her to step out, but she may have held some things in. Did she say something crazier?"

Shyriq didn't want to tell them how she accused him of being a shitty, unavailable spouse, which made it okay for her to mess around.

"Nah. I was just wondering. Almost ten years of my life wasted." He shook his head.

"Nothing in life is a waste, son. Situations end, and life continues. Maybe Xena wasn't the woman for you," Kenny said, licking BBQ sauce from the corner of his mouth.

Maybe she wasn't, and every day, Shyriq wondered if not her, then who?

"You also wouldn't look so stressed if you went out and enjoyed yourself. Get from behind that desk and interact with folks outside of work," Joyce suggested. "Maybe you'll meet a nice woman who appreciates you."

Shyriq smirked. "You'd love that, wouldn't you?"

She smiled. "Only if you do. Your father and I want to see you happy. A marriage ending doesn't mean your life does too. You're more than just a husband. Remember that."

He nodded. Going out didn't sound too bad. The thing was, Shyriq never went out unless he was invited somewhere, so he didn't have the first clue of where to go to enjoy himself.

Was this how the single lifestyle would be?

FOUR

"I DON'T UNDERSTAND WHY you won't get a job that you *actually* like," Jazmyn, Nhuri's best friend, said over the phone.

Rushing around her bedroom, Nhuri almost missed the disdain in her friend's voice. It wasn't that she didn't like bartending. She enjoyed it most days. When the customers weren't belligerently drunk or disrespectful, Nhuri didn't mind mixing and mingling. She wasn't a people person but was skilled in mixology. When times were rough, and she needed some quick cash, the bar she used to work at in her old town provided just enough funds to get by.

"I do like my job," Nhuri confirmed. "Just because I complain about going in doesn't mean anything."

Jazmyn chuckled. "True. I do the same thing. What time do you get off?"

"Two-ish, but I'm hoping sooner."

The lack of sleep she'd gotten throughout the week was catching up to her. Thankfully, she was only working a half shift tomorrow. Working seven days a week, tending to her sister, and trying to keep her mental health intact were a roller coaster of a to-do list, but she was making it happen.

"Hopefully. You need to get some rest, or you'll get sick, girl," Jazmyn said.

"I know. But money ain't gon' make itself, ya' know?"

Jazmyn smirked. "Girl, please. You don't have to work this job. I don't even know how you got hired with your mean ass."

Nhuri stopped to stare at the screen where Jazmyn was on FaceTime. Laughing, she flipped her off.

"See!" Jazmyn exclaimed, laughing.

"You deserved that, and I'm not mean. Just . . . not with the bullshit."

Jazmyn waved her off. "Same thing. I'm glad you're not anymore."

"Yeah," Nhuri mumbled.

Silence echoed around them.

"Have you heard from him?"

"Not in a few months."

Jazmyn was happy to hear that. "Good."

It was great, actually. Not hearing from him gave Nhuri hope that he'd forgotten about her because she had pushed him to the crevices of her mind long ago.

"More than good. Anyway, I have to finish getting ready. I'll text you when I make it home."

"Please do. You forgot last weekend and had me ready to make that drive to come see you."

Jazmyn wasn't bluffing. Nhuri had gotten off of work early, came home, showered, and was knocked out before she could place her low-battery phone on the charger. Thankfully, Jazmyn had Natalia's number and forced her to check on Nhuri because she wasn't answering her phone.

"It won't happen again," she promised.

"Better not. Love you! Talk to you later."

"Love you more."

They hung up, and Nhuri finished getting dressed. She wasn't behind the bar tonight but on bottle duty for the sections at Club Lush. Stepping inside her bathroom, she combed through her shoulder-length sew-in, brushed her lash extensions, and spritzed her skin with perfume gifted by Natalia. She glanced at her phone and noticed she had only five minutes to spare. Making it across the city during Saturday night traffic would be hectic.

After sliding on her tennis shoes, Nhuri swiped up her bag for the night and headed to her car. The night air was warmer than usual, letting it be known that the summer was just starting. After buckling her seat belt, Nhuri cranked up the tunes and pulled out of her complex.

"Please let tonight go smoothly," she said.

The night wasn't going smoothly.

At least, it hadn't been.

One of the bottle girls called in because her dog was sick, a fight had already broken out, and a large party of fifteen wasn't trying to pay their tab. Nhuri was ready to leave. Hell, quit. Jazmyn's words from earlier didn't sound too harsh now.

"Girl, that's damn near a two-thousand-dollar tab. Mindy knew better than not to collect a card to put on file."

Nhuri glanced at one of the twin sisters she had formed a working relationship with. She couldn't remember which one she was, but she wasn't lying.

"You don't know which sister I am, do you?" she smirked.

Nhuri chuckled. "I thought I knew, and then y'all went and got the same color braids. That's just wrong."

The blonde and brown knotless braids they got done the day before were so neat and long. The color combination looked so good against their Godiva complexions. Nhuri loved them but knew she didn't have the patience to sit for a time-consuming style. She'd love the convenience, though.

"I'm Stacy," the woman said. "Stasia is wearing her hair in a ponytail."

Nhuri wanted to tell her that didn't make much of a difference, but instead, she nodded.

"Stacy, right. I got it. I think Mindy has security going over there now."

The manager, Dan, and four burly men in all black headed to the section. The tab was getting paid one way or another.

"That's so embarrassing. If they knew they didn't have the money, they shouldn't have been in here drinking like that," Stacy fussed.

That was just how the game went. Nhuri knew it all too well. People put on a front for those around them but couldn't pay up trying to live up to those expectations.

"Yeah, well . . . You know how it is. I hope nothing else pops off because I refuse to stay late tonight," Nhuri said.

Making her way through the crowd, she was stopped by Dan.

"A customer is requesting your presence," he said.

Nhuri frowned. "What? Who?"

She was still a fresh face in town, so there was no way someone had personally asked for her. Her stomach formed knots, and her heart rate spiked at the thought of the person being her ex. She just knew there was no way he'd located her job.

"I'm not sure. He's in section seven."

Lines of worry creased her forehead as Dan walked away. Tugging downward on her short black spandex one-piece that exposed ample cleavage and her toned thighs, Nhuri sighed. Whoever this was had better been tipping nicely. She weaved through the crowded club with confident strides as Future blasted through the sound system. The quick prep talk she gave herself helped none once she approached the section. It wasn't filled with enough people to occupy the couch, but her head was on a swivel to make eye contact with whoever requested her. Thankfully, Nhuri didn't have to search hard for the man garnering her attention.

Nhuri's steps faltered at the sight of Shyriq.

He stood out whether he wanted to with his eyes trained on her. Still handsome as ever, he looked more casual than the last two times she'd encountered him. Shyriq wore black slacks and a white, short-sleeved button-down in place of a full suit. Nhuri didn't have time to check his footwear because his eyes burned a hole in her.

Shyriq tilted his head upward, beckoning her to come closer. Nhuri rubbed her glossed lips together and invaded his space. Leaning down, she went to speak, but Shyriq beat her to it.

"We have to stop running into each other like this," he said.

Humor laced his tone. Liquor was on his breath and gloss in his brown eyes.

Nhuri took a step back. "This isn't my section."

"It's yours now. Unless that's a problem."

Shyriq's voice was heavy. Thick with the type of masculine energy Nhuri knew only men like him possessed. *You're the problem* is what she wanted to tell him. A handsomely dangerous problem that just so happened to smell deliciously good too.

"It's not a problem. What can I get for you?" she asked.

Nhuri hated that the lights gleamed just right across his face. Shyriq licked his lips and reached for her hand. Gently, he pulled her closer. The high-up sectional made them almost the same height as him sitting down.

"Your name. Can I get that?" Shyriq asked.

Nhuri almost chuckled. "No."

She couldn't get out of her brain the sound of him saying it the first night they met. He'd spoken it like he was trying to commit it to memory, but clearly, he hadn't. Shyriq didn't take offense to her answer. He just smiled.

"Not even a nickname?" he asked.

"Is this what you do in clubs? Hit on the bottle girls?" Nhuri countered.

Shyriq licked his lips. "Nah. Just you."

"Hmm. That's unfortunate for us both because I don't have time for this. Plus, you said my name the first time you requested a drink from me."

"My apologies, beautiful. You're right. That's a mishap for not remembering your name, but I never forgot your face."

His politeness took Nhuri aback and made her concerned. "Are you drunk? We don't know each other, and you requested me as if we do."

Shyriq chuckled, finally letting his hand fall from hers. Nhuri hadn't realized he was still holding it until they disconnected.

"I've been drinking, but I'm not drunk. I spotted you working and wondered if you'd gotten any rest since the last time I saw you."

Nhuri swallowed hard. *Why the fuck is me resting on his mind?*

"That's . . . not weird to you to be thinking about a stranger?" she asked.

"Maybe. But clearly, my brain has a mind of its own. It thought you up, and here you are for a third time. What do they say about those?"

Nhuri covered her grin. Shyriq was too smooth with his conversation, making her forget why she was there and her attitude.

"I say that it is purely coincidence that we're seeing each other for the third time. Had I not been privy to who you are, I'd think you were stalking me," Nhuri said, making a deep chuckle fall from Shyriq's mouth.

The sound decorated Nhuri's skin with goose bumps, and her heart sped up a bit. It wasn't in her nature to flirt with customers, not wanting to give them any impression that she was interested, but flirting with Shyriq came easily.

"You're worth stalking, gorgeous," Shyriq said and smirked. "But that's not my area of expertise."

"Right. Now, what can I help you with again?" Nhuri politely asked.

"Since you decided not to remind me of your name, Nhuri, I'll take a whiskey and Coke."

She smirked. "Impeccable memory."

"You're worth remembering."

Nhuri simply smiled as she retrieved the handheld card reader. She typed in his drink order, sending a notification to the bar. Then she glanced around at the men in their section.

"Will they be ordering as well?" Nhuri asked.

Just as she asked the question, a younger version of Shyriq tossed an arm over Shyriq's shoulder and widely grinned.

"How you doing?" he asked smoothly.

"Good. Just trying to work," Nhuri said, giving him a tight smile.

He stuck his hand out for her to shake. "I'm Rush."

Nhuri looked down at his hand and then back at his face. "And I'm sort of in a rush. So, what can I get you to drink?"

Rush laughed. "Smooth. Real smooth. I know this old man probably ordered whiskey, so let me get a bottle of tequila."

"Any specific juice?"

"Nah. We don't need any chasers, baby," Rush said.

Chuckling, Nhuri replied, "Of course not. I'll have your waitress bring that bottle and your drink right over."

"Are you not able to serve our section tonight?" Shyriq questioned.

The intensity of his gaze made Nhuri stare deeply into his eyes. She could tell he was a man used to getting his way, and that tickled her the most.

"That's not how things work around here," she let him know.

"If it were up to me, you wouldn't be working here at all," Shyriq countered.

They stared at each other until one of the other bottle girls tapped Nhuri on the shoulder. She was needed at the bar, and she was glad to be of service. The longer she stayed in Shyriq's presence, the more she felt something brewing between them. Natalia's words about him going through a divorce rang loudly in her head as she turned to walk away. His married status was just enough to make whatever brewing simmer.

"Who is that?" Rush questioned.

Shyriq kept his eyes trained on Nhuri until she was no longer in his line of vision. "No one you need to be worried about," he answered.

Rush chuckled. "Shit, neither do you. Loosen up some more," he said, patting his brother's back. "There's too many women here to be tripping off one."

That was precisely why Shyriq preferred not to hit the club scene. He didn't mind it in his younger days when the crowd actually danced and enjoyed themselves instead of standing around looking at one another crazily. The women had been eyeing him all night, and a few had even approached him. However, once he spotted Nhuri, all thoughts of possibly getting one of their numbers exited his mind.

Something about her intrigued him, and Shyriq wanted to know more. Maybe it was the liquor talking or the fact that they'd run into each other three times in less than two weeks. Whatever the case was, Ms. Nhuri was on Shyriq's radar.

As the night wound down, Nhuri had stayed true to her word. She stayed away from Shyriq's section, but that didn't stop him from seeking her out as he exited to leave the club earlier than the crew he came with. Stopping at the end of the bar, Shyriq asked the woman close to him to grab Nhuri's attention. Her head swiveled his way, and she shook it. Shyriq licked his full lips and nodded.

Playfully, Nhuri rolled her eyes but walked his way. "Yes, Mr. Man, who can't seem to let me be. Leaving so soon?"

He smirked. "I am, but I couldn't leave without giving you this." Gently, not to alarm her, Shyriq grabbed her hand and placed a large lump of money in her palm.

Nhuri's brows dipped. "Um," she stammered.

"Thank you for your services tonight. The next time we cross paths—"

"The next time?" Nhuri rushed out, flustered by his words.

Shyriq nodded. "Yes. I'm a man who believes in things happening for a reason. The next time we see each other, I'm hoping you've gotten some rest. Not just your body, but your mind as well."

He whispered the last sentence in Nhuri's ear before pulling away. Giving her a once-over, Shyriq tipped his head forward. "Have a good rest of your evening, Nhuri."

"You too," she mumbled, but Shyriq didn't hear her. He was already feet away, walking toward the exit.

Snapping out of her trance, Nhuri glanced at the money in her hand. She unfolded the bills and shook her head as she counted $500. Her services hadn't cost nearly as much, but it didn't matter to Shyriq. He'd taken up her time and had paid for it. Nhuri was just going to have to come to terms with the fact that he was a generous tipper and man.

FIVE

"**I**'M READY TO *come back home,*" *Nhuri mumbled to Natalia over the phone.*

It was the first time she'd said the words aloud, and they felt good.

"You know you always have a room here," Natalia said. "Why the sudden change? I mean, I'm not complaining, just wondering."

They snickered.

"You need me, and Dru is just . . . He's not the same anymore. I don't think either of us are."

"Is he putting his hands on you?" Natalia asked with grit in her tone.

"Of course not," Nhuri reassured her. "He's just extra controlling all of a sudden and manipulative. I don't know what happened, but I'm over it, sis. I miss the old me. The woman who didn't have to tiptoe around her home and wasn't afraid to speak her mind. I just feel trapped. Does that make sense?"

Nhuri was tired. She'd contemplated ending things between them for months now, and she was done being indecisive just to save face and his feelings. Dru no longer seemed to care about hers, so why should she care about his?

"*It makes perfect sense. You don't have to stay anywhere you're not wanted or loved. Come home. I'll pay for whatever you need. Ship some things here a little at a time, and then hop on a one-way flight.*"

Natalia had made it sound so easy. And that's because it was. Two months after their conversation, Nhuri had her things packed and ready to go. Whatever midlife crisis Dru was experiencing, he could go through it alone. Nhuri was no longer his punching bag.

The car she requested to take her to the airport was five minutes away, and Nhuri couldn't believe she was finally doing this. Adjusting the strap of her carry-on and rolling her two large suitcases toward the door, her fingers tightened around the handles. She hated the way her stomach twisted in knots, and the ache in her chest almost made her question if she had made the right decision.

But then, she thought about their last argument . . . and the ones before that. How Dru had spewed words that cut her so profoundly, Nhuri knew it'd take forever to heal. Every concern she voiced was twisted into making her seem like she was attacking him when all she wanted was for them to make it work. Not for Nhuri to feel like a shadow in her own life. That's who she'd become.

Four years.

That's how long she'd poured into him—into them. And now, she was ready to pour into herself. The only way to do that was to leave. She exhaled sharply and slightly turned her head when she heard the garage door open.

"*Nhuri,*" *Dru called out.*

His voice was softer than she'd ever heard it. She didn't turn to face him. Nhuri couldn't stand to see the expression on his face; whether it be regret, anger, or the same smugness that always made her doubt herself, she didn't care. Dru could no longer control her life, and she meant it.

"*You really just gon' up and leave like this?*"

Like this? Nhuri thought, scoffing under her breath as if he hadn't given her every reason to leave. Dru and his audacity. The love they once shared had become suffocating.

"Yes," *Nhuri answered steadily, even though her heart was everything but.*

Dru tried taking hold of her hand, but Nhuri snatched it away. "Don't," *she warned, trying to keep her composure and face him.* "I already know how you want this to go. You'll say all the right things, even though it's the wrong time. Make it seem like I'm the problem, and I stay, hoping things will get better," she said, shaking her head. "But it never does, does it?"

Dru flexed his jaws. "Nhuri, I love you. I'll do better."

"Love isn't supposed to feel like this," *she countered.*

Her phone vibrated, alerting her that her driver was outside. She glanced down at the screen and then at the man she had once planned to spend the rest of her life with.

"Take care, Dru."

His nostrils flared. "Let me at least help you into the car."

"No. It's fine. I got it," *Nhuri said.*

She wanted nothing from him but to let her go in peace. Knowing Dru, he'd use the helping hand he gave her against her if he could. Lugging her belongings that she could fit into two suitcases, Nhuri exited the home they shared. She didn't bother to look back or give any more parting words to Dru once she was in the backseat.

"Hello. Earth to Nhuri," Shareece, one of Nhuri's coworkers, sang.

Snapping out of her daydream of her past, Nhuri glanced her way. "My fault, girl. What'd you say?"

"I asked if you wanted to ride with me to Wingstop for lunch."

They were having a late lunch today, and Nhuri hadn't realized it was almost two o'clock. She wasn't in the mood for wings but decided to ride to get some fresh air.

"Yeah. I'll ride with you. We still have that meeting at three, right?"

Shareece nodded. "Yep. I wonder what it's about."

"Me too," Nhuri mumbled.

Working for one of the biggest retail giant companies had its perks. Some days, Nhuri's workload was as light as a feather; other days, she was ready to pull out her hair. Since her position as a marketing research assistant was part time until she found something she truly loved, Nhuri wasn't too stressed about the hours. The job paid well, but she still chose to bartend on the side and fill in the gaps for Natalia's workload. It was . . . a lot, but Nhuri knew to keep herself busy. Working was a distraction she welcomed.

While scrolling through her emails, Nhuri frowned when a new one from her boss appeared. After clicking on it, her frown deepened at the contents of the email.

"What's the matter?" Shareece asked, noticing her perplexed expression.

Nhuri didn't answer right away. Her eyes read the email again to ensure she wasn't misreading it. Sure enough, she hadn't.

"Ms. Thorsen is trying to send me to another state to work," Nhuri said as if she couldn't believe it.

"What? Why would she want to do that?" Shareece wondered.

Nhuri wanted to know the same thing. Instead of emailing Ms. Thorsen back, she picked up her work phone and dialed her office number. She needed answers immediately and couldn't wait for an email.

"Good afternoon. This is Missy Thorsen."

"Hi, Ms. Thorsen. This is Nhuri. I just read your email. Can I swing by your office to discuss this in person?"

"Of course. Come right on up," Ms. Thorsen instructed.

Nhuri told her she'd see her shortly and hung up. Grabbing her cell phone, she pushed away from her desk.

"You may have to grab lunch without me," she said.

Shareece nodded. "That's fine. Want me to grab you something while I'm out?"

"No. I'm okay. Thank you, though. I'll let you know what she says."

Nhuri was a ball of nerves as she climbed onto the elevator. She'd only moved back home to Kansas City seven months ago. There was no way she was ready to relocate for a job she wasn't even working full time, especially not with her circumstances. She knocked on Ms. Thorsen's office door and was told to come in.

"Hi, Nhuri. How are you?" Ms. Thorsen questioned, greeting her with the type of energy she always gave.

Nhuri smiled. "I was doing okay before I received your email," she said, chuckling.

"I can certainly understand that. Have a seat, and I'll explain everything."

Nhuri slid into the black chair and sat stiffly. The plush leather wasn't uncomfortable, but she was. She felt put on the spot and didn't like it one bit. Anxiously, Nhuri tapped the acrylic nails of her fingers against one another. Ms. Thorsen gathered a few files and a manila folder and met her gaze. She gave her a soft smile.

"You seem nervous," Ms. Thorsen acknowledged.

"I am."

There was no need to beat around the bush.

"No need to be. A high-profile client specifically requested our firm, and I need my best people on it. I consider you one of our best."

Nhuri's stomach dropped. She appreciated the compliment and hoped that'd suffice for her following words.

"Thank you. I appreciate the opportunity, but I—" She swallowed, then tried again. "I can't commit to this assignment."

Ms. Thorsen's eyes slightly narrowed as her blonde brows dipped. "What do you mean you can't commit?"

"The assignment is for two months. I can't just up and leave. I have a family that depends on me."

Ms. Thorsen considered her response before speaking. "I understand family obligations, but you knew when you accepted this job that travel was a requirement. This is what you signed up for."

Nhuri's chest tightened, and she exhaled as her leg bounced. "Yes, it is what I signed up for, but I wasn't expecting traveling duties to happen so soon. I can't leave my sister and niece for that long."

Nhuri thrived at her job and loved it, but not enough to leave for a two-month assignment when Natalia's health fluctuated daily. The thought of something happening again while she was hundreds of miles away made her stomach flip.

Ms. Thorsen's expression shifted into a sympathetic one. "I get it. But we all have personal lives, Nhuri. We all have things that pull us away. When you were first hired, you told me you could see yourself making this your career. My question is, how much are you willing to sacrifice for it?"

Nhuri inhaled sharply. She had sacrificed enough. Long nights, last-minute deadlines, endless projects, and four years without being in the same state as her sister and niece. There'd be other opportunities in her field; there wouldn't be with her loved ones, and she knew that. As much as she cherished her job, she loved her sister and their bond more.

She lifted her chin. "I'm not willing to sacrifice my sanity."

Silence stretched between them, and Ms. Thorsen sighed. "You're damn good at what you do, Nhuri. I don't want to lose you, but I need to know now if you can't fully commit."

Nhuri's heart pounded. She had walked away from one situation with her ex, so it shouldn't be hard to walk away from another, right?

"I need time to think about it," she murmured.

Ms. Thorsen nodded once, though her expression was unreadable. "Very well. Take this evening to think about it, and let me know your decision first thing in the morning."

Nhuri stood on shaky legs. She needed more time than that but nodded instead of asking for more. As she walked out of the office, her heart felt no lighter, and the weight on her shoulders was a ton heavier. Whenever she felt like she was moving in the right direction, something or someone always pulled her back. Again, she was at a crossroads with the curveball life threw her, and no matter the choice she made, there'd be consequences. There always was.

"I promise, that was the last store," Natalia said, pulling out of the parking lot of Home Comforts.

The Black-owned furnishing store was one of her favorites; she had to take Nhuri inside. They were in there for forty-five minutes, and somehow, Nhuri had been convinced to purchase a new console table for her entryway. Leave it up to her sister to persuade her to buy something she didn't necessarily need. At least it was cute.

Nhuri glanced up from her phone and smirked. "Yeah, okay. I thought you needed to go by the grocery store?"

Natalia sucked her teeth. "That is right. Are you cooking tomorrow? If so, we can do all of that in the morning. I'm exhausted."

The fatigue in her voice was evident. Some days, she could get up and be on the go; others, she was completely drained before the day began. They'd been ripping and running for the better half of the afternoon, and a nap was screaming Natalia's name. She flexed her stiff hand as she maneuvered through traffic.

"I'll get them delivered," Nhuri mumbled lowly, in her feelings.

Natalia glanced her way. "What's the matter?"

"Nothing."

"Don't say nothing when I can see it all over your face. We lie to one another now?"

Nhuri exhaled dramatically. "I just hate seeing you like this."

Natalia simpered. "I know. But today was actually one of my good days."

"But every day isn't, and that's what scares me the most. What if—"

"No. Let's not do that, okay?"

"I'm just being realistic. Is it not something you think about?"

Natalia sighed. "All the time. That doesn't mean I want to dwell on it. I try to cherish the good days as much as possible. We only get one life to live, sis. We can't harp on the what-ifs."

Nhuri should've felt relieved by her sister's optimistic personality, but she wasn't. "I wish I felt the same."

"And why don't you?"

"I don't even want to tell you because I know you'll be upset," Nhuri said.

Natalia cut her eyes her way. "Yeah, maybe, but it depends. What'd you do?"

"Declined a two-month job assignment out of state." Nhuri rushed her words as if to make them sound less jarring. That didn't work.

"Why would you do that?" The curiosity in Natalia's voice was so evident.

"I had to."

"No, you didn't." Natalia shook her head. "Don't tell me you declined it because of me."

Nhuri's silence was her answer.

"Nhuri," Natalia grumbled her name with disappointment. "I'll be fine. That could've landed you a great career. Something you've been talking about since you moved back."

"I know, but two months out of state? No. I wasn't taking that with everything you have going on. You and I both know that."

Natalia scoffed. "Everything I have going on? You mean my chronic illness? The one I have been handling for the past three years? You can't keep putting your life on hold for me."

Nhuri's jaws tightened. "That's not fair. Don't say it like that."

"No, what's unfair is you treating me like I'm helpless." Natalia's voice wavered with frustration, and she took a deep breath. "You know I appreciate everything that you do for me, but I didn't ask you to give up on your goals to make sure I'm straight."

"I know you didn't ask, but can't I just look out for you for once?" Nhuri took a deep breath, forcing her tears to stay put. She wasn't trying to argue with her sister. "What was I supposed to do? Leave you by yourself? What about Raniya on the days when you can't get out of bed?"

"I would've managed," Natalia countered. "Like I always do. Like I've been doing. Plus, she has a father, and my friends help when I need them. I always work things out."

Nhuri winced. She'd always viewed her sister as a fiercely independent woman, but that didn't change how she felt. Nor did it stop her illness from crippling her some days.

"You shouldn't have to manage things alone. I'm your sister."

"Yes, you are. And I love you, but you can't babysit me for the rest of your life."

"That's not—" Nhuri rubbed the spot between her brows. "I just want to be here for you and my niece, okay? Fuck the job assignment. I didn't know fully what I was up against when I moved back home, but I'm here, and that's that. You can be upset all you want, but whatever. I'm not going anywhere."

Natalia's tense shoulders loosened. "I don't want you to be here for me like this." Her voice softened, but the sadness in it hit Nhuri harder than frustration. "I don't want to be the reason you don't go after what you want in life."

"You're not, so stop saying that. You're my sister. Anything concerning you matters to me. Whatever job position that's meant to be mine will be. I'm not pressed for it, sis. I promise."

"And I understand that fully, but you shouldn't have had to choose."

Nhuri grabbed her right hand and lightly squeezed it. "But I did, and I'm okay with my decision. I need you to be okay with it too."

Natalia didn't speak for a long moment. So much had changed since she was diagnosed with lupus. Feeling as if she were a burden was the biggest hurdle she still struggled with. Natalia wasn't the type of woman who wanted sympathy, but she also wasn't ungrateful. She didn't expect everyone to put their lives on hold for her, and she still hadn't come to terms with the fact that people would.

The sisters' parents passed away when they were in their early twenties, so they didn't have many immediate family members that they were close to. Their mother passed away first from sickness and their father four years later. He hadn't been sick at all, and the sisters assumed it was from heartbreak, which was a real tragedy when you lost the love of your life. So, Natalia could be upset or feel a way, but Nhuri was here to stay. They were all they had.

Natalia squeezed her hand and glanced her way. "You better not regret it."

"I won't," Nhuri said, smiling.

"So, what did they say when you declined the assignment?" Natalia asked.

Nhuri rolled her eyes. "She seemed so disappointed, but I know for a fact that if something happened to me today, and I could no longer work, my position would be posted online and filled by the end of the week or sooner."

"True," Natalia agreed, pursing her lips. "They'll get over it."

"Exactly."

"Thank you for always thinking of me. I don't know if I tell you enough, and I never want to seem unappreciative of all you do," Natalia said, getting emotional.

"Please don't start crying," Nhuri pleaded, chuckling.

Natalia laughed. "Okay, okay. I won't. But I'm serious. I kinda threw you into taking care of me in the midst of you dealing with a breakup."

"I'd mentally left Dru long before I physically left him. So, please, hush. And stop telling me thank you. What the hell are little sisters for if I can't get my way sometimes?"

Laughing, Natalia shook her head. "I'm glad you know it's only half the time. I'm still big sis around here."

Nhuri leaned over and kissed her cheek. "Yes, you are. And I love you so much."

"I love you more. Now, run this grocery list down to me. I think I'm in the mood for some pot roast."

While Nhuri had been stressed about declining her work assignment, everything had worked out. It had no choice but to because she stood firm on doing things that made sense in her life. She was no longer living to please others.

SIX

SHYRIQ STARED AT his screen monitor, rubbed his eyes, and yawned. His morning coffee hadn't done its job of providing the energy he desperately needed. Going out over the weekend, even though he hadn't done much, had worn him out. Fooling around with Rush and a few of his homeboys had him struggling today.

Huffing, he pushed away from his desk and grabbed his work cell phone. Exiting his office, he bypassed his assistant's desk and went to the main production floor. He spent mostly every Monday at the distillery. Shyriq felt that being surrounded by the scent of aged bourbon that clung in the air motivated him to push through his workweek. And today, he needed that extra push. Otherwise, his mind would venture to the woman who'd disrespectfully taken up space in his brain. Shyriq didn't mind it, but he needed to focus.

He watched through the glass wall as generations of wealth and love transformed before him. Shyriq was humbled to be the main face of GHC. His family's legacy meant the world to him, but he couldn't help but feel like something was missing. Whoever made up the notion that money could buy happiness was somewhat of a liar. Shyriq was frugal with his funds, and he had splurged on more than enough materialistic things to satisfy his cravings, but he wanted more. He wanted what his parents shared.

Since Xena and her conniving ways had put a bad taste in his mouth, Shyriq figured he'd never walk down the aisle again. He didn't see it in the cards for him. All the love he'd given her could've been poured into the business. Or better yet, someone else. *Nhuri looks like she could use some loving.* The thought hit Shyriq so unexpectedly that he drew his head back.

"What the hell?" he mumbled, running a hand over his deep waves.

He shook his head and pushed away from the railing. Again, Nhuri had invaded his thoughts. Their last encounter had done something to him. It altered Shyriq's mind in a way that left him intrigued. Nhuri didn't care about his status or who he was. She stood her ground and kept things strictly professional. That damn smirk she threw his way before walking out of their section was imprinted in his brain.

He walked the grounds for a while, stopping and talking to the employees before returning to his office. Shyriq rolled his bottom lip between his teeth, debating his next move. He knew what he wanted to do to capture Nhuri's attention and keep it, but he wasn't sure if that was how he should do it. Nhuri didn't seem like the type to be easily impressed, so doing something unannounced was off the list.

"I got it," Shyriq said, clapping his hands together.

Going to the employee schedule, he pulled up the log to see if Natalia worked from home today or if she was at the main headquarters. Locating her office number, he punched it into the dial pad but paused before calling.

Shyriq was a confident man. Anything and everything he wanted, he went after. This playing field after being married was new territory for him, though.

Hanging up the phone, he grabbed his personal cell and dialed Rush. He needed some advice. It may not have been sound advice, but Shyriq would take it.

"Yo," Rush answered.

"You're too grown to answer the phone like that," Shyriq playfully scolded.

Rush laughed. "I knew it was you. What's up?"

"Real quick. Would it be crossing ethical boundaries if someone reached out to an employee to get in contact with a friend of theirs?"

The line was silent for a bit. "Nigga, do I look like your HR department?"

Shyriq huffed. "I'm being serious."

"I am too. Is this about one of your employees or you? I know you ain't getting your hand involved with something so minuscule."

Rush was correct. Shyriq was the owner. Unless it absolutely had to come across his desk, he let the people in position do their jobs.

"It's about me. One of my employees' sisters—"

"The fine one from the club?" Rush questioned.

Shyriq smirked. "Yes. Now, like I was saying . . . Her sister works for me. I could easily dial her up and press her about her sister, but is that doing too much? Do men get called thirsty for stunts like that?"

Rush didn't mean to laugh loudly in his brother's ear, but he couldn't control it. Shyriq was acting as if he was an old-ass man instead of a thirty-five-year-old man who was indeed still in his prime. And fine as hell with money.

"I'm about to hang up," Shyriq said.

Rush struggled to get himself together. "A'ight, hold on," he coughed, wiping his eyes. "You just sound old. I get it, though. You ain't really been on the scene like that. Some women like that. It's called applying pressure."

Shyriq nodded. "All right. Got it. Hit up the sister and let her know I want her sister's number."

"Nah, nah. Not like that." Rush chuckled. "You're a smooth talker, but you ain't rude. Be a gentleman. Watch her run and tell her sister to quit playing games."

Smiling, Shyriq nodded. "Look at you schooling me. I owe you one."

"Yeah, yeah. Put me on that fine-ass intern you got, and we're even."

"She's engaged," Shyriq said.

Rush sucked his teeth. "And you're still married to that ho but pursuing another woman. Let's not discuss titles, bro," he said, laughing.

"Get off my phone."

"You call—"

Before Rush could finish his sentence, Shyriq hung up. Back to the task at hand, he placed the office phone on speaker and punched in Natalia's desk number. He hesitated on the last digit, which usually wasn't his style, but something about Nhuri had him moving differently. Only three encounters let him know she was in a league of her own, and he needed to come at her correctly or not at all. Exhaling, he finally hit call.

The phone rang twice before Natalia answered, sounding surprised. She saw his name flash across the phone and almost panicked.

"Mr. Hendrix. Hi."

"What's going on, Natalia? Everything going good on your end?"

She paused. "As far as . . ."

"Your health . . . working for me. Life?" Shyriq questioned and bit back a chuckle. *Can she hear the nervousness in my voice?* he thought.

"Oh," Natalia chirped. "Life's great. You and I both know I love my job, so no complaints there."

She'd purposely left out the update on her health status, but he wouldn't highlight that right now. Shyriq had more pressing matters on his mind.

"That's good to hear," he said.

"Mmhmm. Was there something specific you called me for?" Natalia asked.

He smirked, picturing her arching a brow. "Actually, there was. I need a favor."

There was a pause. "A favor?" she repeated slowly. "From me?"

"You make it sound crazy."

"It is. You don't ask for favors."

"Maybe I'm changing my ways."

Natalia snorted and tossed a hand over her mouth. She'd worked for Shyriq long enough to know he was semistuck in his ways. But if he were changing his ways, that would be good for him. "That'd be a great look," she said. "What do you need?"

Shyriq thumbed his beard. "I just have a few questions about your sister."

There was more silence. "Nhuri?"

"Do you have any other sisters?"

Natalia chuckled softly. "Um, no. But that was random."

"Not quite. Is she single?"

"Wait. You're calling me about my sister's relationship status?" Natalia needed him to fully clarify what this call was about because she didn't play about her sister.

"Yes. You sound as if that's the wildest thing in the world."

"It is . . . coming from you," Natalia admitted. "I just didn't expect it."

Shyriq nodded. "I can understand how I caught you off guard. Your sister, Nhuri, and I have crossed paths a few times now, and I'm interested in her. But I had to see if she was single first."

"Says the man who, by my knowledge, is still married," Natalia said, uncaring that she may have crossed the line.

"Unfortunately, the divorce papers haven't been signed by my ex-wife. Now that we're up to speed on *my* relationship status, I'd love to know if Nhuri is single."

Natalia smirked and chuckled. She wasn't expecting this side of Shyriq at all, but she was amused. "She is and if you have any plans on stepping to her, I'd work a little harder to get those papers signed."

Shyriq smirked, loving how she held nothing back, just like Nhuri. "Dully noted." He let the silence stretch for a few seconds. "Do you mind giving me an address where I can send her something?"

"I'm not comfortable with disclosing her home address, but you can deliver whatever it is to my home, and I'll make sure she receives it," Natalia said.

"Perfect. I'll get on that right away," Shyriq replied.

Natalia smiled on the other end of the phone, picking up on his anxious energy. It was spilling through the receiver. "Was there anything else you needed?"

"Not at the moment. I'll let you get back to work."

She chuckled. "Okay. I won't tell her we had this conversation, but if she mentions your name, then I know you shot your shot."

Shyriq grinned. "Bet. I mean, thank you," he said, trying to go back to being professional.

Natalia snickered. "You're welcome."

The line disconnected, and Shyriq sat back in his chair. He exhaled, and a flicker of anticipation ran through him. He should've asked more questions about Nhuri, but he could tell Natalia was already on the defensive side. That was okay, though. He planned to erase her apprehension and was determined to see where this thing between him and Nhuri could go. First things first, he had to call his lawyer, King. Xena needed to sign those damn divorce papers as soon as possible.

SEVEN

"IT," RANIYA HUFFED, climbing onto the couch beside her head. "Are you going to be sad all day?"

The last thing Nhuri was expecting to happen was for her to be let go from her job. She'd been completely blindsided the following week after turning down the job assignment in another state. Ms. Thorsen seemed disappointed by her decline, but Nhuri didn't think it was *that* serious for her to be fired. Apparently, she wasn't the only one who had declined and wasn't the only employee who had been let go.

So, yes, she was going to be sad all day. It was going on day four of unemployment and Nhuri was sulking at Natalia's house. She'd stayed the night and had no plans of going home anytime soon.

"Maybe," Nhuri mumbled.

"But I don't want you to be sad."

Nhuri glanced at Raniya and almost felt bad for being so short with her. Raniya's poked-out bottom lip, sincere brown eyes, and cute little face always did the trick. Nhuri knew she couldn't be in her feelings for too long; her niece wouldn't allow her to. Sitting up, she yawned and wiped her eyes.

"I don't want to be sad either. You want to cheer me up?" Nhuri asked.

Enthusiastically, Raniya nodded. "Yes! Let's go to the park and get on the swings. Ooh! And then the slide. You know it was a new one built by my school?"

Her energetic mood and suggestion made Nhuri smirk *and* cringe on the inside. Her idea of getting out of her funk didn't involve stepping foot outside, especially to the park where kids were screaming their heads off, exerting all their energy, and having fun. Life wasn't fun for Nhuri right now. Raniya waited for her answer with a smile, blinking her eyes, hoping she'd hurry up.

"Soooo?" Raniya sang.

Nhuri chuckled. "It's too late to go to the park today." Before she could pout, Nhuri added, "But we can always go tomorrow."

Raniya's shoulders sagged. "Okay. But what about today? You're still going to be sad."

"How about you go get me your favorite toys to play with? That'll make me feel better."

Hopping up from the couch, Raniya said, "Okay. I'll be right back, TT. Don't lay down again."

She ran up to her room, and Nhuri chuckled. That's undoubtedly what she had in mind to do. While she waited for her niece to return, she grabbed her phone off the coffee table. Unlocking it, she bypassed the unread text messages and maneuvered to her emails. A coworker, well, an *ex*-coworker now, said they'd email her some job openings they heard about. Sulking in her sorrows was one thing, but Nhuri knew it couldn't last forever, so she was trying to stay optimistic about the future.

The front door opened when Raniya returned down the stairs with a bucket full of toys. Raniya wasn't fazed by the quizzical look her mama gave her. Natalia glanced at Nhuri and squinted, and she shrugged with a small smile.

"What's up, Nhuri," Malik, Natalia's boyfriend, greeted.

"Hey."

"You've been in this same spot since we left?" Natalia asked.

Before Nhuri could answer, Raniya yelled out, "Yes! She's sad."

"Dang. You just gon' tell my business," Nhuri said, laughing.

"My mommy asked. You ready to play?"

Scooting off the couch, Nhuri stretched and yawned. "In a second. Get it all set up for me."

She headed into the kitchen, and Natalia was right behind her. Raiding her sister's fridge and cabinets wasn't anything new. It was the little sister in her. Nhuri considered it a special privilege. While she probably needed to put some food on her stomach, eating was the furthest thing on her mind. Grabbing a can of pineapple juice, she ventured to the cabinet where Natalia stored the alcohol.

"Um," Natalia mumbled, watching her every move.

Nhuri looked over her shoulder. "Yes?"

"Have you eaten?"

That wasn't the question Natalia wanted to ask, but it was one of many that made sense. Nhuri filled her glass with ice.

"I don't really have an appetite. How was your date?"

Avoidance. It was the tactic Nhuri chose when she didn't want to discuss something. Natalia would let her have her moment. She didn't want to talk about her date but also didn't want to be the big sister who nags. Nhuri was going through a rough time, so Natalia gave her some space.

"It was pretty nice, honestly. I'd never been to a candle-making class, but I enjoyed it."

Her smile made Nhuri grin. "Let me find out Malik is a lover boy."

The sisters snickered.

"He is." Natalia swooned. "Like . . . I knew he was, but each date or small gesture proves it even more."

"That's so sweet," Nhuri said, sipping her drink. "And you didn't want to give him a chance."

The pineapple and tequila settling on her tastebuds made her sigh with appreciation.

"I had too much going on, but clearly, he wasn't trying to hear that," Natalia said, chuckling.

Despite her health, having a daughter, and going through a fresh breakup with Raheem, Malik let it be known that he was okay with waiting until she was ready. He didn't pressure her, but he didn't fall to the background as if he were no longer interested, either. He'd left the ball in Natalia's court, and as hesitant as she'd been to bring him into her world, Malik had been one of the best additions.

"You already know he wasn't," Nhuri added, smirking. "Listen to them two."

Malik's animated cartoon voice had Raniya giggling her head off. He was active in her life, and Natalia loved that for her baby. They'd been together a little over two years, and he continued to show up for them in ways Natalia was beyond appreciative of. Raheem did his fatherly duties, but Natalia could see the change in Raniya when he moved out. It was subtle, and she had tons of questions, but thankfully, no love was lost.

"She's about to wear him out," Natalia laughed.

"Better him than me," Nhuri said. She swirled her drink before taking another sip. "I'm glad he's here with y'all."

Natalia swallowed the lump in her throat. "Yeah, I am too."

"So, are you talking to anyone?"

"Natalia," she said, laughing.

Natalia bulged her eyes. "What? Don't say my name like that. I'm just asking."

"Yeah, well, I don't really have time to be *talking* to anyone. Especially not now. What do I look like entertaining a man when I don't even have a job?"

Natalia rolled her eyes. "Please, shut up. You're acting as if you've been jobless for months on end. You literally just got laid off."

"And I feel like shit," Nhuri confessed, downing the remainder of her drink.

"Losing your job isn't the worst thing, Nhuri. It's not the end of the world. You have a degree and skills that will land you something."

"And what am I supposed to do until then?"

Sighing, Natalia walked over, grabbed the glass from her hand, and placed it on the counter. "You continue to live life. That's what the hell you do. It's disheartening and frustrating, I get it, but beating yourself up for something that's a small bump in the road is not happening on my watch."

Nhuri blinked away the tears forming in her eyes. "It's like every time I get ahead, something sets me back."

"That's life. It has no clear direction of where it'll take you or what will happen, but you can try steering it in your favor. Take a few weeks to yourself and figure out some things. Remind yourself who you are. Don't let temporary circumstances become a permanent lifestyle, okay?"

Nhuri nodded. "Okay," she agreed. "Thank you. I swear you're the most positive person I know."

Natalia kissed her cheek. "I have no choice but to be. Now, please, eat something. I'd like to enjoy the rest of my evening with y'all, and I don't need you in here throwing up."

Nhuri turned the faucet on and washed her glass. "There won't be none of that. Let's go see what cartoon character we get assigned to."

Natalia smiled. "Oh, goodness."

No matter what she was going through, Nhuri knew she could count on her sister to get her back into a positive mind-set. Even if only for the moment. She was going to take her advice and hope for the best. Until then, living life was first on the agenda. After all, you only got one, and Nhuri wouldn't let it go to waste.

Nhuri wasn't sure if it was the peach mimosas, the bass-heavy R&B flowing through the speakers, or the fact that she'd gotten out of the house, but for the first time in two weeks, she didn't feel like her head was underwater. Drowning in misery had only lasted for so long, thanks to her girls.

There was nothing like a group of solid friends. And a brunch date filled with laughter until their stomachs hurt. Nhuri's days had turned around drastically, and she was so grateful for the much-needed distraction. When she moved back home, she and her friends picked up right where they left off. They hadn't stopped being friends, but the distance made them miss being in Nhuri's presence and vice versa.

"Girl, you look lighter already," Kendra teased, stuffing a piece of her syrup-drenched waffle into her mouth.

Nhuri smirked and sipped from her flute. She had a slight buzz already.

"Because she is," Jazmyn said, lifting her glass. "No more stressing about these jobs who expect you to break your back for them."

Their other friend, Marie, nodded. "Mmhm. And no more early-morning conference calls that could've been handled through an email."

"Exactly," Nhuri agreed, tapping her flute against Marie's. "Honestly, now that I'm out of my funk, getting fired was probably the best thing to happen to me."

She had some days to think about her situation and realized how tired and stressed out she'd been. Not having to wake up early, talk to rude customers, have restless nights, and have practically no time for herself was something Nhuri wouldn't miss. She'd gotten out of her woe-is-me mind-set.

"You think so?" Kendra asked.

Nhuri nodded. "Yes. My sister was mad at me for not accepting the assignment out of state, which was never happening. I couldn't just leave her and my niece. Too much is going on, plus I still have my bartending job."

"The one you should've been quit," Jazmyn fussed, playfully rolling her eyes.

"You must've had a bad experience at Lush or something," Marie chuckled, pushing her plate aside. "You're so against her working there."

"Right," Nhuri chimed.

Jazmyn took a sip of her water and cleared her throat. "It's nothing against them at all. I just know Nhuri is settling."

Marie glanced to her right, where Nhuri sat. She shrugged.

"If that's what she wants to call it," Nhuri said.

"You know, sometimes we settle out of fear or the unknown," Kendra added, and they nodded.

"Yep. And that's exactly what she was doing. Which, I guess, was fine at the beginning, but not anymore."

Nhuri knew her best friend wasn't trying to throw shots at her, but the champagne and tequila shot they'd taken had her thinking otherwise. Her brain was a bit foggy, so she needed her to clarify what she meant.

"There's a problem with being a bartender?" Nhuri asked, her tone defensive.

Jazmyn sucked her teeth. "No. You know that's not what I mean or what I said. All I'm saying is that *you* have more potential than being a bartender. Is that a lot of people's job title? Yes. There's nothing wrong with that. Get your money by any means. But as for you, my girl . . . You're doing exactly what Kendra said."

Nhuri leaned against the cool cushion. Thankfully, they were seated at a round booth near the window, so no one could hear how Jazmyn just read her. It was out of love; it always had been and would be. And Nhuri couldn't say she was bluffing because it was the truth. Though she loved bartending and the few outside jobs she worked, clocking in at Lush every weekend wasn't what Nhuri wanted to do. It helped pay the bills, but at what cost?

"And that's okay," Kendra added. "You act like she has to have everything figured out right now."

"No, I'm acting like a friend who knows that she's worth so much more than wasting time mixing fucking drinks as if she needs that job. If you had absolutely no other option to fall back on, cool. That's not the case, though. And if you don't start acting like the boss bitch that you are, I'm not giving you the gift I brought," Jazmyn said, pursing her lips.

Nhuri couldn't help but laugh. "Wow. I never knew you to be an Indian giver."

"Technically, she hasn't given it to you yet, so that name doesn't fit," Marie concluded.

Nodding, Nhuri polished off her mimosa. To someone who didn't have real friends, it would've sounded as if Jazmyn was being a hater or on Nhuri's case for no reason. She loved her friend beyond measure and wanted the best for her. Jazmyn witnessed people becoming stagnant in situations, including jobs that stressed them out. In her eyes, holding on to things that no longer serve a purpose in your life showed how less you thought of yourself, as if you didn't deserve more. That's all Jazmyn wanted Nhuri to grasp.

"I'm not," Jazmyn said, handing her an orange gift bag with sparkly white tissue paper tucked inside. "Here you go."

Squinting, Nhuri glanced around the table. "What're the gifts for?"

"Just a little something to let you know that we love you and have your back, no matter what," Kendra said.

"Awww. Y'all are trying to make me cry," Nhuri cooed, poking out her lip.

"Please don't, friend," Marie laughed. "Your makeup looks way too good to ruin."

Knowing she was right, Nhuri pulled herself together and opened her first gift. It was a $150 gift card to QuikTrip for gas and a bottle of Tiffany perfume. Nhuri collected perfume like Infinity stones. She never needed much convincing to buy a new perfume, body oil, or mist. Some purchases were blind buys that she regretted, but they'd become gifts.

"I've been meaning to snag this perfume," Nhuri said. "Thank you."

"You're welcome," Jazmyn said. "Your income may look a little funny for a while, but your collection doesn't have to. And you'll have some gas for those interviews you go on."

The table laughed, but Nhuri was truly touched. The simple things meant the most to her.

"As high as gas has been these last few weeks, I'll definitely be using it."

Nhuri grabbed Marie's bag and wondered what was inside. It seemed a bit heavy. The first item she pulled out was a plant. Glancing at Marie, Nhuri bunched her brows.

"Now, you know me and plants don't get along," she said seriously.

Marie laughed. "I know, but this one is pretty easy to take care of. It just needs a good balance of water and light. Mainly indirect sunlight."

Nhuri nodded, reading the tag. "A money tree," she read aloud.

"Mmhm. It attracts good luck and prosperity," Marie explained.

"I love that, Marie. Thank you so much. Let's see what else is in here."

Nhuri pulled out a gift card to the spa and a manifestation journal for her to write in. The thoughtfulness behind each gift made her so emotional that her eyes began to water.

"I just thought we were coming to brunch to get me out of the house. I wasn't expecting anything," Nhuri said, sniffling.

Their waitress stopped by just in time for refills. They had another hour to enjoy bottomless mimosas and were taking full advantage. Nhuri ordered two at a time, grateful she'd ridden with Jazmyn.

"Well, you have one more, so don't cry yet," Kendra teased, handing over her bag.

Kendra's gifts were just as nice as her friends'. She bought Nhuri a gift card to Sam's Club, a weighted lavender-scented eye mask since she was having trouble sleeping, a new pair of comfy house shoes, a pack of edibles, and a small white poster board. Nhuri knew what everything was for except the last item.

"A poster board?" she questioned.

Kendra nodded. "Yes. I'm hosting a vision board party. I had to buy a small one to fit inside the bag, but that's my other gift."

Nhuri was excited. She'd never done a vision board, let alone had a party for one. Leave it up to her girls to put her onto something new. It was perfect timing too. Nhuri had goals in life, and just talking about them would no longer work. She needed to put some action behind her words and was grateful for friends who made her want to keep going even when times got rough.

"We're not trying to overwhelm you or anything," Marie said. "Just know that we love you and are here to help in any way we can."

"Even if that means snuggling up on the couch, taking a nap, and binging our favorite TV shows," Jazmyn added.

Nhuri patted the dampness underneath her eye and nodded. "I love y'all so much."

Not only had they comforted her by being a listening ear all week, but they also validated her feelings and were a source of support Nhuri needed at the time.

"We love you too, girl," Kendra said, smiling.

"The time I planned on taking off doesn't sound too bad now," Nhuri chuckled.

Marie couldn't agree more. "Not at all. Let's not think about another job right now."

"Okay, okay. But one more thing," Nhuri said.

The friends eyed one another and smirked.

"We're listening," Jazmyn said.

"Maybe this was the sign I needed to stop playing around with my gifts. I missed out on an opportunity that may have elevated my career, but that just means it wasn't meant to be mine."

"Amen!" Marie said, clapping.

"So, I just want to thank y'all for putting up with my mood swings this week and even before then. I don't know what's next for me on this journey, but I'm done crying . . . well, maybe not completely done crying about it."

They all laughed because one thing Nhuri did when frustrated was cry. A good, soul-cleansing cry never hurt anyone.

"But I'm prepared to take on whatever is next like the boss bitch I clearly forgot that I am. It won't be easy, but what's the fun in that?" she concluded with a smile.

"I heard that!" Jazmyn said.

Kendra picked up her flute. "We love seeing you step into your purpose!"

"Yes! Cheers to Nhuri and her new journey. I just know it's going to be amazing," Marie declared.

They clinked glasses, this time with even bigger smiles. Positive energy floated through their booth, and Nhuri felt it all. She wasn't sure where this next chapter would take her, but right now, sharing drinks and good food with her girls hyping her up was all that mattered. Laughter and talks about their upcoming plans for the week filled the space as they swayed to the music and enjoyed the atmosphere.

Nhuri leaned back against the plush booth, feeling the warmth of the liquor settling in her veins. She knew the nap she'd take once she got home would be everything. It was the perfect Sunday vibe, and she reminded herself to get out more often. Thankfully, she didn't have to work at Lush tonight.

She was in the middle of responding to a text from Natalia when their waitress appeared at the table, balancing a sleek black tray lined with four shot glasses filled with tequila.

"Okay, ladies," the waitress said with a grin as she set the tray down, "These are for you."

Nhuri exchanged a look with her girls before addressing the waitress. "Oh, we didn't order these."

"I know. Compliments from a gentleman who wanted to celebrate with all of you," she explained.

Her eyes flickered across the restaurant, and Nhuri instinctively followed her gaze. Patio, the name of the restaurant where they were dining, is a relatively new soul food and R&B lounge that received numerous positive reviews since its opening. Naturally, it attracted a crowd. A table full of beautiful women receiving shots was not uncommon. However, the sender increased Nhuri's heart rate.

Shyriq sat comfortably at the bar, his gaze already locked on hers. His full lips tilted into a smirk, and his dark brown eyes silently called to her from across the room. He gave Nhuri a subtle bow that lifted her cheeks. Like every other time she'd crossed paths with him, Shyriq was amazingly dressed.

A black-and-white-patterned short-sleeved silk shirt stretched over his broad chest, paired with black jeans and a silver watch with diamonds shining so brightly that they competed with the sun. His fresh haircut, impeccably groomed beard, and glowing, cinnamon-hued skin made him even more dangerously handsome than Nhuri could remember. She felt the low tremble in her stomach that she'd felt the last time they were in close proximity.

We have to stop crossing paths like this, she thought.

Kendra let out a low whistle. "Whew. Now, *that's* a man."

Jazmyn snorted. "He looks familiar. Who is he?"

Nhuri cleared her throat, picking up one of the shot glasses. "Shyriq."

Kendra squinted. "Wait . . . The owner of that whiskey you like?"

Nhuri nodded, trying not to let the heat in her face show.

The three friends shared a look while Nhuri tried ignoring their questioning gaze.

Marie snickered. "Okay, friend. I see you. You know the man on a first-name basis."

"So does Kendra. That doesn't mean anything," Nhuri countered.

"I only know it because my daddy and uncles have been drinking their family's whiskey for years. Every time they see one of the family members out, they stop and talk like they've known each other for years."

Nhuri smirked. She could see that happening, seeing as though almost every encounter with Shyriq had turned into him wanting to hold a full-blown conversation with her. It was nice to know he and his family were hospitable.

"So, what's your excuse?" Jazmyn teased.

"I don't have one," Nhuri said much too quickly. "I may or may not have run into him a few times over the last month. Maybe he's just being nice."

She shrugged it off, but her friends knew better. Kendra and Jazmyn exchanged sneaky glances, wanting to press her for more information, but Nhuri lifted her shot glass before they could. "Are we taking these or what?"

"You ain't said nothing but a word," Jazmyn grinned.

The foursome clinked glasses before tapping them against the table, then tipped them back. The liquor burned, but it was smooth. It was a type of tequila none of them had tasted before, but would be willing to try again. Nhuri ran her tongue over her teeth, savoring the lingering taste of agave.

Kendra licked her lips. "Oooh, that's good."

"Mmhm and smooth," Nhuri agreed. Her eyes landed on Shyriq again, but he was now talking to the men beside him. She remembered one introducing himself as Rush, but she wasn't familiar with the other man.

"You gonna go say thanks?" Jazmyn wondered.

Those weren't in Nhuri's plans, but it felt right to do so. She hesitated, pulling up the camera on her phone to check for eye boogers and make sure she still looked good.

"You still fine, friend," Jazmyn complimented, garnering a smile from Nhuri.

"Thank you. I'll be right back."

She adjusted her cropped white tank top before sliding out of the booth. Her high-waisted loose denim jeans were slightly oversized but relaxed, showing off a sliver of her midsection. Her strappy nude heels would have gotten Shyriq's attention, but her nearing presence did it all on its own. Nhuri approached the bar with the utmost confidence, which was needed with a man like Shyriq.

As if he'd been expecting her, he smirked once she slid beside him. Shyriq pulled out the stool for her to sit on and noticed the sweet floral scent of her perfume before taking her in. Nhuri wasn't intimidated by his intense stare, and she halfway blamed it on the liquor and the fact that he was so damn fine. Smiling, she tilted her head to the side.

"I didn't take you for an R&B lounge type of guy," Nhuri said, earning a full smile from Shyriq that made every nerve ending on her body come alive.

His deep chuckle made her heart flutter. "Is that right?"

"Mmhm," Nhuri hummed. "It is."

She studied him, trying to ignore how his presence filled the space and felt so heavy. Even in a crowded restaurant, he was the only one she wanted to focus on. Shyriq made it easy for her to do so, giving her his full attention. His eyes were on her, trailing her face, and he licked his lips.

"There's more to me that doesn't meet the eye, gorgeous." He let a few seconds pass. "You look nice."

She tried not to blush. "Thank you."

"Let me introduce you to my folks," Shyriq said, leaning back on his bar stool so they could see her.

He patted Rush on the arm. "You remember Nhuri," Shyriq said.

Rush grinned. "I do. You look like you're enjoying yourself," he said, noting the slight glossiness in her eyes.

She smirked. "I am. Nice to see you again."

"You too."

"This is Cane. You probably remember bartending his engagement party," Shyriq said.

Nhuri nodded and smiled. "I do. Congratulations."

"Thank you," he said. "What's your name?"

"Nhuri."

"Good to meet you, Nhuri," he said.

She waved. "Nice to meet you too."

He and Rush got back to the conversation they were having, leaving Nhuri with her thoughts. A man who didn't have manners or any plans for things to progress between them wouldn't have introduced her. At least, that's how Nhuri saw it. *Or maybe he's just showing he has manners*, she thought.

"A round of shots for me and my girls? I must be special."

Nhuri was teasing. A round of shots was nothing, but she wanted to check Shyriq's temperature. See why he seemingly had it bad for her. She was sure a man of his caliber had a fair share of women in rotation, including a wife, according to Natalia. So, adding her to his list isn't something Nhuri wanted to be on. He decided against sending a gift to Natalia's home, figuring it'd be weird, so a round of shots for her girls was his next step. He'd gotten Nhuri's attention, so it was safe to say he'd made the right choice.

"Do you want to be?" Shyriq asked.

Her stomach flipped, but she masked it with a dry laugh. "I'm special whether you approve or not, sir. Thank you very much."

Shyriq chuckled. "You are. I'm glad you know that."

"Is this your first time here?" Nhuri asked, letting her eyes scan the room.

Her friends pretended they weren't staring and quickly looked away once her eyes landed on their table. Nhuri could feel their anticipation from across the room.

"It is. Wanted to show some love for a new Black business in the city," he answered, resting his forearm on the bar.

Nhuri noticed the tattoos and something about them brought even more intrigue. Tipsily, she ran her fingers over the intricate ink. The hair on Shyriq's arms stood up, and his dick almost followed suit from her touch. But he had restraint.

"These are nice," she said.

"If you wanted to touch me, all you had to do was ask."

She snatched her hand away. Her eyes shot up to his, and she exhaled, seeing the playful glint in them. He smirked, and she playfully rolled her eyes. A smile tugged at her lips.

"Whatever."

"Y'all out enjoying the day or celebrating something?" Shyriq asked.

"I guess you could call it a celebration. I'm no longer employed," she said and chuckled.

Shyriq's brows dipped as confusion settled in. He didn't find that amusing but knew people coped with loss differently. He asked his next question with caution.

"Are you good?"

Nhuri's expression changed. She cleared her throat. "Yeah … I'm fine. My friends just wanted to do something nice for me since I've been in a bad mood. I'm okay, though. Thank you for asking."

Shyriq nodded even though he didn't fully believe her. "No problem. It's good to have friends in your corner who want to make your days better. I know I would."

Nhuri reached for the glass of water the bartender placed before her. Taking a small sip, she composed herself. Shyriq's question had thrown her off, and she didn't know why. Maybe because outside of her friends and Natalia, she didn't have anyone else who truly cared about her well-being. Most people would've accepted her casual response at face value, but he seemed to care about the hidden truth behind her words.

She wasn't used to that.

Especially from a man.

"You would what?" Nhuri mustered up the courage to ask.

"Would want to make your days better. Make them the best."

He answered her question without hesitation and with pure confidence. It was as if he was testing her to let him do exactly what he said. Nhuri was flustered and even more intrigued. She ran a hand over her warm neck and rubbed her glossed lips together while maintaining eye contact.

"You're bold."

Shyriq chuckled. "Is there any other way to be?"

"I guess not for a man like you."

"And what type of man do you think I am, Nhuri?"

Shyriq leaned closer, invading more of her personal space, but she didn't mind. Hearing her name roll off his tongue and the smell of citrus and musk on his body had Nhuri in a trance. He could stay in her space, in her face, for as long as he pleased.

"The type that knows exactly what he wants and gets it."

Shyriq's head bobbed forward. "That would be true only under one condition."

"And what is that?"

"Knowing what I want and getting it is one thing. Who and what I want has to be willing to get got."

He was smooth. Too damn smooth, and Nhuri felt herself giving in.

"As long as you're up to the chase, I'm sure you'll be just fine," she said, teasingly patting his muscular arm.

Shyriq smirked. "Yeah. A bit of chasing never hurt me. So, what's next for you?"

"After we leave here?" Nhuri questioned.

Surely, he wasn't asking her to leave with him. Not that she hadn't run the idea through her mind since perching beside him. Shyriq chuckled, hearing the apprehension in her tone. She'd misinterpreted his question.

"No. As for work," he explained.

Nhuri let out a breathy laugh. "Why does everyone keep asking me that?"

"Probably because you don't strike me as the type of woman to sit around and do nothing," he answered, studying her over the rim of his glass before taking a sip.

Nhuri held his gaze. "Do I?"

"You do," Shyriq replied confidently. "Correct me if I'm wrong, though."

"You're not. I do want to take a break from work, though. At least for a few weeks to just enjoy life, you know?"

He wish he could agree with her. "I haven't been able to do that in a while, so enjoy it for both of us."

"I sure will."

"What type of work are you looking to get into?" Shyriq asked.

Nhuri didn't want to talk about jobs, working, nine-to-fives, or none of that. She was looking to get into him, and the more she watched his mouth move, the more she wanted to feel his lips on her. But he kept the conversation light for now so she'd play along.

"Something in marketing, but I'm not sure which direction yet. I'm still trying to decide if I want to work for someone else or start a business of my own."

Intrigued, Shyriq lifted a brow. A smile spread across his face. "Yeah? That's solid. I like that."

"Do you?" Nhuri jested.

"Yeah. Nothing wrong with working for someone else, but if you can build your own empire, why not go for it? That's a smart move and some boss shit."

Nhuri bit her bottom lip, suppressing the unexpected warmth his words sent through her body. There he went again, talking as if he wanted the best for her, and Nhuri was eating it up.

"Strong on the word *if*," she chuckled. "Starting your own business is a lot."

"But it's worth it. I'm sure you'll figure it out. You just need the right people in your corner to keep giving you that push."

Nhuri tilted her head. "Are you one of those people?"

"I could be," he said and smirked.

She scoffed, but her lips curved into a smile. "I'm going to call you Mr. Smooth from now on."

"Oh, we get nicknames now?" Shyriq chuckled, making her laugh.

He got caught up in the sound but more so in her beauty and couldn't tear his eyes away. Nhuri laughed from the heart, not expecting him to say that.

"You're the one with a slick mouth. Not me," she said.

"I'm not trying to be smooth at all, gorgeous. That's just who I am. How I converse."

Nhuri shook her head, laughing under her breath. "I bet that works out so well for you, huh?"

He didn't answer right away. Shyriq held her gaze with that intense look that returned, then said, "What do you think?"

"I'm still sitting here, aren't I?" Nhuri replied, getting a smirk out of him.

"Indeed, you are. Let me make the best of our time before you get back to your girls. They've been eyeing me since you sat down."

Nhuri laughed. She wanted to look over her shoulder at them but didn't want to make it obvious that they were talking about them.

"They'll be fine," Nhuri said, waving her hand. "They're probably glad I'm over here running my mouth with you. I've been in my own little bubble and haven't had the energy for much else but sulking around the house."

She wasn't sure why she felt the need to explain, but opening up to Shyriq was easy for some reason she hadn't figured out yet. He didn't seem like the type to judge her, and Nhuri appreciated that, plus the attention he continued to give her.

"I get that. Losing a job will make you isolated, but you have good people around you. That makes a huge difference."

"Yes, it does," Nhuri agreed. "They haven't stopped checking on me."

"What about you? You the type to check up on your people like that?"

Nhuri pursed her lips. "Of course. I'm a drop-everything-and-pull-up-if-and-when-they-need-me type of friend," she said confidently.

"Yeah, I figured you were."

"And what made you come to that conclusion?" Nhuri questioned.

"The day I popped up at your sister's house. You were ready to beat my ass thinking I disrespected her," Shyriq said and chuckled. "That's not even how I get down."

Nhuri laughed. "Listen. I don't play about my sister, okay? The quickest way to piss me off or get cursed out is to come for her."

Shyriq licked his lips. "I can tell. I love that. It means you were raised right."

The underlying mention of their upbringing made Nhuri think of their deceased parents. For a moment, she could only stare at him, feeling a strange but pleasant heat settle in her stomach—the good kind. She cleared her throat, reaching for her water again.

"What about you?"

"What about me?" Shyriq asked.

"You quick to go to war about your people?"

Shyriq nodded. "Always."

Nhuri narrowed her eyes. "Okay . . . That wasn't vague at all," she said, making them chuckle.

"My fault. But yes, I will go to war about my people. I don't let too many get close to me, but the ones I do can come to me for whatever and are well cared for."

Nhuri swallowed, realizing he meant every word he said, from him showing up at Natalia's home to tipping her the two times she'd served him and now. Although they were just talking, Shyriq made her feel comfortable and cared about her, even though he didn't know much about her. That . . . was an art. The type of skill a man who didn't bluff about anything could only possess.

Before she could respond, the bartender appeared with two shot glasses. One was filled with the same amber liquid Shyriq had in his glass and tequila for Nhuri.

She eyed the glass, then Shyriq. "Are you trying to get me drunk?"

He chuckled. "Nah. Not at all. Just figured you could use a little more celebrating."

She hesitated, then picked up the shot. "In that case, cheers to us."

Shyriq lifted a brow. "Us?"

"What you're celebrating with me, right?"

He smirked and lifted his glass. "I am, gorgeous. Cheers to you and the much-needed rest from work you're about to take and every future endeavor with your name on it. It's already yours."

Nhuri hesitated, letting his words sink in. They were much more heartfelt than she expected, but what was new? Shyriq had been surprising her with his words since day one. Nothing would change now. They raised their glasses, their fingers brushing before tapping the bar and tossing them back.

Nhuri exhaled, setting down the glass. "Damn, that's smooth."

Shyriq nodded. "Had you not already been drinking clear, I would've had you drink some whiskey."

"Some whiskey or your whiskey?"

Shyriq leaned to whisper in her ear. "Not anyone else."

The warmth of his breath against her ear made Nhuri shudder. He could whisper sweet nothings in her ear for the rest of the day, and she wouldn't have minded at all. He settled back into his seat, and she shook her head while smiling.

"I don't know what you're up to, but I feel like I should be concerned."

He smirked. "You're worried?"

Nhuri met his gaze. "Not yet."

Shyriq chuckled, his eyes never leaving hers. "Good. You never need to worry with me."

Nhuri wasn't sure what he meant by that, but it sounded good. She wasn't sure what this was or where it was going, but she wasn't in a rush to leave. And judging by the way Shyriq was looking at her, neither was he. Nhuri almost got caught up in it all until she remembered one detailed thing. Glancing down at his left hand, she noticed his bare ring finger and exhaled. Her eyes shot up when he addressed the elephant in the room.

"I'm not a taken man, Nhuri."

"And what exactly does that mean, Shyriq?"

It was the first time she said his name, and he loved hearing it.

"It means that I'm separated and have been for a while now. Legally, I'm still married, but I couldn't be single any more than I am right now."

Nhuri snorted. "Well, until those papers are signed . . . You belong to someone else."

He nodded. "Understandable. What about until they get signed?"

Again, it was an unexpected question that Nhuri didn't have the answer to, but she didn't let him see her sweat.

"I guess we continue to bump into each other," she said, curling her fingers to mimic quotation marks.

Shyriq shook his head. "Nah. I'm not really feeling that."

She lifted a brow. "Oh. So, what I say doesn't matter?"

"It does, and I heard you, but let's compromise," he said, grabbing his wallet.

Nhuri looked on with curiosity as he pulled out a card and handed it to her. She glanced at the details before locking eyes with him.

"What's this for?"

"For you to call me on your terms, but you can also use that when you're ready for a job. That's my office number."

Nhuri drew her head back. "You think I'm going to work for you?"

"Why do you sound so defensive?" Shyriq asked coolly.

Nhuri shook her head, clearly having misread the time they just spent talking. She didn't know this was a damn interview process.

"You look upset and shouldn't be," Shyriq said, leaning closer. "I told you . . . I take care of mine, Nhuri. And when those papers are signed, that's exactly what you'll be. *Mine.* So, take my card and call me when you're ready . . . for whatever."

Nhuri gulped. His straightforwardness made her nipples tingle and the seat of her panties damp. She felt lightheaded but even bolder, knowing he indeed wanted her. Sweetly, Nhuri kissed his cheek and gave him a quick side hug that Shyriq didn't have time to reciprocate. He held his hand out to help her stand and stood with her.

"That was sweet of you to offer. Just remember what I said if I call," Nhuri reminded him.

Shyriq licked his lips. "I will. Enjoy the rest of your afternoon, gorgeous."

Nhuri walked off without saying another word. Had she, they would've been lewd, and her next actions wouldn't have been suitable for the public. Shyriq had given her a lot to think about, mainly him. Nhuri was pissed that she'd locked herself in the house for so long. Who knows, maybe she would've rerun into him before now. Shyriq was the extra pick-me-up she didn't realize she needed but was more than grateful for.

EIGHT

SHYRIQ HAD BEEN waiting for this day to come.

For months, and even before talks of a divorce were mentioned, Xena had made Shyriq's life miserable. He couldn't pinpoint when the annoyance began, but it hadn't always been. She wasn't the woman he had once fallen and been in love with.

As he sat back in the sleek leather chair, his hands clasped in front of him and his expression neutral, Shyriq looked over Xena's appearance. He hadn't seen her in a while but was shocked to see her wearing a blunt-cut bob with a part down the middle. Long bundles down her back were more of Xena's style, but she decided to switch it up today. She wanted to make a statement that matched her attitude: bold. She'd already made up her mind that she was going to win this battle.

The tension in the room was thick, but Shyriq was relaxed. Xena tried throwing her weight around, demanding they meet at her lawyer, Kelsey's, office, but she forgot who was in control. They met at King's office, and Xena's entitled attitude filled the air before they could sit down. She sat across from him with a smug expression, perched in her seat as if she owned the place and had the upper hand.

However, she was sadly mistaken.

"Gentlemen," Kelsey began. "Good morning."

Shyriq tipped his head. "A good morning it is indeed."

Xena gave a devious grin. "You're saying that now."

"Shall we begin?" King said, getting to the point. Though he was Shyriq's lawyer, he was also a friend and wanted to wrap this up today. Xena had worked his last nerves, and she wasn't even his client.

"Of course," Kelsey said.

As she flipped through divorce settlement papers, Shyriq couldn't help but wonder how they'd gotten to this point. Having been married to someone for five years after being in a relationship for two and then seeing them transform into another person before his eyes was jarring to Shyriq. He wondered if loving her as much as he had, wanting to be the absolute best husband he could be, had blinded him to her wickedness.

"Mrs. Hendrix is—"

"Ms. Lewis," Shyriq corrected Kelsey before she could complete her sentence.

Xena rolled her eyes. "Was that necessary? I'm still your wife."

"On papers and not for long," Shyriq replied.

The perks of being tied to the Hendrix name were why she still enjoyed being addressed by it. It made no sense to Shyriq, who saw it as a sign of disrespect. She could do whatever she wanted and be called whatever name she pleased, except any name tied to him. Xena was coming up off of it today, regardless of whether she wanted to.

Kelsey glanced at Xena before continuing. "Ms. Lewis is seeking spousal support for five years—"

Shyriq laughed. He wasn't trying to disrespect Kelsey, and he wasn't that type of man anyway, but they had him fucked up.

"It's not happening," he said calmly but firmly.

Xena exhaled loudly, dramatically, like she seemed to do most days. She tilted her head as if he was being unreasonable.

"And why not? Were we not married for five years? I was with you when you expanded your business. I sacrificed just as much as you, and I deserve to be compensated."

"Sacrificed?" Shyriq chuckled. "Xena, let's be serious here. I'd hate to continue wasting everyone's time."

"I *am* being serious," she ranted.

Shyriq shook his head. "What exactly did you sacrifice? Your body that was supposed to only be shared with your husband to another man?" His tone was smooth, but his words cut deep. He wanted them to. "Is *that* the sacrifices you're talking about? Because if so, save it."

Xena's smirk faltered, but she recovered quickly. "We had our problems, and you know it. You worked long days and even longer nights. Business trips that left me at home waiting for you. You weren't exactly the present husband, nor were you perfect."

Shyriq knew what she was doing. Trying to play the victim in a situation she caused had been Xena's go-to for months.

"While that may hold some truth, I wasn't the one who stepped out on our marriage. You were. I was handling business while another man was handling you."

They stared at each other long and hard. Shyriq wanted to clarify that despite what she may have felt he lacked in their marriage, he'd never stoop as low and cheat. She did, and now, she meant nothing to him.

Kelsey cleared her throat. "Let's please remain professional."

King finally spoke up. "My client is being incredibly professional considering the circumstances. Now, let's be clear. There is a legally binding prenup in place, which waives spousal support in the event of infidelity. We have undeniable proof that Ms. Lewis violated that clause."

Xena curled her fingers in her lap. "Is that so?"

"It is," King clarified.

"So, that's it? I get absolutely nothing. You're that damn bitter and heartless?" Xena sneered.

Shyriq leaned forward, resting his forearms on the table. His voice dropped an octave but remained steady. "No. Bitter and heartless is running around like you're still entitled to anything with my name attached after disrespecting me. Bitter is thinking you could do what you did and still come out on top." He shook his head. "Me? I just want to wash my hands of you and move on with my life."

Xena's chest rose and fell in anger and frustration. His words didn't hurt her, though they should have. The villain in her wouldn't allow them to or for those emotions to surface. Her right leg bounced as she squeezed the armrest and smiled.

"And let me guess, this has something to do with the bitch you were all cuddled up with at brunch," she said with a grit in her tone.

Her accusation almost threw Shyriq off, but he recovered just as quickly as her jab was tossed. He didn't react or even blink. Shyriq refused to give her the satisfaction of knowing she'd gotten under his skin. Nhuri had nothing to do with this. Instead of calling out her jealousy, he tilted his head slightly.

"You're worried about the wrong things. Focus on right now and what you *won't* be getting out of me," he said callously, uncaring about her feelings.

Xena scoffed, rolling her eyes. "My point proved. You want to spend the money I rightfully deserve on some new ho."

"Why is what I do with *my* money any of your concern? Haven't you spent enough of it on your fake *girls'* trips?"

While Shyriq thought he was funding an experience for Xena and her friends to share, that was far from the truth. Sloppily, she'd used money from their shared account to fund her affairs. Hotels, trips, gifts, lunch dates, and who knows what else she had splurged on were on Shyriq's dime. That was the proof he needed to get out of paying spousal support, and thanks to his financial advisor, he'd gotten it.

"Actually, the girls and I enjoyed plenty of trips. I don't know who this heartless man is you're trying to portray, but I know better."

Shyriq sat back, exhaling through his nose. "You *knew* me. Past tense."

Kelsey had clearly gotten in way over her head and knew that with the proof they had, there was no ground to stand on. But she wasn't leaving out of there without Xena getting something, regardless of whether or not she was in the wrong.

"Okay. Since you aren't willing to agree on five years of spousal support, how about four?" Kelsey countered.

Shyriq shook his head. "Nope."

"You *are* aware that your client violated the prenup?" King asked Kelsey.

"I'm aware of what you're accusing my client of. We can go before a judge with your proof, but we both know they'd like to avoid the courtroom if possible."

Xena's smirk returned. She was one hell of an actress and knew that if this were taken to court, the judge would likely rule in her favor of receiving something. She wasn't sure what proof Shyriq had, but she didn't care. Shyriq, on the other hand, knew if this went to court, she'd look like the fool she was.

"So, it's best if you just agree. I mean, what's five years to a wealthy man such as yourself?" she said tauntingly.

Okay. So, she wants to play. Game on, Shyriq thought before ending all possibility of her trying to run game.

"Imagine standing before a judge and a room full of people, and you get denied alimony all because you couldn't keep your legs closed. How embarrassing," he said and laughed.

Xena's face heated with embarrassment. "Fuck you, Shyriq."

"That's what you could've been doing instead of cheating," he said and shrugged. "Your loss."

She was trying to uphold an image; if they went to court, it would be shattered. No one except those close to them knew the details behind their separation, and Xena wanted to keep it that way.

"Are you willing to come to a compromise?" Kelsey asked.

Shyriq's nostrils flared. He was tired of going back and forth. The longer he was legally married, the longer he had to endure Xena's bullshit. Leaning toward King, he whispered something in his ear. King thought for a second before nodding.

"We'll agree to a one-time settlement," King said.

Xena sucked her teeth. "Of course you would."

"Are you okay with that?" Kelsey asked her, and she gave a curt nod.

"Sure. Let me write down a number."

King and Shyriq shared a look, already knowing that she was about to be on some bullshit. Xena scribbled a number on a notepad, showed it to Kelsey, and slid it in Shyriq's direction.

"You done lost your damn mind. I'm not giving you $2,000,000 for fucking another man."

He was trying to keep his cool, but Xena had really taken it there.

"For my pain and suffering," Xena smirked.

"It looks like we'll be seeing you in court," King said, gathering his belongings.

Xena panicked as he began neatly stacking paperwork. She was sure Shyriq would agree to the amount. He had it to give, but that didn't mean he would hand it over willingly. Going before a judge and having her affair broadcasted would be more shameful than the act itself in her eyes. Coming to her senses, Xena leaned in Kelsey's direction. She whispered a number in her ear.

"Seven hundred thousand," Kelsey countered.

Shyriq sucked his teeth. "Two hundred fifty thousand, and that's my final number before I show you how heartless I can really be in this motherfucka," he hissed, staring into Xena's eyes.

Xena hated how aroused she got from his words alone, and it annoyed her to no end, knowing that he still had that effect on her.

Rolling her eyes, she said, "Fine. I guess that'll do."

"Wait," Kelsey said. "Are you sure? That's not—"

"She made her decision, and we've made ours. Two hundred fifty thousand dollars is the settlement we agreed upon, and King will have the paperwork drawn up and emailed by the end of the week," Shyriq said, cutting off Kelsey.

He no longer cared about being respectful to either of them. He came up with that option because it avoided long-term financial obligations, kept Xena from returning for more money later, and cut all ties with her. Having to pay her a monthly sum would give her the upper hand, but that wasn't happening on his watch. It was either the settlement or embarrassment, and he was glad she had chosen wisely. Either way, he was about to be a free man.

Xena laughed bitterly while shaking her head. "I should've drained your ass for much more when I had the chance."

Shyriq's nostrils flared. "You're pathetic. I hope it was worth it."

Xena stood from her seat. "Trust me . . . I've never felt freer in my life."

She grabbed her designer purse off the table just as Kelsey stood.

"I'll be on the lookout for your email. Nice doing business with you, gentlemen. Enjoy your day," Kelsey said, keeping it professional.

"Girl, fuck them and their day. Let's go," Xena spat.

Shyriq shook his head and scrolled his emails as her six-inch heels clicked sharply against the marble floor. She stormed out, muttering under her breath as if *she* were the one who had been wronged. Shyriq waited a beat after the door closed to look up at King.

"Can you believe her?" Shyriq asked. "Two million? She must think I'm a sucker for real."

King chuckled. "She was so confident too. That's a damn shame, man. If anything, she owes you. Has she even apologized after all this time?"

"Nah, but you know what? I don't even care. It won't change anything, and I'm over blaming myself for her fuckup. Once we get those papers signed, she'll be a thing of the past."

King nodded. "She will. So, you celebrating tonight?"

"Not yet. Wait until it's official and throw me the biggest damn party the city has ever seen," Shyriq joked.

He'd never put his business out there like that. Their wedding was over the top, and that's not how he wanted it to end. He was relieved and could finally begin moving on with his life as he saw fit. Less worries meant more time to focus on his business. Shyriq may not have been a good husband in Xena's eyes, but he damn sure knew how to get money. That was how he was about to celebrate.

NINE

NHURI SAT CROSS-LEGGED on her couch with her MacBook perched on a table tray in front of her. She'd been lounging around her house all day and had finally decided to be somewhat productive. The half glass of wine she was sipping on was her motivation. It wasn't quite five o'clock in Kansas City, but it was five somewhere.

Releasing a heavy sigh, she continued scrolling through job listings on Indeed while an episode of *The Jamie Foxx Show* played on the TV. It was the only sound throughout the apartment besides the clicks of her mouse and occasional typing. Her eyes glazed over the redundant descriptions, and she rolled them.

"Why does everything have to be a fast-paced environment," she mumbled.

That wasn't her style of work. Nhuri was strategic. A thinker. All of this corporate jargon in every description was the same, and it started to get on her nerves and made her consider entrepreneurship. At least then, she'd know what she was getting herself into. She exhaled sharply and took a swig of her wine, clicking out of yet another listing that didn't hold her interest. When her phone buzzed beside her, she barely glanced at the screen before answering.

"Yeah," she grumbled.

"Girl, don't answer the phone like that," Jazmyn laughed. "Who pissed in your coffee?"

Nhuri smirked. "I'm actually sipping some wine."

"Yeah, well, it doesn't seem to be doing the job of relaxing you. You sound tense."

She didn't just sound tense; she was. Leaning her head against the back of the couch, Nhuri rubbed her temples.

"I'm over searching for jobs already. They either have these ridiculous expectations, want you to have twenty years of experience for an entry-level position, or pay you pennies for a damn senior role. It's ridiculous."

"It's sad, honestly," Jazmyn said, her blinker sounding in the background. "But you just started looking again. Give it some time. Something will pop up when you least expect it."

"I need something to pop up now," Nhuri muttered. "If they ask me to pick up another shift at the club, I'm going to quit."

Jazmyn couldn't help but laugh, knowing how serious she was. "I believe you. But that's your only income now, so don't mess it up 'cause you're frustrated. Do you need help with bills or anything?"

"No. Plus, you just hooked me up with some food stamps. You don't have to do anything else," Nhuri reassured her.

Jazmyn sucked her teeth. "Girl, please don't do that. Those food stamps weren't even mine. You know my cousin gets like eight hundred a month."

"Damn. They giving them out like that?" Nhuri chuckled. "Maybe I need to apply."

"You should. You are unemployed. You'd get approved the same day too. It might not be much, but it'll save you some money in your pocket."

Nhuri nodded. "Yeah. I'll see. Gotta apply for a job before I can apply for some damn food."

"You know what your problem is?" Jazmyn asked in a playful tone but laced with the truth. "You don't like asking for help—ever."

Nhuri smirked slightly. "That's not true."

Jaz scoffed. "It's very true. You'd rather stress yourself out than admit you need help. There's nothing wrong with that, boo. I promise."

Nhuri didn't feel that way but wouldn't tell Jazmyn that. And she didn't have to. Jazmyn knew her best friend better than anyone. They'd been friends for eighteen years, so there wasn't much they could get past each other.

"I'm not going to confirm or deny that," Nhuri grumbled, making Jazmyn chuckle.

"You don't have to. I confirmed it for you." The line fell silent for a second, and then Jazmyn shouted, "Wait!"

"What?" Nhuri panicked. "What's the matter?"

"Didn't you say something about that man from brunch offering you a job?" Jazmyn asked.

Nhuri squinted as if trying to recall the day. They left brunch, headed to another spot, and then linked up with a few of Jazmyn's cousins at a day party. By the time Nhuri got home Sunday night, all she could do was take the quickest shower ever and climb into bed. It'd been a while since she had that much fun, and trying to recall every conversation she had that day was a bit fuzzy. But she did vividly remember Shyriq and her holding a lengthy conversation.

"Shyriq?" Nhuri questioned.

"Yes, girl. The way y'all were so deep in conversation, you'd think he offered you a kidney," Jazmyn teased.

Nhuri snorted and laughed. "Jaz, please."

"I'm for real. You probably don't even remember him giving you his card. When you came back to the table, you were like, '*That fine-ass man talking about call him if I'm interested in a job. Sir, I'm interested in riding your face and wetting up that luscious-ass beard.'*

Nhuri blinked, her mind rewinding to the weekend. The brunch spot had been loud, the drinks strong, and the conversation had flowed easily. Shyriq had slid her his business card near the end, and she had tucked it into her purse without a second thought. Between job hunting and life's little stresses, she had completely forgotten about it.

Nhuri's jaw dropped. "I did *not* say that."

"Yes, you did, ma'am. And was proud too."

Smiling, Nhuri tilted her head to the right. "Hmm. You might be right. He does have such a sittable face and lips. Whew."

"Girl," Jazmyn screeched through laughter. "Focus! Worry about sitting that unemployed coochie on his face *after* you find his card."

Cackling, Nhuri scooted the table tray out of her way and stood up. She grabbed the purse she wore on Sunday from the bench near the front door and sat back on the couch.

"I swear I forgot all about it," she muttered, digging through the small pockets.

Her fingers brushed against the matte black card beside a folded twenty-dollar bill before pulling it out. Nhuri stared at the embossed gold letters that the sun from her patio window hit just right. Shyriq's name was there, along with the number to his office.

For you to call me on your terms, but you can also use that when you're ready for a job. That's my office number.

Nhuri recalled that part of their conversation. His offer had been unexpected almost as much as his presence, which shouldn't have been anything new at this point.

"Did you find it?" Jazmyn asked.

She flipped the card through her fingers. "Yeah, I still have it."

"Okay," Jazmyn dragged. "Are you going to call?"

Nhuri glanced at the time on her MacBook. It was only 4:37. Still business hours, but she wondered if she should wait until tomorrow. As if Jazmyn could read her mind, she interrupted her thoughts.

"Nope. I already know what you're thinking."

"Do you?" Nhuri teased.

"I do. You're trying to think of a way to get out of calling him."

Nhuri playfully rolled her eyes. "You swear you know me," she chuckled and sighed. "He was cool, but maybe he was just being nice, Jaz. I'd feel like I'm taking advantage. Plus, I'm sure the *real* reason he gave me his card was to get to know me better."

"Okay. There's nothing wrong with that. Get to know him and see what he has to offer personally and for a job. Men with money love helping women they like, and he offered. You didn't beg the man for a job, but shit . . . You do need one."

The friends shared a laugh, easing some of the unwanted tension Nhuri felt creeping in.

"I hear you. But," she mumbled, thinking about Natalia and what she might say. Mixing business with pleasure, especially so close to home, was a dangerous game.

"But what? He was feeling you, and if he weren't, you wouldn't be holding his card in your hand. I'm sure he's been waiting for you to call."

Nhuri wondered if that was true. It was Wednesday, three days later, and surely, Shyriq hadn't been sitting around waiting for her to ring his line. *A man like him doesn't have time to sit around waiting*, she thought.

"You know I hate mixing business with . . . whatever this is," Nhuri said.

Jazmyn huffed. "You always act like taking an opportunity is the same as owing somebody your firstborn. Just call the man."

Nhuri smirked but didn't respond. Instead, she stared at the card a little longer, tapping it against her knee.

"Fine," she finally gave in. "Should I wait for tomorrow? It's almost five."

"No! Do it now, or I'm disowning you. Stop being scary."

Nhuri chuckled. "Okay, okay."

"I'm serious, Nhuri. You had better hang up this phone and call him, then call me right back and let me know how it goes. I have to get ready for this date."

Nhuri's brows dipped. "Wait. A date with who?"

"One of my coworker's cousins. He's fine, so we'll see."

"Don't embarrass us," Nhuri joked.

"Me?" Jazmyn laughed, then added, "Never. You need to focus on securing this job. Don't be awkward either. I know how you get when you overthink shit," she teased.

"Girl, whatever. I'm calling now before it hits five."

"Okay. Good luck."

Nhuri thanked her and hung up. Exhaling an audible breath, she typed the number into her keypad. She paused before calling, letting her mind replay Shyriq's deep voice. He'd been so caring that day, and his generosity prompted her to press the green phone icon. She stood up and stretched, needing to move her body to rid herself of the nerves building up. The sound of the phone ringing was all she heard until the line clicked, and a friendly voice answered.

"Good afternoon! This is Michelle with Great Hendrix Co. How can I help you?"

Nhuri was taken aback. She was sure she'd called Shyriq's main office number. She cleared her throat, trying to keep her voice steady.

"Hi. My name is Nhuri. I was trying to reach Shyriq. This is his office number, correct?"

She needed clarification.

"Yes, it is. Mr. Hendrix is currently in a meeting, but if you'd like, I can take a message for him and have him return your call as soon as he can."

Nhuri hesitated, weighing her options. "Can you just let him know Nhuri called?"

"Yes, of course. What's your last name, and what does this call pertain to?"

Oh, they're real professionals around there, Nhuri thought proudly. She loved it!

"My last name is Coleman. It's a follow-up to a conversation we had Sunday afternoon. Let him know I'm interested."

Nhuri heard keys clicking, and then they stopped.

"Got it! I'll make sure he gets the message," Michelle assured her.

"Thank you. Have a good day," Nhuri said.

Michelle told her to do the same, and the call ended. Nhuri flopped down on the couch, sliding her phone onto the table tray. She'd built up all the courage to call, only to be prompted to leave a message. Well, it was better than nothing. His offer couldn't have come at a better time. She had no job or clear direction on where she wanted to go; this was the only thing that made sense so far. Taking a chance on something or someone with more ambition than she did at the moment wasn't the worst.

Figuring she'd hear from Shyriq tomorrow, Nhuri tuned into her show on TV. She laughed at Jamie doing something ridiculous when her phone vibrated along the wooden tray, startling her. Her brows dipped at the unknown number, and she knew it couldn't have been Shyriq. It'd only been twenty minutes since she called. Her heart skipped a beat as she swiped to answer the call.

"Hello."

"Hey, Nhuri. It's Shyriq. I got your message." His voice was calm and oddly warming through the receiver.

Nhuri tried to keep her tone casual. "Hi. How are you?"

Shyriq chuckled. He was stressed out, but that wasn't something she had to worry about. "I'm good now that you finally put my number to use."

He was teasing her, and Nhuri's nerves settled some.

"Let me find out you were waiting by the phone for me to call." Her words came out a bit more flirty than she intended for them to, and Shyriq ate them up.

"Would that be a problem if I was?" he questioned, making her smile drop and her nipples pebble.

Something about his words in that husky tone led her to believe him.

"I guess not, considering you did offer me a job," Nhuri said, veering the conversation to why she'd called in the first place.

"I did. That's if you're interested."

Nhuri squinted. She was trying her hardest not to blur the lines, but Shyriq wasn't making his approach any clearer. *Was I interested in the job or him? Hell, is doing him the job because I'll take that too?* Nhuri thought and chuckled.

"You there?" Shyriq asked.

She cleared her throat. "Yes, I'm here, and I'm interested. Can you provide me with details of the position?"

"My assistant."

His answer was so plain and direct that Nhuri thought he was joking.

"I'm sorry . . . *your* assistant?" she questioned.

"Yes. You spoke with Michelle earlier. She's currently my assistant but will be taking maternity leave shortly. I'd need a permanent assistant to pick up where she's leaving off. Is that something you're interested in?"

His explanation sounded believable, but Nhuri wasn't sure it was a position she wanted to take. She was overqualified for the job, and she knew it. Chewing her bottom lip, she thought about what it could mean if she accepted his offer. Maybe it wasn't the smartest or the safest thing to do, but then again, what was safety when she was already out of her comfort zone?

"Honestly, no," she admitted, and Shyriq chuckled. "I'm not sure I'm the right person for that position. I have an MBA in international business. What could I possibly do as your assistant with my skills?"

"You could do much more than what I'm sure is running through your mind. Answering calls and taking messages isn't the only thing Michelle does. It gets pretty hectic around here, but in a good way," Shyriq explained. "I could use someone on my team with your drive and attitude."

Nhuri's pulse quickened at the easy confidence in his words. He seemed confident in her skills, but she hadn't shown him any qualifications yet. Deep down, she knew where this was headed, and Nhuri wasn't sure if she was ready for the risk. But something about Shyriq made the danger feel like it might be worth it.

"Okay," she agreed.

"Yeah?" Shyriq asked, shocked.

Nhuri chuckled. "Yes. You sound surprised."

"I am. I didn't have to do much convincing."

"Well, that's where you're wrong. Once the interview takes place, I can decide if being your assistant is something I want to do."

The underlying message and tone in her words made Shyriq smirk. He had no plans to have an interview. If Nhuri wanted the job, it was hers. But he decided to follow protocol.

"Of course. Swing by the office tomorrow for an interview."

"Um," Nhuri hesitated. Tomorrow was much too soon, and she wanted to prepare. Testing to see if Shyriq would be a lenient boss, she said, "I can't make it tomorrow, but Friday works perfectly."

"Friday it is then," Shyriq agreed more quickly than she thought he would. "Does three o'clock work?"

That was much later in the day than she'd like, but Nhuri agreed. "Yes. Three o'clock is fine. Adding it to my calendar now."

"Michelle will also add it to mine," Shyriq chuckled. "You've been good?"

"Yes," Nhuri answered quietly.

"Getting that rest you need, I hope."

Nhuri smirked. "More than enough sleep with so much time on my hands."

"I bet. Those were the good ol' days," Shyriq said. "Let me not hold you up any longer. I'll see you on Friday."

"See you then."

"I look forward to it."

Before he could hang up, Nhuri said, "And, Shyriq . . . Thank you."

He felt her gratefulness through the phone. "You're more than welcome, gorgeous."

Nhuri blushed as they hung up. If he was going to be her boss, he'd have to keep the compliments and pet names to himself. Maybe Jazmyn was right. It wasn't about owing anybody or taking advantage. Perhaps it was just about taking an opportunity when it was handed to her.

TEN

FRIDAY HAD COME around quicker than Nhuri thought it would. She'd spent most of yesterday preparing her resume and trying not to talk herself out of going. When Natalia called to see what she was doing, it took everything in her not to spill the beans. It wasn't that she didn't want her sister to know she had an interview with Shyriq, but more so how it came about. An interview was one thing. Flirting with a married man was another. Separated or not, Nhuri knew Natalia wouldn't approve of her behavior or actions.

Nevertheless, Nhuri had kept her plans for today to herself. If she accepted the job, she would gladly tell Natalia what she'd been up to. Nothing was final until she saw the extent of her duties and pay. Those two outweighed everything when considering this position. As nervous as she was, Nhuri didn't let that stop her from showing up fifteen minutes early. Her mama always taught them that being on time was late and to respect people's time because they'd want the same courtesy in return.

Nhuri smoothed her hands over her high-waisted, wide-leg black slacks as she entered Great Hendrix Co. headquarters' sleek, modern lobby. She had chosen the outfit carefully. It was polished but not too corporate. Her fitted white blouse was tucked in neatly, accentuating her waist without being too form-fitting, and the cream-colored blazer she wore over it provided just the right amount of structure. Her stilettos clicked against the polished floors, and her steps were steady even though her stomach disagreed.

She was nervous, but she wouldn't let it show.

The distillery's main office was impressive. The kind of space that felt both luxurious and powerful. Floor-to-ceiling windows let in an abundance of natural light that bounced off the marble reception desk in the center of the room. A few plush chairs were in the waiting area, but Nhuri didn't sit. She wasn't about to look unsure of herself before she even got started.

A young woman at the front desk, dressed in a navy blue dress with a name tag that read Ashley clipped on the left, glanced up from her computer and smiled politely.

"Good afternoon, welcome to GHC. How can I help you?"

Nhuri adjusted her purse strap on her shoulder and cleared her throat. "Good afternoon. I have an interview today. Nhuri Coleman."

The receptionist nodded, clicking away at her keyboard before checking something on her screen. "Got it. Give me just a second."

Nhuri exhaled slowly, forcing herself to relax. She had prepared for this and even spent yesterday evening researching the company. GHC was spoken of highly by various people in different careers, and the company's work ethic and environment were praised. That was a good sign, and Nhuri felt ready.

Or at least she thought she was. She spotted a tall, curvy woman with a lovely silk press striding toward her in grey slacks and a cream top that accentuated her belly. Even while carrying a child, she moved confidently, silently telling Nhuri she wasn't anything to play with.

"Nhuri?" the woman asked, her voice smooth and professional. Nhuri nodded. "Yes, that's me."

"Hi. I'm Michelle, Mr. Hendrix's executive assistant. I'll be taking you back."

Nhuri blinked. "Oh, I thought I was meeting with HR?"

Michelle gave her a soft smile. "No. Not at the moment. That will hopefully all come later."

Nhuri exhaled and nodded. "Okay. Sounds good. Mr. Hendrix told me that I'd be filling your position. I'm sure you're ready to kick your feet up."

Michelle blew out a deep breath and rubbed her belly. "I most definitely am, so please kill this interview," she pleaded teasingly.

"I'll try my best."

"And that's all you can do. Please follow me," Michelle said with a wave of her hand.

Nhuri's heels clicked against the hallway floors as they moved deeper into the building. The glass walls and doors gave a glimpse into different offices. Some were occupied by people locked into meetings, others empty but immaculately designed. This wasn't just some random whiskey company. Shyriq and his family had built something profound. A business of opulence that operated at a high level.

Michelle stopped at a door near the end of the hall, tapping twice before pushing it open.

"You can go in," she said, stepping aside.

Nhuri hesitated for only a fraction of a second before squaring her shoulders and walking through. Floor-to-ceiling windows cast natural light over the office. Shelves were lined with a mix of books, awards, and bottles from the distillery's premium collection. Behind a dark wood desk, Shyriq sat casually yet with an air of quiet dominance.

Unlike the suited executives she expected to meet, Shyriq wore a black crewneck that hugged his broad frame and a gold watch gleaming against his deep brown skin. His beard was freshly groomed, and his cologne instantly hit her. It was warm and rich, with a subtle spice that made her head swim for a second.

He didn't look up immediately, focusing on whatever was on his phone. But then, with an exhale, he set down the device and leaned back in his chair, finally locking eyes with her.

Nhuri swallowed, and Shyriq smiled as if he'd missed seeing her face.

"Thank you, Michelle. You can head out for the day," Shyriq said.

Michelle mumbled *Thank God* under her breath, and it took everything in Nhuri not to chuckle. When the door shut, they stared at each other for a few seconds before he gave her instructions.

"Please, have a seat."

His tone was casual, but there was an underlying authority in it that had her legs moving before she even realized what she was doing. Shyriq watched her the entire way. Mainly her hips, that would surely be a distraction. He shook his head and focused on her face, which was even more taunting than her body. When Nhuri finally sat down, Shyriq exhaled. He'd been holding his breath, trying to control his tongue since his mind ventured to unprofessional thoughts.

"So," he said, resting his elbow on the arm of his chair and dragging a hand down his beard. "You made it."

Nhuri frowned slightly. "I was invited to an interview."

He smirked at her response. "That you were. You sounded a bit apprehensive on the phone is all."

"I was, but for a reason. I'm technically overqualified to be an assistant," Nhuri said.

She wanted to let him know she was taking a risk even considering this position.

"You are, but I hope you can consider your options. I'm sure Natalia has mentioned what a joy it is to work here," he said.

Nhuri gave him a tight smile. "Actually, she hasn't said much about the company or you."

Shyriq's brows dipped. "Interesting."

He was sure Nhuri had given her the rundown about him pushing up on her at Patio, but it was clear she hadn't. Nhuri found it amusing that he thought they sat up gossiping about him. That wasn't the case at all, and Shyriq sensed it. He could also tell that Nhuri was serious about this interview, so he planned to tone down the informality.

"I have my resume prepared if you'd like to take a look," she offered, wondering why that wasn't the first thing he asked for.

Going along with it, Shyriq stuck out his hand. Nhuri opened the shiny black folder and handed the papers to him. Though he didn't need to read it, he was highly impressed with her skills. From his quick scan alone, Shyriq had no doubt that she'd excel on his team . . . in more ways than one.

"An MBA in international business." Shyriq wasn't asking a question.

"Yes," Nhuri replied, keeping her voice steady.

"Fluent in Spanish and French," he continued. "Worked in market expansion, competitive analysis, even handling strategic partnerships overseas."

As he read her credentials, Nhuri checked herself. She had no reason to be nervous, and this was more of an opportunity for Shyriq than it was for her. He needed her, *not* the other way around, even though she needed a job. His tone was smooth yet firm, leading her to believe he was evaluating her.

Finally, Shyriq set the papers aside and leaned back in his chair, leveling her with a gaze that pinned Nhuri in place. "Why did your last job fire you?"

The bluntness caught her off guard. She hadn't been expecting that.

She straightened her shoulders. "Because I wasn't willing to uproot to another state and leave my family for two months."

One brow lifted slightly. "That's all?"

Nhuri nodded. "Yes, unless you're privy to something I don't know."

He'd asked as if he had the inside scoop on her termination. Shyriq didn't, but he found it strange that a company, one of such success, would let go of someone with Nhuri's credentials. It was baffling, to say the least.

"I was just wondering. Your duties here will be slightly different than what you did there. Is that something you're willing to take on?" Shyriq questioned.

Nhuri wanted to tell him it was his decision, but instead of smarting off, she answered his question.

"Yes. Being an assistant can't be that hard, can it?"

Shyriq smirked. "You tell me."

Nhuri wished Michelle or somebody would have warned her about Shyriq. He was somewhat arrogant, which frustrated Nhuri *and* turned her on. Instead of trying to win her over with what he had to offer, Shyriq wanted her to understand that much more came with being his right-hand man. Well, his right-hand woman in this case.

"I have the experience to make an impact here and know how to move in high-stakes environments. This job might be titled 'assistant,' but we both know it's more than that," Nhuri said.

Shyriq leaned back, tapping his fingers against the desk. "It is."

Nhuri nodded, wanting him to delve deeper.

He exhaled, glancing at her resume once more before pushing it aside. "This isn't a run-errands, grab-coffee, schedule-meetings type of role. I need someone who can anticipate what I need before I ask for it. Sure, you'll manage my schedule, but you'll also handle vendor contracts, investor meetings, and overseeing projects directly affecting GHC's growth."

Nhuri nodded, absorbing the weight of the responsibilities. "Okay. Doesn't sound excruciating."

Shyriq continued. "Depends on your tolerance. You'll be working with distributors, tracking market trends, and making sure I'm not walking into any bullshit deals. That means long hours, last-minute changes, and me being on your ass every step of the way."

His gaze was unwavering, wanting her to understand fully the extent of her role.

She didn't waver. "I can handle it."

A slow smirk ghosted over his lips, but it disappeared just as quickly. Shyriq nodded once. "Okay. Good. Any questions for me?"

"Yes. What would my salary be?"

"One hundred five thousand. You'll receive a $5,000 sign-on bonus and full benefits. The welcome packet will include all other details, including sick leave, PTO, and other incentives."

Nhuri was pleased with his response but didn't let it show. A sign-on bonus was right up her alley, and she couldn't wait to go shopping for a new wardrobe, stationery, and add some to her savings account. But she had to play it off as if she had other options. Make Shyriq on edge about her decision since he wanted to play.

"That all sounds good," she said, sounding unimpressed.

"So, you accept the offer?"

She twisted her glossed lips side to side. "Possibly. GHC sounds like a good home, but I have to weigh my options. Thank you for offering me this opportunity to—"

Shyriq shook his head, stopping her midsentence. He wasn't falling for her games. "You don't have to do all that."

Her brows knitted. "Do all what?"

"The rehearsed speech," he said, shaking his head. "You don't have to sell me on anything you bring to the table."

Nhuri pressed her lips together, irritation bubbling in her chest. "I was under the impression this was an interview."

"It is." He tilted his head slightly. "But not in the way you think."

She took a slow breath, forcing herself to read between the lines. Shyriq was a confusing man.

"Then how exactly should I be thinking about it?"

"That you already have the position because you did before you stepped foot inside this building or my office."

Nhuri let her guard down some. "Okay," she said slowly and evenly.

Shyriq rested his forearms on the desk, leaning forward slightly. "I was never planning to let you go through HR."

That caught her off guard. "And why is that?"

You know why, he thought.

"This wasn't about them," Shyriq continued. "It was about you. Whether you were serious enough to walk through that door."

He told her to use his card for two reasons, but Nhuri wasn't trying to discuss that here. Or ever again, for that matter.

She stared at him, processing his words. "So . . . What? This wasn't a real interview?"

He shrugged. "Depends. Do you really want the job or not?"

A rush of frustration mixed with confusion flared inside her with his underlying message. "I wouldn't be here if I didn't."

He smirked again, leaning back. "Well, okay. Then it's yours."

Her stomach flipped, but she refused to let the surprise show on her face. "And if I say no?"

"Then you wasted both of our time," he said, shrugging like it didn't matter. But something in his eyes told her he already knew her answer.

Nhuri exhaled slowly, glancing down at his ring finger before locking eyes with him again. "And if I say yes?"

Shyriq's smirk deepened, knowing what was on her mind. His answer would confirm the question she wasn't willing to ask just yet. "Then you start Monday."

"And *all* the paperwork is filled out and ready to go?"

She finally hinted at what Shyriq had been waiting for her to mention since she sat down.

"It is."

Smiling, Nhuri said, "Monday it is then."

"Perfect. Ashley will have a welcome packet waiting for you at the front. You'll need to give her your ID and some other information so you'll be able to enter the building come Monday. Your office is two doors down from here on the right, with a nice courtyard view. Take my number down in case you have any questions or concerns before then."

As if he knew she'd accept, Shyriq had an entire speech ready. Nhuri smirked at his eagerness to get her settled in when he'd just been throwing mixed signals minutes prior. Working for him wouldn't be a walk in the park at all. Especially with the way he kept staring at her.

"I have your office number. Isn't that the one on the card you gave me?" Nhuri answered.

"No. As my assistant, you need my personal cell number so you can contact me directly. This line will transfer to you when I'm out of the office."

Nodding, Nhuri pulled her phone out of her purse and unlocked it.

"Okay. What's your number?"

Shyriq rattled off his cell number, and Nhuri saved it under *Mr. Hendrix.*

"All locked in?" he questioned.

"Yep. I'll contact you *directly* when you're needed. Do I get a tour today?"

Shyriq chuckled. She was testing the boundaries, but that's what he liked about her. She toyed with him just as much as he did with her.

"Unfortunately, you don't. I have another meeting, and Michelle has gone home for the day. She'll show you around on Monday. Be here at seven thirty."

"Is there anything specific I should have waiting upon your arrival?" Nhuri questioned.

Shyriq's eyes darkened some. Her question sounded innocent. One that an assistant had to ask, and he was trying to convince himself that she wasn't fishing for him to step out of character and tell her what he really wanted. Nhuri saw the fire blazing in his eyes and smiled.

"Coffee or tea?" she continued, urging him to break.

Shyriq swallowed. "Sure. A chai latte with almond milk from Sip."

Nhuri took a mental note and nodded. "Got it. I'll see you bright and early on Monday."

She stood, and Shyriq followed suit. He stuck his hand out for her to shake. His large hand swallowed her dainty one, and Nhuri could've sworn she felt him caress her fingers.

"Welcome to GHC, Nhuri. It's a pleasure to have you aboard. Enjoy your weekend."

"You as well."

Nhuri stood on steady legs, much steadier than the ones she entered his office with. She didn't have to see his face to know Shyriq was looking at her ass as she walked to the door; she could feel him. Before she walked out, his voice cut through the air.

"Oh, and Nhuri."

She glanced over her shoulder.

His eyes locked on hers. "Don't make me regret this."

She met his stare with her chin lifted. "You won't."

Nhuri wasn't sure if he meant giving her the job or whatever journey they were about to embark on. Either way, her pulse quickened at the idea of stepping into something much bigger than her role as his assistant.

ELEVEN

NHURI GRIPPED THE steering wheel of her Hyundai a little tighter as she pulled onto Natalia's street. Stopping to grab food and making it to her house during rush-hour traffic should've come with an award. Especially knowing what she was about to tell her. Nhuri's stomach twisted at the thought.

She had run the conversation through her mind a dozen times since leaving Shyriq's office, yet it still didn't feel like she had the right words. It wasn't that she didn't want to tell Natalia; she did. But something about saying it out loud, admitting that she had accepted a job she had never even applied for, didn't sit right with her.

Maybe it was because everything had happened so fast. One moment, she was unemployed, navigating the anxiety of losing her stability, and the next, she was sitting across from Shyriq, being offered an opportunity she hadn't seen coming. It wasn't that she didn't think she deserved it. Honestly, she deserved more and had the skills and the experience. She wasn't worried about that.

What unsettled her was the uncertainty of it all.

What if it didn't work out?

What if this role wasn't what she thought it would be?

What if she'd only accepted because she was desperate to feel grounded again?

Imposter syndrome was on her heavy. Uprooting back home after a breakup was enough to make Nhuri question everything coming her way. It was a feeling she'd grown to accept and hated that she needed something . . . someone to validate them. Exhaling sharply, she pushed the thoughts away. She knew she was overthinking. It was a bad habit of hers that Jazmyn called her out on, but it didn't change the fact that she had to break the news to Natalia.

Natalia would be happy for her, no doubt. She had been one of her biggest supporters, constantly reminding her of how capable she was and how much she deserved to be in rooms where her intelligence and skills could shine.

But what if I let her down? Nhuri thought.

She couldn't help but wonder if things went left that she would have to sit across from Natalia in a few months, explaining why she was back to square one . . . the same way she had to explain what happened between her and Dru. Nhuri hated disappointing people, but more than that, she hated feeling like she had set herself up for failure.

Her fingers drummed against the steering wheel as she parked in front of Natalia's house, staring at the front door as if it'd magically open and spill out all the answers she was looking for. Finally, taking a deep breath, Nhuri grabbed her purse and the food from her passenger seat and stepped out of her car. Using her key to enter, the familiar scent of vanilla and something faintly herbal filled the air. She stepped inside, closing the door behind her. Upon entering the living room, her eyes immediately landed on Natalia with her feet propped up in the recliner and a thick blanket draped over her legs.

"Finally," Natalia exhaled, lowering the footrest. "I was about to send out a search party."

Nhuri rolled her eyes, dropping her purse onto the couch. She set everything on the table before heading to the kitchen to wash her hands.

"You texted me thirty minutes ago, and I said I was on my way."

"Thirty minutes feels like three hours when you're waiting on somebody to bring you food," Natalia said, pouting playfully.

"Well, I'm here now. Let me wash my hands and grab us some real silverware."

She returned with two forks and spoons. Nhuri pulled out the containers of soup, rice, plantains, jerk chicken, and cabbage she'd picked up from their favorite Caribbean spot.

"You're acting like you haven't eaten all day," Nhuri teased, watching Natalia pile up her plate.

"I haven't," Natalia answered, peeling the lid off the soup container.

Since it was hers, she didn't hesitate to dip her spoon into the steaming broth and indulge. She briefly closed her eyes in appreciation of the flavors hitting her tastebuds.

"Mmmm. This is *exactly* what I needed."

"You feeling better?" Nhuri asked.

Natalia nodded. "Yeah. I've been sipping tea since this morning."

Nhuri didn't want to bring up the obvious, so she didn't. Some days were good, and some days caught Natalia by surprise. Thankfully, Raniya was with her daddy for the weekend because Natalia had no energy to parent. They ate in silence for a few minutes before Nhuri broke it.

"So . . . I accepted a job."

Natalia paused midchew, her spoon hovering over the container. "Really? When?"

"Today. That's where I just came from."

"Wait. We talked this morning, and you didn't mention anything about an interview."

Nhuri bit into her bottom lip. "I know. I was waiting to tell you until I made a decision."

Her sister narrowed her eyes playfully. "Mmhm. So, where at? This is exciting. No more hiding out in the house."

Nhuri chuckled to mask her nervousness and prepare for her reaction. "GHC."

Natalia blinked. "GHC?"

Nhuri nodded.

"As in Great Hendrix Co.?"

"Yes."

Natalia's brows lifted in surprise as she set down her fork. "Okay. Back up some. Since when have you been trying to work there?"

"I wasn't," Nhuri admitted. "I had no plans to. You know the girls took me to brunch the other week, and I ran into Shyriq. He bought us shots, we ended up talking at the bar, and I guess I mentioned celebrating my unemployment."

Natalia snorted with laughter. "You're so friendly when you drink."

"Obviously," Nhuri laughed and continued. "He gave me his card and told me to call if I was interested."

Natalia's lips pressed together like she was trying to suppress a knowing smile. "Oh yeah? In him or the position?"

Nhuri chuckled. "Both. But it's not like that. I promise."

"I didn't say anything," Natalia said, but the way her eyes twinkled with mischief told a different story.

Nhuri ignored it, focusing on the food in front of her. "It's a good opportunity. The assistant position is solid, the pay is great, and it's real work more in my field. It's not just busywork. I'll do more than schedule meetings, answer calls, and take notes."

Her excitement made Natalia's expression soften. "I know. Being an assistant is more than that, especially for a corporation like GHC. I'm happy for you, for real. You deserve this."

Nhuri exhaled, some of the tension in her shoulders easing. "Thank you. I thought you'd be upset."

Natalia eyed her carefully. "No. I would've been pissed if you missed out on yet another opportunity because of me. Just because I work there doesn't mean you can't. I'm hard on you because I love you and want the best for you."

"I know you do, and I guess I didn't want to disappoint you. Had me sitting in my car with the bubble guts."

They shared a laugh and ate some more of their food.

"So, whose assistant are you?" Natalia asked, sitting back on the couch while rubbing her stomach.

"Shyriq's."

Natalia coughed harshly, making Nhuri's eyes widen before she reached over to pat her back. Nhuri grabbed her tumbler of ice water, holding the straw out for her to sip.

"I'm good, I'm good," Natalia repeated once her coughing simmered.

Nhuri stared at her and cleared her throat before continuing to eat. "What do you have to say?"

"Nothing. I can't lie and act like I'm not shocked by the position because I am, but you're grown," Natalia said.

"What do you mean?"

"On one hand, I think you're way too qualified. You do my work tasks with ease, Nhuri. I'm talking about in hours when some projects and assignments take days or weeks. I don't know. I guess I'm trying to figure out the motive of it all."

Nhuri nodded. "I know what you mean, and I had second thoughts too, but after reviewing the description and listening to him explain everything, I'm okay with it. There's always room to grow."

"There is, so I won't harp on what I think you should do. I'm just glad you found something I know you'll enjoy and not because you get to be around him," Natalia teased.

"Oh, whatever," Nhuri said, chuckling.

"On another more serious note, is he still married?" Natalia asked.

All the perks about the job were cool to hear, but she needed to know if this man intended to try to play her sister. Job title be damned. Nhuri couldn't be 100 percent sure, and asking in the interview would've been so unprofessional, but she read between the lines. That was enough not to make Natalia flip out.

"No. The papers were filed," Nhuri answered.

"Okay. Good. I know you're not a home wrecker, but you're not exempt from temptation. I'd hate to have to whoop someone's ass for playing with you."

Nhuri grinned. "There won't be any of that. What is Shyriq like as a boss?"

Natalia thought back to her first days of working for GHC. Shyriq had always been kind to her and was spoken of so highly for treating his employees with respect. Not just them but everyone he interacted with. He wasn't Natalia's main boss, but she had been around him enough to know he was a stand-up guy in and out of the office.

"He's not some hard-ass that will make working for him miserable," Natalia said.

Nhuri blew out a deep, exaggerated breath. "Well, thank God for that," she said, and they laughed.

"Just from attending meetings with him and interacting over the years, I can tell he's serious about his company. He comes off as a bit chill and laid-back, but I've witnessed him snap at a few people," Natalia said.

"Comes with the territory," Nhuri concluded.

"Yeah, it does. He's loyal, though. He looks out for those under his wing."

Nhuri nodded, recalling his pop-up at the house that day. As an owner, he didn't have to go out of his way, but he did and ensured Natalia was okay. Back then, Nhuri didn't understand why he did it, but she didn't know the type of man Shyriq was. Slowly, he was showing her.

"That's a good trait."

"It is," Natalia agreed, sipping her water. "He respects your ideas, especially if you can prove they're beneficial and not some mess you just threw together."

Nhuri listened and smirked. "So, he wasn't just being difficult with me for no reason?"

Natalia chuckled. "I'd say no, but he may have been acting that way with you for reasons I don't know about."

She eyed Nhuri, who was blushing. "Maybe, maybe not."

"Mhm," Natalia grinned. "Seriously, though. He's cool. We get great bonuses, have the best company parties, and he makes sure everyone, including family, is cared for. It's not a messy work environment, either. He doesn't play that. He wouldn't have wasted his time if he didn't think you'd fit in or were incapable of the position or something better. He sees something in you. He might push you to be the best or frustrate you with deadlines, but trust me . . . If Shyriq hired you, it's for a reason."

"Yeah, because Michelle is going on maternity leave," Nhuri said, trying to sike herself out of the real reasoning.

"Or because he wanted you," Natalia said. "Own that shit, sis. You can handle a little pressure," she teased.

"I can," Nhuri replied confidently.

"And you will."

Nhuri cleaned up their plates and trash before settling back on the couch. Natalia adjusted the blanket around her legs and got comfortable.

"I'm glad you told me," she said softly. "I know you like to keep things to yourself sometimes, but this is huge, and I'm so proud of you."

Nhuri felt a pang of guilt as her eyes watered. "Thank you. And I know. I just . . . needed to sit with it first."

Natalia nodded in understanding. "Well, now that you have, we need to celebrate. Even if I'm sipping on ginger tea instead of champagne."

Nhuri chuckled, shaking her head. "You're a mess."

Natalia grinned. "And you love me."

Nhuri smiled. "More than you know."

TWELVE

"**I** PROMISE TO GET by there tomorrow, Mama," Shyriq said, pulling into the parking lot of the cigar lounge.

It was packed, but that was to be expected for a Saturday evening. He managed to find a parking spot somewhat near the door when a car pulled out. Backing in, Shyriq could hear his mama's next words before she said them.

"Mmhm," Joyce hummed. "I sure hope so. I'm starting to think you have a woman who's been keeping you hostage."

Shyriq chuckled. "Not quite. When I get one and decide to settle down again, you'll be the first to know."

"Now, *that's* what I like to hear. I'm glad that hussy didn't scare you off from finding a wholesome woman who actually loves you and isn't out to get your money."

"Yeah," Shyriq agreed, knowing Joyce would keep him on the phone if he said any more or fed into the conversation.

She liked Xena at one point in time. Joyce even loved her, but she rubbed her the wrong way one too many times, so now, she doesn't care for her at all. Once she found out she'd been cheating on her son, Joyce gave Xena an old-fashioned cursing out and blocked her number.

"And who doesn't mind starting a family? I want grandchildren at some point in my life, Shyriq," Joyce said.

"You're going to live a long life, Mama. So, that means I have time," he teased.

"Between you and your brother, I don't know who's worse."

Shyriq felt insulted. "C'mon now. You know Rush and I are nothing alike. He doesn't even *want* to settle down."

The line was silent for a half a second. "True. You got me there." They shared a laugh. "Don't worry, though. I'm calling him next. Enjoy your night, and I better see your face tomorrow, or I know something."

Shyriq smirked. "You will. Love you, woman."

"Love you too."

The call disconnected from his Bluetooth, and Shyriq grabbed his phone from the cup holder. Stepping out of his truck, he straightened his khaki-colored shirt, closed the door, and hit the locks. A night out with the fellas was just what he needed. Getting out of work and husband mode was hard when it was all he knew, but he was adjusting slowly but surely. Unlike the club, the lounge was more his speed. Entering the building, the host, who he was familiar with, greeted him.

"Shyriq. What's going on, man?" Luke greeted. "Good to see you."

"You too. Everything been good?" Shyriq asked.

Luke nodded. "For sure. Just holding down the fort."

"That new baby and the wife got your skin glowing," Shyriq jested, but highly impressed.

"Aye, man. What can I say? Happy wife, happy life. Our baby girl just added a lot more," Luke said.

His happiness was radiant, and instead of feeling like he was missing out like before, Shyriq was optimistic that he'd experience those same emotions one day.

"Right on. Can't do anything but respect it. Let me get in here with these fools."

"A'ight. Enjoy your night."

Shyriq walked down the dimply lit hallway and entered the lounge area. A smooth jazz tune filled the speakers, making him nod his head. Thankfully, the place wasn't overly packed, and he quickly spotted his crew. Cane was the first to shake his head as he approached.

"Damn, look who made it," Cane joked, raising his glass.

Shyriq slapped hands with him, Travis, and Bleek. "I can't even get comfortable before he's on my case," Shyriq said. "What's up, fellas?"

"What's good?"

"What's going on?" Travis and Bleek replied.

Shyriq eased back into the plush booth, stretching his arm over the back as he scanned the dimly lit lounge. The scent of whiskey and cigars was thick in the air. It had been too long since he'd visited the spot, and he welcomed the aroma.

Travis was already sipping his drink, a dark amber liquid swirling in the glass. Cane leaned back with his signature grin, ready to dig into Shyriq's business. Bleek looked content and chill like he always was.

"Heard you were a free man," Bleek said. "How you feeling?"

Shyriq huffed out a dry laugh. "Not free yet. You know how that shit goes. Paperwork needs to be signed off on, and then it's a go." He rolled the tension out of his shoulders just as a waitress came by.

"Welcome. What flavor cigar and drink can I get for you?" she asked Shyriq.

"What's your name?" he questioned.

She looked a bit flustered by his question. "I apologize. My name is Shar."

"No need to apologize, sweetheart. I just like to know the name of the person who'll be servicing me," Shyriq replied. "I'll take the CAO Cherrybomb and Nine Oak neat."

Shar typed in his request and looked up. "Any food for you?"

"Not at the moment. Thank you, though, Shar," Shyriq said.

"My pleasure. Gentlemen, any refills?" she asked, and they shook their heads.

Travis replied. "We're good for now."

"Okay. I'll be right out with your order," Shar said and walked off.

"This guy," Cane chuckled, tossing his thumb in Shyriq's direction.

"What now? You got a lot to say tonight."

"I'm just happy to see you out and in good spirits, is all," Cane said seriously, and the men couldn't help but agree.

It'd been a while since they could all kick back and relax with one another. Cane's days were filled with cases as a highly sought-after attorney. Travis kept busy cutting hair at his barbershop, and Bleek owned a mechanic shop. Their lives were always on the go, and to know what Shyriq had been up against had Cane in good spirits to joke around.

"I feel you. I appreciate that. It's been a minute," Shyriq said.

"Wifey was telling me the other night how Xena has been talking ridiculous on social media," Travis said, shaking his head.

Shyriq shrugged. "That ain't got shit to do with me. She was no longer my concern once she walked out of that office the other week."

"She really tried to get two million up off you?" Travis questioned in a whispered tone.

He and his wife Toya were good friends with Shyriq and Xena. The women introduced the men to each other when they first started dating. Shyriq was still somewhat private about what had gone down, but it was clear Xena no longer cared about her business being exposed. Once it left the mouth of one person, the news was sure to spread.

Shyriq nodded. "Yeah. Crazy as hell if she thought I was agreeing."

"She was ready to travel the world with another man on your dime," Bleek scoffed, shaking his head. "That shit is sad."

"Very. I handled her like a business transaction, though. There wasn't much else I could do," Shyriq said.

Before he found out about the cheating, he suggested marriage counseling and tried communicating with Xena about what the problem could be. She didn't like his suggestions and hardly wanted to talk. Those late nights at the headquarters were for a reason. She either complained or had her hand out if she wasn't speaking to him. What man wanted to come home to that? And she wasn't having sex with him, so Shyriq knew something was up, and thankfully, he wasn't the type of man who believed his woman couldn't step out.

"You feel this was the best decision?" Cane asked.

"For sure, and the prenup came in handy too. I wasn't trying to go before a judge, and I know she damn sure wasn't. Hashing it out with our lawyers saved me from an even bigger headache."

The fellas all nodded, knowing how stressed he'd been.

"Hell yeah. At least it wasn't messy," Bleek said. "What business looking like? I be so proud to walk into the stores or turn on the TV and see Nine Oak."

Shyriq smiled. "Man, who you telling? It's a blessing, for sure. Business is solid. Expanding distribution overseas. Got a few deals in the works. Hired a new assistant," he said as Shar circled back.

"Here you are," she said, placing his glass down and then the tray with his cigar and a lighter. "How would you like your cut?"

"V-cut," Shyriq answered.

Skillfully, she used the cutter to trim his cigar before handing it to him. "Enjoy. Need any refills?"

The men mumbled off their requests, and she walked off. Shyriq lit his cigar and exhaled. The V-cut in his cigar allowed a tighter draw to pull the flavors and smoke in. Plus, the sweet notes of cherry, black current, and creamy vanilla paired deliciously well with the smooth caramel pour of the Nine Oak bourbon.

"This is nice," Shyriq acknowledged.

"Yeah, I'm a fan of their brand too," Bleek said.

Travis cleared his throat. "You got a new assistant?"

"Yeah," Shyriq answered, sipping his drink.

Cane's brows lifted. "What happened to Michelle?"

"She's about to have the baby soon. Someone had to fill her spot," Shyriq said.

Cane nodded. "True. I heard that maternity leave pay is real nice. I should tell Autumn to land a job before we have kids," he teased, making them laugh.

Shyriq smirked. "Hey, what can I say? I look after my people. Michelle damn near runs the place, which is a good thing 'cause she's going to be training Nhuri before she leaves."

Pausing midsip, Cane tilted his head. "The chick from Patio?"

Travis leaned in. "Who is she?"

"Gotta be someone special. This man was booed up for damn near thirty minutes with her when we stepped out the other weekend," Cane divulged.

Shyriq gave him a "yeah, right" look. "You're exaggerating."

"Shiiiit," Cane dragged and laughed.

Travis scratched his head. "So, that's what Toya was talking about," he said.

"What you mean?" Shyriq asked with a frown.

"She was running down what all was going on with Xena, and she said she mentioned something about getting a video of you and some woman hugged up at the bar. Ol' girl must've been who she was talking about."

Shyriq set his glass down. "A video . . . of me and Nhuri?"

He was confused. That afternoon at brunch, he'd been much too occupied to notice if someone was recording him. The real question is why. All they were doing was talking. Furthermore, he was a single man.

"Yeah, Xena was saying something about she knew you were cheating too or something like that," Travis explained.

Shyriq laughed. "Imagine that."

"I mean, shit . . . You did hire the girl," Bleek added.

"Hiring someone means I'm fucking them?" Shyriq questioned, swiveling his head to look at them.

"Nah, man. I know you were never on that, but I guess that's what she thinks," Travis said.

Shyriq downed the remainder of his drink. He couldn't care less what Xena thought. She wasn't on his mind at any time of the day, and he wished it was the same for her. He didn't know who this person was recording him, but Shyriq hoped he never found out, not for his sake but for Nhuri's. She had nothing to do with their divorce and surely wasn't a part of his life before it.

"That's on her. I hope whatever I'm doing haunts her ass at night," Shyriq said nonchalantly.

The men howled in laughter.

"That's cold, man. But she had it coming," Cane said.

"So, how y'all meet?" Travis asked.

He was trying to make it sound like he was interested, and he was, but he really wanted to pillow talk with Toya later on. She may have been friends with Xena, but she didn't condone her behavior or how she treated Shyriq during this entire ordeal. Morally, she was in the wrong, and it rubbed Toya the wrong way, so Shyriq's business was safe with her . . . and her husband.

"Cane's engagement party," Shyriq answered.

"Awww shit. I get to give the best man speech at the wedding and tell everyone how it was because of me that you met the *real* love of your life," Cane said, making them laugh.

Shyriq waved him off. "Man, grow up. You moving a bit too fast."

"Am I? You the one who hired her as your assistant," Cane said.

"She got let go of at her job, and I had a position open," he shrugged.

"A few positions open," Bleek said, coughing under his breath.

Shyriq was single and needed an assistant. It was the perfect setup.

"Y'all not gon' let me live, huh?" Shyriq asked, amused by their nosiness.

"We are. We're just trying to see where your head is at. Is she even qualified?" Travis asked.

Shyriq's jaws clenched. He didn't like Travis questioning Nhuri's capabilities, and something in his chest tightened by him doing so.

"What, you think I brought her on to fuck off?" Shyriq questioned. "Of course, she can handle the position."

Cane and Travis exchanged looks before Travis nodded. "A'ight. No need to bite our heads off."

Shyriq waved them off just as Shar refilled his glass. "Thank you," he said. "Y'all need to stop acting like I don't know what I'm doing. Nhuri is in good hands."

Cane chuckled. "I bet. I know she ain't expecting your ass to be so damn serious. You got that 'boss mode' switch that throws people off."

"Good," Shyriq said evenly. "It keeps people on their toes."

Travis studied him for a beat. "You see her moving up in the company?"

Shyriq exhaled, thinking about it. "Honestly, yeah. If she wants to, she has the skills. Just gotta see if she got the drive."

Cane's grin widened. "You really like her, huh?"

Shyriq side-eyed him. "What you mean by that?"

"You ain't just hiring anybody, Shy," Cane said, puffing his cigar. "You see something in her."

Shyriq shrugged. "I see potential. That's it."

Travis smirked. "Hmm. We'll see."

Shyriq ignored them, taking another sip of his whiskey, but the conversation lingered in the back of his mind. He most definitely saw something in Nhuri besides what she had on her resume. Only time would tell if he was willing to figure out exactly what it was.

The night began to wind down for the fellas, but the flow of occupants in the lounge remained steady. A younger crowd who enjoyed the atmosphere had gotten hip to the location and started visiting in the last few months. Shyriq loved to see that. He was all for seeing a business be supported and flourish.

"A'ight. I'm out. Got get home to the missus," Cane said while stretching and rolling his shoulders.

"She ain't your wife yet. Wedding planning stressing you out yet?" Shyriq asked, finishing his whiskey. He let the smooth burn settle in his chest before pushing his glass to the side.

"Not yet, but I can feel it brewing. It's whatever for my baby, though," Cane said, smiling.

Love looked beyond good on him.

"I hear that," Travis said, sliding out of the booth.

Bleek and Shyriq were up and out of their seats next. A hefty tip was left behind for Shar, and she was more than grateful for them. Fresh air entered their lungs as they exited the building. Shyriq inhaled, feeling as relaxed as ever.

"Y'all be easy," Cane said, and they all slapped hands.

"Shy, you good?" Travis questioned, watching him closely.

He nodded. "Yeah, just enjoying the nice weather. You know how KC gets. One day, you can wear shorts, and the next, you'll need a coat."

"Or a boat. It rained for forty days and forty nights the other week," Bleek griped.

Business at the car shop had been slower than ever those days. It rained for a good five days straight. The city hadn't seen anything like it.

"Man," Travis chuckled. "Tell me about it."

Cane and Bleek headed to their rides while Shyriq and Travis stayed back.

"Aye, man," Travis began, "I ain't mean to be negative on whatever you have going on with another woman."

Shyriq shook his head. "I didn't take it that way. I know y'all are just some nosy mothafuckas," he said, chuckling.

"I can't deny that. We were just worried, that's all. I've never been through a divorce, so I can't speak on how to feel, but I've been betrayed before. Don't let what Xena did make your heart cold. If Nhuri is who you want, forget what anyone has to say."

Nodding, Shyriq took in his words and nodded. "I 'preciate that, and I won't. Xena didn't do anything but make me want to find the woman truly meant for me."

"And that's her loss, bro. You're a good guy," Travis said as they embraced. He patted him on the shoulder. "Be safe, and don't get too lost in those thoughts. They can cripple you."

"I hear you. Good looking out," Shyriq said.

They parted ways, and though Shyriq wanted to act as if his words didn't affect him, they had. He didn't want to turn his heart cold. He had so much love to give, and Xena had played with his heart. Shyriq scolded himself as he walked to his vehicle. *How didn't I see the signs?* The question entered his brain as he started the ignition. His drive home was filled with what-ifs and his next steps in life.

Going from married to single was a jump scare, and if you weren't prepared, because who could be ready for that type of thing, you'd be lost in who you were. Or who you were meant to be. By the time Shyriq pulled into his driveway, the thoughts of his past had quieted, but the ones of his future were loud.

His house was big but not excessive. It's a nice mixture of modern and minimal. It was the kind of home built for someone who valued order over unnecessary clutter. Entering through the garage, Shyriq tossed his keys onto the kitchen counter, pulled off his watch, and went upstairs. Slipping off his shirt, he yawned. His body was tired, but his mind was in overdrive.

He tried to shake it, but one thought kept circling back. One person specifically. Shyriq couldn't shake Nhuri for shit. He wasn't the type to dwell on people, but something about her kept scratching at the back of his mind. Maybe it was how composed she was during their meeting, even when he'd thrown her mixed signals. Or how she subtly made him hand over some of his control with her comebacks.

Shyriq smirked. He loved a woman who could stand on her own no matter who she was up against. Nhuri carried herself with a quiet confidence that shined through when it needed to. Hiring her was going to test every patient bone in his body. After showering off the night, Shyriq brushed his teeth and did his skincare before moisturizing his body. Inside his bedroom, he slipped on a pair of briefs and climbed into bed.

Without thinking too much about it, he grabbed his phone. What he was about to do was probably against the policy somewhere in the handbook for GHC. *But was it really considered rule-breaking if she hadn't started yet?* Shyriq smirked and shook his head.

"It's not. Plus, I'm the owner. A little background check is needed," he said, trying to convince himself.

Opening Facebook, Shyriq ignored the hundreds of notifications and went straight to the search bar. He typed Nhuri's first and last name in. Her profile popped up, and he tapped it. Scanning her picture, Shyriq smiled. Nhuri's warm, brown complexion, tantalizing eyes, and high cheekbones had him stuck. She had the type of face and beauty that made you get lost and forget your train of thought.

Shyriq scrolled her page, noticing she wasn't the type to flood her page with selfies or long statuses. Each post was days or weeks apart, as if she were never on the app, which Shyriq found attractive. Compared to Xena, who lived for a social media moment and posted every intimate detail of her life, except her cheating, Shyriq found Nhuri's page refreshing, just like her. Her profile was clean and carefully curated, leaving much to the imagination.

Curiosity got the best of him as he continued scrolling. Most of her posts were light, random thoughts, shared articles, some pictures of her and Natalia, and glimpses into her personal life without giving too much away. Then he stumbled across a post from a few months back. Shyriq sat up in the bed.

"Sometimes life reroutes you for a reason. I'm just going to trust God and this process."

There was no extra explanation, and the comments didn't give up any context clues. Just a bunch of people telling Nhuri they were proud of her and that she had this. Shyriq tapped his thumb against the screen, wondering what had happened around that time. He looked at the date and realized it was around the same time he and Xena split.

"Damn. What a coincidence," he mumbled.

Too caught up and feeling like he needed to solve a mystery, Shyriq kept scrolling further. He caught a picture of her at some event, dressed in a sleek black gown, looking poised and elegant. She was smiling brightly, and Shyriq peeped the bystanders in the photo's background. All eyes were on her. He smirked slightly. Nhuri didn't seem like the type who wanted attention, but she got it anyway.

Based on the pictures he saw, she had friends, but her circle looked small. She had a lot of love for her sister and niece, though. That made him wonder where her parents were. Natalia was all over her page, laughing in videos, celebrating milestones, and just being siblings. Shyriq's mind quickly ventured to Rush, but then he wondered.

How much had Nhuri sacrificed for her?

The more he saw, the more he realized he wasn't figuring out much about her at all. He knew her qualifications and knew she'd be able to handle the tasks he handed her way, but *who* was Nhuri? And why the hell was he so damn intrigued?

Shyriq huffed and locked his phone before sliding it onto the nightstand. He didn't do this. Sit up and scroll a woman's page, wondering how her life came about. This was new. Nhuri had him acting out of character in more ways than one, and Shyriq didn't know whether to drop his interest in her or lean into it. He hired her because she was competent, not because he needed another distraction.

But maybe Nhuri was the exception, regardless of whether Shyriq wanted to admit it.

THIRTEEN

NHURI'S FIRST DAY of work hadn't gone exactly how she had planned.

Her alarm would've dragged her from her sleep at six a.m., but she woke up at five forty-two and just lay there with her eyes closed. She was grateful.

Not just for the job but for life in general. No matter which route it took her, she seemingly navigated toward the right track. She wasn't sure if working at GHC was right or wrong, but her body said otherwise when she climbed from bed eighteen minutes later. Surprisingly, she wasn't nervous.

She was just a bit anxious to see what all was in store. Nhuri took her time in the shower, letting the scalding hot water fully wake her. While she washed her face, she thought about what outfit was fitting for her first day. Standing inside her closet wearing a silk robe, she debated her outfit much longer than she cared to admit. She wanted to look professional but not stiff. Not too revealing but still flattering.

Knowing she needed to put a move on it, Nhuri settled for a sleeveless V-neck taupe dress that cinched at the waist, a black blazer, and gold accessories, but not over the top. Just a watch and stylish hoop earrings. She slipped her feet into black high heels but grabbed a cute pair of loafers in case she needed to change. She pulled the look together by styling her hair in a low bun at the nape of her neck.

Breakfast was out of the question because she knew her stomach wouldn't agree with it. Plus, it was much too early. By the time she was in her car, Nhuri declared that whatever happened today was for the best. It had to be. This was the start of a new journey, and she hoped she was making her parents proud.

After stopping by Sip and ordering a hazelnut iced coffee for herself and a chai latte with almond milk for Shyriq, she headed toward the main office. Nhuri found parking rather quickly, thanks to her assigned spot. She smiled at the extra perks and grabbed her things. Then she strolled through the doors and was greeted by Ashley at the receptionist desk.

"Hey. Good morning, Ms. Coleman," Ashley said brightly.

Nhuri smiled. "Good morning. Please call me Nhuri. Ms. Coleman is so formal," she chuckled.

"Noted. I'll let Michelle know you're here," she said, picking up the phone.

Nhuri gave her a soft smile and took in the lobby. Many people were arriving at work. Some of them stopped to introduce themselves, while others gave a polite wave. GHC was welcoming, and Shyriq made sure it felt like one big family. Michelle walked her way a few minutes later, smiling brightly.

"First day on the job, and you're looking like that?" Michelle questioned, smirking.

Nhuri's mouth opened in surprise as her eyes widened. "Is . . . Is something wrong with my outfit?"

"Absolutely not. You look good, girl. Me and this belly can't squeeze into a dress like that unless it's a muumuu," Michelle said, laughing.

Nhuri exhaled and chuckled. "Whew. You had me scared. My dress is okay, though, right?"

"Yes, Nhuri. I was just complimenting you. No worries. You'll more than likely be the first contact for Shyriq besides Ashley, so looking good isn't a problem. Now, the roaming eyes of the men might be, but all they better do is admire."

Nhuri blushed. She liked Michelle's energy. It was much different from the first day they met, but Nhuri wouldn't hold that against her. She was doing her job while carrying a life in her womb.

"Okay. Good," Nhuri said, relieved.

"Ash, can you please hold all of my calls for at least the next hour? I'm going to get Nhuri settled in," Michelle said.

"Of course. Have a good day."

"Come on. Let's get you all set up. How are you feeling?" Michelle asked as they walked through the lobby that led to the elevator.

Nhuri followed behind her. "Blessed."

The elevator pinged, and they climbed on.

"That's a great feeling. Today will honestly be a drag or overwhelming, depending on how you intake things. Lots of paperwork, system setups, introductions, and busywork that stresses me out."

Nhuri sighed. "Sorry. I know getting me acclimated isn't something you really want to do."

"No, no. Don't take what I said as an insult. I'm more than happy to bring you into the flow of things. Trust me. It's just I know how meticulous Shyriq can be and how fried my brain is," Michelle snorted. "No one prepared me for pregnancy brain, so forgive me if I repeat myself or forget something today."

"You're fine. I'm sure I can keep up," Nhuri assured her.

"Good. That's what I like to hear."

Their first stop on the executive floor was her office. Nhuri entered and inhaled the fresh scent. It had been deep cleaned the night before, emitting the air with a cozy laundry and lemon fragrance. The floor-to-ceiling windows bathed the space in natural sunlight. The courtyard view was breathtaking, and she knew she'd be spending most of her days gazing outside. The walls were painted a soft cream, making the rich wood tones of the floor and bookshelf pop. It was filled with reports she'd need, decorative accents, industry help books, a small potted plant, and a framed abstract painting that added a touch of personality.

"This is a new desk and chair," Michelle explained. "If you want to change anything out, email Ashley, and she'll get on it."

Placing her things on the glass-top desk, Nhuri swiveled the plush ergonomic chair so she could sit. Her body immediately sank into it, and she smiled.

"Nope. This is good," Nhuri said.

To the right of the desk, two caramel-colored leather chairs were positioned as a sitting area for guests. It was cozy but not cozier looking than the plush love seat on the opposite side of the office. A sleek floor lamp stood nearby, but Nhuri knew it'd hardly be needed, especially if she kept her shades open. The space was soft but professional, and she already felt at home. Despite only being inside the office for a few minutes, Nhuri felt like she belonged.

"You'll get to come back in here later. Let's make our rounds," Michelle announced.

Nhuri stood and grabbed the warm cup off her desk. "This is for Shyriq."

"You can leave that for now. He's not here yet," Michelle said.

"Oh. Okay," Nhuri said, setting it down. She thought he'd be here just as early, if not earlier than her.

However, she didn't harp on his absence as they exited the office.

"I'll walk you through the basics, but most of this is learn-as-you-go," Michelle explained.

Nhuri nodded slowly. She'd already learned so much, so that technique was fine with her. The next few hours flew by and were a blur of information. Michelle was efficient, introducing Nhuri to a few employees she'd need to know, showing her how to set up scheduling and internal systems, and throwing in hints about Shyriq's work habits.

"He's big on structure but open to ideas that may help things flow smoother," Michelle explained, clicking through the scheduling software. "Right now, meetings are tight, and his schedule is packed. If it isn't urgent and you can handle it on your own, don't disrupt his workflow."

Nhuri absorbed it all, forcing her mind to catalog every detail. "And what about emails? Is he hands-on with his responses?"

Michelle snorted. "He skims. I'll give him that. I filter the fluff and flag what needs his attention. More recently, especially with us launching overseas soon, his time is spread thin. But you'll learn what he cares about real quick."

Nhuri wasn't sure if she was relieved or nervous. She was already overloaded with information but soaked it all up gracefully, not shying away from a challenge. Next on the agenda was receiving a work cell phone. Then Michelle explained the different parts of the building and which floors belonged to which part of the company.

They made a detour to HR, where her professional headshot picture for the website and company directory was taken. By the time Michelle freed her, Nhuri was worn out, and it was only a little before noon.

"I leave today at one, but I'll drop by to see how things are going," Michelle said.

"Okay. I'll try to knock out a few assessments before lunch."

Michelle smiled. "Have at it. I'll see you in a little bit."

When Nhuri finally returned to her office, her feet were killing her. But not enough to notice that Shyriq still wasn't in his office. She bypassed it with curiosity, wondering where he was.

It's not like he didn't know it was my first day, Nhuri thought, stepping inside her office. Exhaling, she flopped into her chair and slid off her heels. With a contented sigh, she leaned her head back and closed her eyes. She tried to relax before jumping back into work mode, but she couldn't shake the slight irritation that crept up on her. Nhuri figured he wouldn't be the one showing her the ropes today, but it also felt like he'd just thrown her in the deep end.

Nothing against Michelle. She's a sweetheart, Nhuri thought, swiveling her chair toward the window. Nhuri tried quieting her thoughts, watching the rippling waves from the pond. She didn't know what irritated her more: the fact that she was pressed to see him or the fact that he hadn't checked in at least once. After all, he was the one who hired her and had the audacity to move as if her presence didn't shift a single thing in his day.

"Maybe it doesn't," Nhuri murmured.

She exhaled slowly, rolling her shoulders. *It's fine. You don't need him to hold your hand.* Just as her gaze locked in on a group of ducks, the office phone blared, cutting her daydream short. Nhuri jumped, swiveled in the chair, and reached for the receiver.

"Hi, this is Great Hendrix Co., and I'm Nhuri. How can I help you?" she answered, almost flustered, hoping she answered correctly.

There was a slight pause before a deep, authoritative voice filled her ear. "Hello, Nhuri. This is Domino. I need to speak with Mr. Hendrix. Is he in?"

Nhuri straightened and glanced at the caller ID. She recognized the name flashing on the phone's screen as one of the distributors Michelle had mentioned earlier.

"He's unavailable at the moment," she said smoothly. "Can I take a message or assist you?"

A heavy sigh came through the line. "We need confirmation on the barrel shipment for next week. There's a discrepancy on the invoice we received, and we can't move forward without it being cleared up."

She hesitated, wondering if she'd have to call Michelle for assistance or try to solve the problem at least a little bit. Deciding on the latter, Nhuri asked him for his company name and the invoice date. Her fingers flew across the keyboard as she logged into the system and pulled up the shipping details. It took her a few seconds to locate the invoice in question. Quickly, she scanned the numbers.

"I see the issue," she said, keeping her tone professional. "It looks like the deposit amount was misapplied. I can notify accounting to have it corrected immediately. I'll also flag this for Mr. Hendrix, so he's in the loop."

Domino let out a relieved sigh. "I appreciate that. Just need it squared away before the end of the day."

"Understood. I'll make sure it is."

"Thank you," Domino said. "Are you new?"

Nhuri smirked. "Yes. I'm the new assistant, so if you can't contact Mr. Hendrix, you'll speak with me."

"Very well, then. I'll store that information for future use. I'll be on the lookout for the email. Thanks again, Nhuri."

She smiled brightly. "You're welcome. Have a great day."

Wrapping up the call, Nhuri leaned back in her chair. She couldn't help but give herself a small clap for handling the call like a skilled professional. Even though her heart was beating fast, she'd gotten one task marked off. Now, it was time to reach out to accounting. Nhuri woke up her monitor and prepared an email when there was a knock on her office door. She glanced upward and was thankful that the door was open so she could see his face and not be alarmed once he walked in.

"Hello," she greeted him with an edge in her tone as Shyriq crossed the threshold.

He nodded once and smirked. "Good afternoon. I see you're getting settled in."

Nhuri blinked twice. "I am."

Shyriq licked his lips, and she wished he hadn't. It was bad enough that he filled her space with his energy and intoxicating smell. He was dressed in slacks and a white button-down, looking just as good as Nhuri remembered him. Strangely, all the nervous jitters she didn't have came to the forefront in his presence. Nhuri intertwined her hands together to keep from nervously running a hand down her neck.

Shyriq's eyes flickered to her hand before lifting back to her face. "How was your morning?"

She swallowed hard, sitting up straighter. "As good as it can get."

His brow quirked. "Is there an issue?"

Nhuri knew she was being a brat for no reason, so she gathered herself. "No," she answered. "Here's your chai latte. Well, iced chai latte now."

Shyriq smirked. *So, that's her problem. I wasn't here when she arrived.* He had a great eye for reading people and saw right through Nhuri. Her cute pout made him want to kiss it off her face. His gaze swept over her desk, noticing she had already taken a few notes.

"Thank you. I'll still drink it cold," he said as she handed it to him. Shyriq twirled the liquid and then took a sip. "You're sending emails already?" he asked, concerned and impressed.

Nhuri nodded. "I was about to when you walked in. Domino had an issue with the invoice, but I figured it out. I was going to reach out to the accounting team."

Shyriq nodded, more than impressed with her efficiency. "You let me handle that. There shouldn't have been any mix-ups."

"Okay," Nhuri said slowly. "Do you normally handle that, or does Michelle?"

"She does, but I'll take care of it today. You don't have to worry about it."

All Nhuri could do was nod. She expected him to take a seat at least, but he continued standing. Shyriq drank from his cup, and Nhuri finally had to break the silence.

"Are Mondays your late days?"

He smirked. "Usually, yes. I'm at the distillery for most of the morning into the afternoon."

"Hmm. Okay. Noted."

"You seem to be doing just fine."

Her eyes narrowed slightly. "I am. I just would have preferred a heads-up, a have-a-good-day, an ETA—something."

"You're right, and I apologize. I'm used to a schedule, and though I knew today was your first day, business still had to be handled accordingly. If I recall, you have my cell number," Shyriq said.

"You wanted me to reach out to you on my first day? Who's the assistant?"

He laughed, and Nhuri dropped her frown. Shyriq met her playful gaze.

"No, I didn't expect you to call or text me. I knew you were in good hands. I'm not a fan of micromanaging. I hired you because I knew you wouldn't need me to hold your hand."

Nhuri held his stare. "And you don't, but common courtesy still works like a charm."

They just stared at each other momentarily, battling on who would break first. Nhuri may have been taking things a bit personally, but Shyriq didn't find her observation wrong. The distillery had been so hectic this morning that he didn't have time to check in on her. Shyriq figured he'd just wait until he could get away and now realized a quick call or text would've been appreciated. He understood her completely.

Shyriq exhaled first, breaking their eye contact. A part of him liked being in control, especially of his feelings, and Nhuri was making him relinquish some of that power on day one. He glanced around her office before walking to the window and taking in the view as Nhuri had done earlier.

"You're right, it does," Shyriq said. "Next time, I'll call."

Behind his back, Nhuri smirked. "Okay."

He turned to face her. "Let's go to lunch."

Her nose bunched. "Huh?"

"Lunch. I know you haven't eaten yet."

"I haven't, but—"

"But nothing. We both need to eat, and I want to see how your morning went since I wasn't here. Meet me in the lobby in five minutes."

Nhuri stared at him, waiting for more of an explanation about why he wanted to treat her to lunch besides the logical one he gave. But all Shyriq gave her was a subtle head nod before walking out of her office with his chai latte in his hand. Her lips pressed together as she watched his strong back, and she shook her head. A smirk teased the corner of her lips.

"It's just a friendly lunch with your boss, girl. Get it together," Nhuri told herself and stood up.

Even though she'd uttered those words, she had a feeling that working for Shyriq would be nothing like she expected . . . plus a lot more.

FOURTEEN

SHYRIQ WASN'T SURE what he'd gotten himself into with Nhuri, but he knew that leaving her office for the day and sticking to business wasn't in the plans. She'd checked him about his absence, and he had to make up for it. Lunch was the perfect solution, or so he thought. Watching Nhuri enter the lobby put him in a trance and had him wanting her to be on the menu instead.

She strutted his way with strides that enticingly swayed her hips. Shyriq knew she wasn't trying to tease him, but it didn't take much. Nhuri was effortlessly beautiful and possessed this sureness about herself when up against him.

"You ready?" Shyriq asked once she reached him.

Nhuri bobbed her head, and he led them out of the building to a sleek, black Suburban. He opened the passenger door so she could climb inside before going to the driver's seat. Nhuri hated how her eyes fluttered at his smell surrounding the interior. She was quiet for the quick drive and glad he had received a call.

"Yeah, I'll be back in the office in about an hour," he said.

An hour? Nhuri questioned herself.

Shyriq entered the parking lot of a small building tucked between two high-rises. She didn't know what to expect, but she definitely didn't expect this. She was sure he would've taken her to some high-end restaurant with an overpriced menu that served small portions. They entered the place, and a woman greeted them whose face lit up. She welcomed Shyriq by name, leading Nhuri to believe he was a frequent visitor.

"Shy, it's always so good to see your face," she smiled, leaning in for a hug.

"Yours too, Aunt Jackie. You have something open for us?"

"Of course. And who do we have with you today?"

Shyriq faced Nhuri. "This is my assistant, Nhuri. Nhuri, this is my aunt Jackie."

She stepped Nhuri's way and embraced her in a warm hug that she melted into. She hadn't had a woman besides her mother hug her like that in quite some time. Feeling too much at once, Nhuri cleared her throat.

"Hi. It's nice to meet you."

"You as well, sweetie. My goodness, you are pretty," Jackie gushed.

Nhuri blushed. "Thank you."

"You better take care of her," Jackie said, patting Shyriq on his arm.

What the hell? Shyriq and Nhuri both thought, stealing a glance at each other.

Jackie grabbed two menus off the podium. "Let me get you all settled in. Follow me."

The spot was quiet and laid-back, with a few customers occupying the tables. Nhuri's stomach growled as they passed a man cutting into a crispy piece of fried chicken. She didn't realize how hungry she was until the aromas from the food reminded her she hadn't eaten.

"Thanks, Auntie," Shyriq said once they were seated at a table near the back. The table provided some privacy but still gave a clear view of the establishment.

"You're welcome. Tessa will be right over to get y'all orders."

She walked off, and Nhuri immediately grabbed her menu. The Spot was coined and named after so many described it as "You know, that spot right between the two high-rises? Yeah, *that* spot. The food is incredible." Jackie owned the place, which had been passed down from her aunt years ago. Knowing what he wanted, Shyriq didn't bother looking over the menu. Instead, he watched Nhuri. The way her lips tooted out as she read a new item or the way her eyebrows dipped reading over the sides made him smirk.

"You know, staring isn't polite," Nhuri said, still reading the menu.

Shyriq chuckled. "Even if it's done politely?"

That got her to lift her head. "Politely . . . or intensely? The eyes can be misleading."

"Both," he answered, licking his lips. He didn't want to mislead her in any way. He was letting it be known that he was staring for a reason.

Nhuri cleared her throat. "Everything sounds so good on here."

Chuckling under his breath, Shyriq took the hint. She wasn't trying to go there with him today. That was cool with him.

"Everything is good too," he clarified.

"Is Ms. Jackie your real aunt?"

"Not by blood, no. She and my mom are best friends, practically sisters."

Nhuri smiled. She loved seeing a close-knit bond between women as friends who become family. She felt the same about her relationship with Jazmyn.

"That's so sweet. So, I'm assuming you get special treatment around here?" Nhuri asked.

He smirked. "I wouldn't say all that."

As soon as he said that, Tessa appeared to take their order. "Hey, Mr. Hendrix," she greeted before speaking to Nhuri. "Hi. Welcome to The Spot. Is this your first time dining with us?"

"Hey, yes, it is. I was told everything on the menu is good, so I'm not quite ready to order yet. Still trying to decide."

"That's perfectly fine. I'll get you all's drinks started and come back. What can I get for you?"

Nhuri scanned the beverage section, and before she could make her decision, Shyriq intervened.

"Do you drink pop?" he asked.

"Yes," Nhuri answered, nodding.

He faced Tessa. "We'll take two Shirley Temples and some fried pickles to start us off."

Tessa didn't bother scribbling their request in her notepad. "Gotcha. We figured you'd be in today, so we have your favorite ready to go."

"Y'all treat me so good around here," Shyriq jested.

Tessa chuckled. "We treat everyone good. Ms. Jackie just loves on you a lil more. I'll be right back."

Nhuri stared at him and smirked.

"What?" Shyriq asked.

"No special treatment, huh?"

Shyriq's head fell back, and a deep chuckle resounded around them. The sound made a chill creep up Nhuri's back. The way his straight teeth peeked from behind those lips, and the way he filled the chair had her squirming in hers.

"A'ight. You got me," he admitted.

"Exactly. What's your favorite?" Nhuri asked.

"The braised oxtail grilled cheese sandwich."

Nhuri's eyes lit up, and her stomach rumbled. "That sounds so good. I was leaning toward the sweet heat chicken and waffles, but now I don't know."

The whine in her voice made Shyriq's chest feel funny. It was adorable, and the kind of sound he knew would make him give her whatever she wanted without asking. He shook his head.

"Get both, or you can taste some of mine."

Nhuri blinked slowly. She wasn't expecting him to say that, but then again, every moment leading up to Shyriq had been unpredictable.

"Okay," she mumbled as Tessa placed their drinks down.

The Shirley Temples were made with real cherry syrup and were highly requested by customers. Ms. Jackie's mix of soul food, American food, and unique dishes kept her doors open. The menu was plentiful, the food was beyond delicious, and the warm hospitality customers received was why The Spot was rated one of the best in the city.

Sticking her straw inside the glass, Nhuri swirled the drink and sipped. "There's no way this tastes this good."

Shyriq chuckled. "Same thing I've been saying for years. It's real cherry syrup."

"I can tell," she said before taking another generous gulp.

"How'd everything go with Michelle this morning?"

Pushing her drink aside, Nhuri cleared her throat. "Things went good. It was mainly busywork, but she taught me so much in a short time."

"Yeah, she's thorough," he agreed. "You'll get the hang of everything."

Nhuri remained quiet for a second, taking in the building. Its warm lighting, exposed brick walls, and large windows gave the place a serene vibe. It felt homey and smelled it too.

"How long has she been your assistant?" Nhuri asked, wondering how much more pressure would come her way.

"For years, but I don't want to talk about business, though."

Her brow lifted slightly just as Tessa brought out the fried pickles. "You don't?"

"Nah. Hold whatever thoughts you have real quick," Shyriq said.

"You all ready to order?" Tessa asked.

Nhuri glanced at her and then Shyriq. He bobbed his head once, encouraging her to go ahead. "I'll take the sweet heat chicken and waffles. Does it come with eggs?"

"It doesn't, but we can add them as a side. Would you like to do that?"

"Yes."

Tessa scribbled down her order. "Got it. And for you? Even though I'm sure what you're going to say."

Shyriq smirked. "You know I'm going with the braised oxtail sandwich. Honey mustard for the fries. What's the dessert of the day?"

"Pineapple upside-down cake," Tessa answered.

"I will definitely be taking a slice," Nhuri said.

Shyriq laughed. "You don't even know if it's good."

"I trust that it is. You wouldn't have asked about it if it weren't."

Tessa smiled. "She has a point. Enjoy your fried pickles, and your lunch will be out shortly."

Nhuri wasted no time dipping a pickle into the ranch before popping it into her mouth. She nodded her head in appreciation.

"Good?" Shyriq asked.

"Mhmm. I can tell this is a homemade ranch."

"I believe it is," he said, dipping one of his own and eating it.

They ate a few more in silence before Nhuri picked back up on their conversation. She wanted to know why he didn't want to discuss business when that was the sole reason she was here.

"So, you don't want to know how my day was so far?" Nhuri asked.

"I don't mind hearing about your day, just not business right now. I'd rather know more about you. The Nhuri outside of work and not my assistant."

Nhuri pursed her lips, amused. "Are you sure that's appropriate? You know . . . as my boss and all."

Shyriq smirked. "I'm sure there's some things you'll learn about me that aren't work-related. You don't have to share, though."

"I don't mind, but I'd rather get to know you better. So, you first. Why'd you bring me here?"

A bit taken aback by her question, Shyriq thought carefully about his response before answering. He narrowed his eyes a bit, trying to gauge where this conversation was going. Nhuri could tell he was waiting for her to ask something else or explain why she asked that, but she refused to give him that satisfaction. Bringing her to a spot where he and his wife more than likely visited had red flags flying around her head.

"Because we both needed lunch, and I love the food," he answered.

"Hmm," Nhuri hummed. "Okay. That simple of an answer?"

"Some things in life are simple. Did you want another answer?"

Did I expect a different answer? Nhuri asked herself. Truth is, she was in her head again. Shyriq was blurring the lines once more and not clearing them up.

"No. I was just curious," she answered.

"That's fair. What other questions do you have for me?" Shyriq asked.

Nhuri placed a pickle into her mouth. "Since I'll be working closely with you, I think it's safe to ask about your marital status."

With every encounter they've had, Nhuri hadn't come right out and asked. Shyriq was glad she had today because he could give her an answer that sufficed. At least, he hoped so.

"I am a single man, Nhuri. The divorce papers have been signed, and within the next few weeks, no woman will have my last name besides my family."

He held eye contact, making sure she heard every word he said. Xena didn't matter in his life, and she wouldn't matter in Nhuri's if he had his way.

"That's good to know. Thank you for answering," she said.

"No problem. If you ever want to know anything, especially about or from me, all you have to do is ask."

Nhuri nodded. "Will do."

"What about you?"

"What about me?" she wondered.

Shyriq's gaze flickered to something that made Nhuri's stomach swirl. "Since we'll be working so closely together, tell me something about you."

Nhuri blinked, pondering how much she should share. And if she even wanted to share much anyway.

She chuckled. "Your request was vague."

"What do you like to do outside of working and hanging with your friends?"

It was the safest question. What he really wanted to ask was if there was a man in her life he needed to know about. Shyriq wasn't concerned, but working for a man like him while in a relationship could cause drama if the person wasn't secure. He didn't need any more drama than he already had.

Nhuri hesitated, seeing the look in his eyes transform into genuine curiosity. "You know . . . regular things. My niece loves the park, going out for ice cream, and making me play with her dolls, so most of my weeknights are with her and my sister."

Shyriq smiled. "Enjoy those young days while you can. That's all?"

"I like to read and travel when I can. I'm truly a homebody, and I love to bake when I have time."

"For real?"

She nodded, sipping her drink. "It's therapeutic."

Shyriq's lips quirked. "What's your specialty?"

Nhuri smirked. "Why? You placing an order?"

"I might. Depends on if you got skills."

Nhuri scoffed. "I'm pretty good."

"A'ight. We gon' see."

She narrowed her eyes. "You don't believe me?"

"I didn't say that," he said as Tessa and another waiter approached with their meals. "But if I'm trusting you with my desserts, I need proof."

Nhuri shook her head with a soft laugh, moving her glass out of the way. "You're something else. But I'll make you a believer."

"All right. We have the sweet heat chicken and waffles with a side of eggs," Tessa announced placing plates down in front of Nhuri before grabbing the other two from her coworker. "And your favorite with a side of honey mustard." She grabbed a warm bottle of syrup for Nhuri's waffle and placed it on the table before stepping back. "Everything look good?"

Nhuri glanced her way. "Yes, and it smells even better. Thank you."

"No problem. Enjoy," Tessa said, walking over to another table.

Shyriq watched Nhuri bow her head in prayer, and his heart swelled. When she looked up, he was still staring.

"What's the matter?" she asked, hoping nothing was wrong because she was too hungry to talk right now.

"Nothing. Did you bless my plate too?"

"I did."

Shyriq tipped his head. "Thank you."

Nhuri smiled at him but said nothing else. She cut into her meal before lathering it with syrup and taking a bite. Her eyes fluttered closed, and she shook her head.

"Mmm, mmm, mmm," she mumbled, chewing.

Shyriq didn't have to ask her if it was good. The satisfaction on her face and the way she cut into another piece before swallowing the first bite was all the proof he needed.

"I knew you'd love the food," he said, biting into his sandwich.

Nhuri watched in pure lust, not bothering to get caught for staring. The grease from the beef coated his lips, and he slowly licked it off. Nhuri's chest heaved as he kept eye contact.

Yeah, this man isn't playing fair at all, she thought, looking down at her own food.

"You want a taste?" Shyriq asked.

Her eyes shot up, and she blinked slowly. "Of your sandwich?" She needed to make sure they were on the same page.

Shyriq smirked. "Yes."

"Oh. Um, sure. Yes, if you don't mind."

"I don't," he said, stretching his arm across the table.

Nhuri looked uncertain, confused about why he didn't just cut her a piece, but he gave her a nod. She bit into the buttery, toasted bread, smoked Gouda, and caramelized onions before getting to the beef. It melted in her mouth, and she clasped a hand around his wrist. Shyriq laughed loudly, garnering them a few stares, but he didn't care.

"Give me my sandwich and arm, woman," he said through laughter.

Grinning, Nhuri chewed and finally released him. "Listen, I will never doubt your restaurant choice again."

"Damn. You doubted me?"

She inched her index finger and thumb together. "Just a *little*, but I was wrong. Lesson learned. That is absolutely delicious. My goodness."

"I'll order you one to go."

"No, that's okay. I'll already have the itis, plus my dessert is coming. We can always come back another day."

Shyriq grinned, loving how she included him. "Yeah, we can do that."

For a moment, they fell into a comfortable silence and ate. Nhuri was so full by the time half of her meal was gone; she just knew the piece of cake would have her looking as if she were with child. But she wasn't going to pass it up.

Shyriq took a sip of the water that Tessa brought them. "Where you from originally?"

"Kansas City. Born and raised."

His brows lifted. "Yeah? And this is our first time crossing paths. I'm surprised."

"Why is that? We don't hang in the same places."

"That's not necessarily true, considering we've run into each other more than a few times."

She cocked her head to one side. "Okay, yes. That is true, but not surprising."

"Your sister has worked for me for years. I've never seen you at any events or heard her mention you, is all."

Nhuri swallowed. This was the part of the conversation she didn't want to have. Her past. It wasn't horrible, but she didn't feel the need to share it with him. So, she kept it simple and surface-level.

"I lived out of town for a while and moved back."

Shyriq nodded, putting two and two together. The status he read on Facebook about rerouting made sense now. He wondered what caused the move but didn't want to make her discuss something he could tell she wasn't ready to talk about.

"A move well worth it," he said.

Nhuri sipped her drink. "That's still up in the air," she jested.

"You said you like to travel," he said, steering the conversation back to her. "What's your favorite place you've been?"

Nhuri thought for a second. "Santorini. Hands down."

"Why?"

She smiled, thinking back. "The views were unreal. The water was the clearest I'd ever seen, and I could stare at the sunsets all day."

Shyriq nodded, taking a sip of his drink. "I'll have to check it out."

"You've never been?"

"Nah."

Nhuri's brows lifted. "You strike me as the kind of guy who's been everywhere."

"I travel, but I've never been to Greece," he smirked. "Guess you got one up on me."

She laughed. "I'll take that as a win."

"You should."

There was something about how he said it that made Nhuri believe her win wasn't just this one. His low, smooth voice made her stomach tighten a little. She ate a few more bites of her eggs and wiped her mouth. To say she was shocked by their lunch date would be an understatement. She walked in this morning thinking it would be all work, but he'd flipped the script. Her working for him was personal . . . Nhuri could see that now.

Shyriq wanted to get to know her on levels she knew would be a conflict of interest. And what was worse was that she didn't care.

She liked him.

She looked back up, catching him watching her again, and she blushed.

"You should bring me something next time you bake," he said casually.

"We'll see."

Shyriq chuckled, shaking his head. "You just can't let me have it, huh?"

"Nope."

"A'ight. I see how it is. I put you on my favorite food spot, and this is how you treat a brotha."

Chuckling, she didn't break eye contact. "I'm just saying trust has to be earned."

Shyriq caught the underlying message and nodded. If trust is what she wanted, that's what she'd get. Professionally *and* personally.

FIFTEEN

FOR THE FIRST weekend in a while, Nhuri was in the house. Jazmyn was trying to make plans and hit the city since it was warming up outside, but Nhuri just wanted to chill inside. After realizing how tiring it'd be to keep her bartending job, she ended up quitting. Thankfully, she had connections with the owner, and if she ever needed to come back to work or take on a gig, she could. Nhuri didn't see that happening any time soon and was honestly grateful. The void of uncertainty in her life was somewhat nonexistent now.

And right now, she was stretched across her couch with a Netflix series on pause because Natalia had called.

"Wait. Slow down. He said *what?*" Nhuri asked Natalia.

She called her so upset that Nhuri thought she would have to make a trip to her house. Though she was still dressed in pajamas and lounging around, Nhuri would gladly leave to see about her niece and sister.

Natalia sucked her teeth. "Raheem accepted a job out of state, so he's moving. He asked if he could get Raniya every other month."

"For the *entire* month?" Nhuri questioned with wide eyes.

"Yes! Is he crazy or stupid?"

Nhuri's sputtered laughter came out of nowhere. She didn't mean to laugh, but when Natalia got serious like this and started talking crazy, it was the funniest thing to her. Not much could rattle her sister's nerves, but playing with her child would get her out of character every time. The thing was, she was so serious about Raheem being crazy or stupid, and that's what made her question funnier.

"Sorry. I didn't mean to laugh. Maybe he meant for a week out of every other month," Nhuri said, trying to calm her down.

"No. I know exactly what he said because I made him repeat himself. He wants her for an *entire* month, Nhuri. No. Hell no. What am I supposed to do without my baby for that long?"

Natalia was losing it, and Nhuri knew it was for a good reason. Raniya hadn't been away from her for more than a few days since birth. Raheem wasn't a bad father by far, and Raniya loved him to death, but sending her baby across the world for a month had Natalia panicking at the thought.

"Hey," Nhuri said softly. "First, I'ma need you to calm down."

Natalia audibly inhaled and exhaled. "Okay."

"Next, think about what he's really asking you. Raheem is a good father. You and I both know that. Him getting Niy for one or two months during the summer is feasible, considering there are twelve months in a year."

"I know how many damn months are in a year," Natalia scoffed.

Nhuri snickered. "Well, *act* like it. Are you scared she'd get down there and act out?"

"No. Not really. Niy is a good kid. I just . . ." She paused, and Nhuri felt the weight of her words before she mumbled them. "I guess I'm scared of something happening to her, and I'm not there to protect her or vice versa."

Nhuri swallowed the lump in her throat. Those were the same emotions she felt when Natalia first revealed that she had lupus. All she had were scary, negative thoughts until Natalia reassured her that everything would be okay. Now, Nhuri knew it was her turn to make her sister feel at peace with whatever she decided to do.

"You always tell me that I can't live in fear. That if I want something, go after it. Sending her across the country will be scary for everyone, but imagine the experiences she'll miss out on if she doesn't go. The memories she'll make with her daddy. You have her full time now, and he gets her on the weekends and some days during the week, but I know you sometimes wish things were how they used to be a few years ago. And that's okay. You can still want and have that, but what're you willing to sacrifice?"

Natalia never talked much about her breakup with Raheem anymore. It happened right before she told him she was sick, and by then, Natalia decided that maybe they were better off apart. Her earlier stages were the roughest, and Raheem tried reclaiming his role as her man, but Natalia shut him down. In her eyes, learning about her health condition shouldn't have prompted him to want to be with her.

She was in a new relationship now and loved Malik but sometimes wondered what her life would've looked like had she taken Raheem back. Going through changes was scary. Natalia had been through enough of them in the last four years to know that. Every day, it felt like she was up against a new one, but Nhuri's words centered her. She didn't operate in the spirit of fear. She moved like God was in control because he is and will always be.

"You're right," Natalia sighed. "I don't want the relationship with him back; just how we worked together so well for our child, you know? He was here, and I didn't have to worry about what she was doing, eating, watching on her iPad, any of that."

"And you still don't. His parenting skills didn't change because y'all aren't together. I mean, unless there's something you haven't told me."

"No, they haven't," Natalia confirmed. "I'm just being emotional."

"Awww, sis. I know you are. How about this? You ask Niy what *she* wants to do and then go from there. Ultimately, it's up to her, even though y'all are the adults."

Natalia planned to do that anyway but was glad for her sister's input. Parenting was hard, and sometimes, Natalia cried at the thought of not having her parents there to help her, but she was so grateful for her small community. They were few in number but strong, and they had unwavering love for her and Raniya.

"I will. She's going to be so hyped and have a million questions," Natalia said.

Nhuri chuckled. "You already know she is. Do whatever is on your heart and go with your gut."

"Like always," she sighed. "Enough about me, though. How was your week? We only saw you one time."

Nhuri sat up on the couch and tossed the cover off her legs. "It was long."

"I bet," Natalia replied teasingly. "You officially survived your first week. How do you feel?"

Nhuri's lips curved slightly as she glanced up at the ceiling. "Honestly? Not bad. It wasn't what I expected, though."

"Meaning?"

"I don't know. I thought I'd be running around all day or stressed out, but it wasn't like that." She exhaled, lowering her head. "It's structured but not overbearing. Shyriq is particular, but I can respect it."

"Hmm."

Nhuri rolled her eyes at the sound. "Here we go."

"I didn't even say anything."

"You didn't have to."

Natalia chuckled. "I'm just making sure you remember what I told you."

Nhuri sighed. "Yes. Keep it professional."

"And?"

Nhuri pressed her lips together, already knowing where this was going.

"And don't put all my eggs in one basket."

"Exactly."

Nhuri shook her head. "You really think I'd do that?"

"I think you're intrigued by him."

Nhuri sat up a little. "And?"

"And you need to be careful." Natalia's voice was calm but firm. "You just got this job, Ri. You don't need unnecessary stress or drama in your life, especially not at work."

Nhuri sighed, tucking her feet beneath her. "I hear you."

"But are you listening?"

"I am," she admitted, but a part of her still wanted to push back. "I'm not naïve. I know how to keep things separate."

Natalia let out a knowing hum. "And yet, you're already calling him 'particular' like you admire it."

Nhuri groaned. "Please, don't start."

"I'm just saying."

Nhuri sighed, rubbing her forehead. "It's not even like that. We had lunch, that's all."

Natalia paused. "Lunch?"

Nhuri could already hear the judgment in her sister's tone. "It was nothing."

Natalia scoffed. "Girl, you went to lunch with your boss during your first week? That's *not* nothing."

Nhuri frowned. "It wasn't a date, Nat. He just wanted to talk."

Natalia sighed. "Look, all I'm saying is, don't make things more complicated than they need to be."

Nhuri heard her, and she was really trying not to, but Shyriq didn't make it any better. They had lunch again, but in his office after a quick meeting, and he didn't discuss work. The lines had already been crossed, blurred, and flipped. Nhuri felt like it was too late to turn back. And she wasn't wrong. Before she could respond to Natalia, her doorbell rang.

"Hold on," she said, pushing off the couch.

She reached the door and peeked out of the peephole before pulling it open. A deliveryman stood on the other side holding a large, elegantly wrapped basket.

"Hi. Can I help you?" Nhuri asked.

"Yes. I have a delivery for Ms. Coleman," he said.

Nhuri blinked. "That's me."

He handed over the package, along with a second bag that Nhuri immediately recognized as a designer brand. Her face screwed up as the man checked a few things off on his device.

"Have a good day," he said before walking off.

Nhuri stepped back inside, lightly kicking the door shut with her foot. She placed the bag down and locked the door before carrying it and the basket to the couch.

"Who was that?" Natalia asked.

Nhuri stared down at the packages with her heart thudding. "I . . . just got a delivery."

"From who?"

"I'm not sure."

Nhuri wasn't sure if the gift was from her ex or someone else. She didn't know why Dru was the first person to enter her mind, but he was the only option, considering he'd been her last real relationship. But that didn't explain how he'd gotten her address.

Instead of torturing herself more, she plucked the attached card from the clear pin.

Congratulations on your first week. Looking forward to what's ahead. Enjoy your gifts.
—*Shyriq*

Nhuri's stomach did a small flip seeing his name. *This man got something delivered to my house.*

Natalia's voice pulled her out of her thoughts. "Well? Who is it from?"

Nhuri cleared her throat. "It's from Shyriq."

All she heard was silence on the other end until she heard her name as if she were in trouble.

"Nhuri."

"What?"

"I *know* you're not about to tell me this man sent you something. What is it?"

Sighing, Nhuri ran her fingers over the gift basket, eyeing the items inside. An expensive box of chocolates you could only get out of the country let Nhuri know he'd put thought into this. Shyriq moved with intention, and Nhuri was trying to figure out if the gift was truly because he appreciated her first week or if he had sent it for another reason.

"It's just a gift basket with some flowers."

"And what else?" Natalia knew Shyriq and his generous pockets.

More than once, she and her boss, Cara, were shocked by the expensive gifts they received during the holiday season or when they closed on a big deal. She knew he hadn't just sent a gift basket. Nhuri hesitated before pulling the satin bow loose on the bag. Removing the neatly placed tissue paper, she grabbed the bag's handles, pulling it out.

"This is *so* nice," Nhuri cooed.

"Girl," Natalia fussed, making her sister smirk. "You know what?"

Nhuri giggled. "Hold on. Let me call you on FaceTime."

She tapped the video icon, and Natalia picked up. Flipping the camera, Nhuri showed her.

"Oh," Natalia chirped. "That's just not *any* bag. That hasn't even come out yet."

"I know," Nhuri whispered in awe.

Shyriq spared no expense when he picked out Nhuri's workbag. Meloré, the Black, woman-owned brand for luxury handbags and accessories, was one of Nhuri's favorites. It was founded in Chicago in 2012 and quickly became a well-known staple in the fashion industry, selling out collections in minutes.

The exquisite brown and cream python leather tote screamed luxury. It wasn't set to release until the fall, and already had a huge buzz about it. Nhuri didn't know how he was able to snag it already, but she wasn't complaining. The bag's structure was sophisticated yet functional and was designed to hold everything she'd need for the office without sacrificing style.

"You know . . . I wasn't going to ask about the lunch date at first—"

"It wasn't a date," Nhuri said, cutting her off.

Natalia cocked her head to the side. "That bag is telling me something different."

Chuckling, Nhuri ignored her and continued examining her gift. The glossy, hand-textured python skin added a touch of opulence with natural scale patterns that subtly caught the light. What Nhuri loved most was the gold hardware. It was minimal but striking and still caught your eye. A discreetly embossed Meloré logo sat near the top, giving the bag a hint of exclusivity.

You couldn't find this one in the store just yet, and not everyone was privy to the brand.

Inside, it was just as luxe, lined with plush suede in a deep cognac shade. Multiple compartments, including a padded laptop sleeve, ensured organization without clutter. A hidden zipper pocket provided extra security for essentials, while reinforced top handles and a detachable shoulder strap gave her versatile carrying options. It wasn't just a bag; it was a statement. A reminder that Shyriq believed she deserved nothing but the best.

Nhuri wasn't used to gifts.

Especially not from men like him.

"I think he was just being thoughtful," she murmured, more to herself than Natalia.

Natalia sighed. "I know you, Ri. And I know that tone."

"What tone?"

"The one that says you want to be stubborn and not admit that this man is trying to blur the lines."

Nhuri exhaled. "He's my boss."

"And yet, he's sending you luxury gifts after *one* week?"

Nhuri pressed her lips together, staring at the bag before her.

She wanted to brush it off, to act like it wasn't a big deal. But deep down, she knew Natalia wasn't wrong.

Shyriq wasn't the type to do something without reason. She was quickly learning that. His purpose was intentional, which Nhuri found attractive. Same with taking her to The Spot. He could've taken her anywhere, but he'd chosen somewhere to make a statement. She was his assistant, but he also wanted her to mean much more.

Nhuri bit her lip, contemplating her next move. *Should I send a thank-you text?* she thought, and, of course, Natalia read her mind. It was those sisterly instincts that always got her caught up.

"You're thinking about texting him, aren't you?" Natalia asked, amusement laced in her tone.

Nhuri groaned. "Can I live?"

Natalia laughed. "I *knew* it! Girl, he got you wrapped already."

"No, he doesn't," Nhuri argued, not sounding convincing at all.

Natalia sighed. "I just don't want you getting caught up in something that's gonna make work messy. You deserve all the good coming your way. Don't let a man, no matter how fine or charming, get in the way of that."

Nhuri exhaled, rolling her shoulders. "I know."

"Do you?"

"Yes, I do."

"Good. Because the moment I see you acting crazy, I'm coming up there to personally knock some sense into you."

Nhuri chuckled. "Duly noted."

A slight pause settled between them before Natalia spoke again.

"But for real, though . . . How was the lunch date?"

Nhuri grinned. "It felt natural. Initially, I was kind of nervous, but he's so easy to talk to."

Natalia smiled. "I love that for you. I just hate that he's your boss."

"Girl, he's your boss too," Nhuri laughed.

"No, he isn't. He's the owner. Truthfully, he needs to think about taking a step down and enjoying life. I know I would."

Nhuri nodded, agreeing. "I would too. But I get it. GHC is his baby."

"And you're going to be his baby next."

"You don't know what you want for me," Nhuri laughed. "One minute, it's leave him alone; the next, you're talking like I should be his woman."

"I know," Natalia sighed. "After the shit you went through with Dru, I just want you happy. If that happiness comes from Shyriq, then so be it. I'd never want anything less for you."

Nhuri's eyes watered. "I know you wouldn't."

Shyriq drummed his fingers against his desk as he held his phone to his ear. The blinds in his office were slightly cracked, letting in a warm afternoon glow, mimicking how he felt at that moment. He'd just received the documents finalizing his divorce, and King was the first person he called. Shyriq was sure it would've taken the full thirty days or more to receive something, but it'd only been twenty-three days.

"You should have the documents that finalize the divorce and the settlement paperwork," King explained.

Shyriq scrolled through the PDF files and downloaded each one. He scanned them while nodding. "Yeah, they're all here."

"All right, good. So, it's over, man. How you feeling?"

Shyriq slowly exhaled, rolling his shoulders. Truthfully, he wasn't sure yet. He didn't feel any regret and knew that, as a man who valued what marriage meant, Xena had to go. Yet, he still couldn't wrap his mind around Xena's betrayal. It wasn't even how she played him but that he didn't see the signs. Or couldn't save his marriage. As a man, Shyriq felt that the worst feeling was knowing he lacked in an area of his life where he had vowed to always be there.

He let out a dry chuckle. "Ask me again in a few days."

"I hear that. You're a free man, though. Enjoy it," King said.

Shyriq nodded, letting the word *free* roll around in his head, but it didn't hit him like he thought it would. Xena had spent the last year making the process more difficult than necessary, stretching things out longer than needed. His marriage had been long over before he received that email, but seeing it in writing made it all real. Shyriq ran a hand down his face and over his beard.

"You're right. I appreciate you, King."

"You know it's nothing. You gon' be good, though?"

Shyriq smirked. "Yeah, I'ma be good. It ain't like I'm heartbroken. I been checked out of the marriage."

King laughed. "Yeah, yeah. I just know how shit can feel when it's set in stone. Ain't no going back now."

"There wasn't going to be anyway."

King hummed in agreement. "That's facts. But what's next? What's up with that celebration?"

"You niggas just want something to get out of the house for," Shyriq laughed.

Cane and the fellas had been on the same time. They were happy for him.

"Aye, man. This is worth getting out of the house for," King chuckled. "Whatever you decide, go do something for yourself today. Clear your head," he advised.

"Nah, bro," he muttered. "I ain't in the mood for all that."

"Man, you always acting like you above turning up."

"I didn't say that," Shyriq corrected, leaning forward. "I just don't see the point in throwing a party 'cause my marriage failed."

King chuckled. "Fair enough. You probably just need it to settle in."

"I hear you."

"But are you listening? Don't sit in that office acting like it's just another workday. This is a reset."

Shyriq didn't take his words lightly. King was being more than just his lawyer; he was being a friend. One who had saved him a bunch of money, so Shyriq didn't mind taking his advice. He hadn't steered him wrong yet.

"A'ight, bro. Get off my phone preaching," Shyriq jested.

"Whatever, man. I'll check in later. If you need anything, hit my line. I'll be in and out of the office."

"Bet. I'll hit you up if something comes up."

Shyriq ended the call, dropping his phone onto the desk before looking at the ceiling. He was in a weird mood, and though he should've had celebrating on his mind or pouring up a drink and booking a flight, he just wanted to take the day off. But he couldn't. He had meetings lined up and couldn't move them around.

He took a slow, deep breath before printing the documents and grabbing them off his printer. A knock at the door made him glance up. Before he could respond, Nhuri stepped inside. Shyriq blinked, straightening slightly as she walked in.

"Hey. Sorry to interrupt," she said, her voice smooth and calming.

It was just what Shyriq needed to hear to calm his nerves. She was just the face he needed to see. Nhuri's outfit highlighted her curves in a way that made his jaws tense, and eyes focused. She looked good. *Too* damn good and distracting.

She was dressed in an olive-green fitted, long-sleeved dress, with her hair pinned back neatly, making her features stand out even more. She looked put together, but there was something about her expression that seemed like she had something on her mind and wasn't sure how to get it off.

Shyriq cleared his throat. "You're not interrupting. What's going on?"

"Just wanted to let you know I made it back."

A smirk tugged at the corner of his lips. "That's all? You could've texted me."

"I could've, but I figured you'd want to see me in person before this meeting. You know . . . as your assistant and everything," she teased.

"Oh, so you're claiming the title now?"

Nhuri's eyes narrowed slightly, but amusement danced in them. "I mean, that *is* my job, *right?*"

Shyriq leaned back, his gaze slow and deliberate as it moved over her face. "Good to know you remember that."

Nhuri arched a brow. "Did you think I forgot?"

Shyriq exhaled, shaking his head as he gestured to the chair across from him. "I didn't. Have a seat."

Nhuri hesitated momentarily before sinking into the chair and gracefully crossed her legs. Shyriq watched her adjust the iPad on her lap before she looked up at him. Something about her presence made the weight of what he'd just finalized and his conversation with King feel a little less suffocating.

"How was your first week?" he asked, shifting the focus.

Nhuri tilted her head. "You mean before or after you abandoned me on my first day?"

Shyriq let out a short chuckle, shaking his head. "I see you're still in your feelings about that."

"I'm just messing with you," Nhuri smiled. "It was good. I couldn't have asked for a better trainer."

Michelle was thorough, just like Shyriq said she was. She made sure Nhuri knew all the steps if something complex needed to be explained. If Nhuri had questions, Michelle had the answers. In addition to giving her work advice, Michelle also gave her womanly advice. Michelle had seen and experienced some things that Nhuri could relate to, and having her encourage her without judgment felt good. Nhuri planned to get a bunch of gifts for her baby girl, who would grace the world soon.

"That's good to know. You're still here, so I guess I didn't scare you off," Shyriq said.

Nhuri smirked. "Not yet."

Shyriq chuckled lowly. "Good. I'd hate to go through the process of finding someone else."

Nhuri smirked. She'd hate that too because she actually liked her job. Now, she was trying to figure out how to address him about sending her the gift basket and bag. She sent him a text, but thanking him in person seemed the right thing to do as well. A comfortable silence settled between them before Nhuri's gaze flickered toward his desk. Her eyes caught the heading of the papers, still resting near the edge.

"So, how's *that* going?" she asked, her tone shifting slightly.

Shyriq met her gaze, noting the curiosity behind it.

He exhaled, glancing at his screen before returning his attention to her. "Everything was finalized today."

Nhuri's brows lifted slightly. "Oh."

He nodded. "Yeah."

A beat passed before Nhuri spoke again. "How do you feel?"

Shyriq huffed a quiet laugh, rubbing a hand over his jaw. "That's the million-dollar question, huh?"

Nhuri tilted her head. "I guess so."

He considered it for a moment before speaking. "Relieved. But also . . . not as much as I thought I would be."

Nhuri nodded slowly, taking that in. "I get that."

Shyriq's gaze lingered on her. "Yeah?"

Nhuri exhaled, looking down briefly before meeting his eyes again. "Uh-huh. Endings are weird. Even when you know they need to happen."

Shyriq studied her for a long moment; something about her words sitting deeper than he expected. She got it . . . maybe more than she was letting on.

"Sounds like you know a bit about letting go too."

Nhuri rolled her eyes, but a small smile played on her lips. "You'd be surprised."

Shyriq nodded. "Maybe I would."

Nhuri cleared her throat. "Yeah, but that's not why I stopped by. Before the day ends and before we go into this meeting, I wanted to thank you for the gift basket and bag. You didn't have to do that."

Shyriq shrugged, placing his hands on the desk. "It was nothing."

Nhuri scoffed playfully. "A Meloré designer workbag is *not* nothing, Shyriq."

He smirked and licked his lips, and his voice dropped slightly. "It is to me. Do you like it?"

"Yes. I love it. The bag doesn't come out until the fall. How did you even get it?"

"A know a friend that knows a friend," he replied as if it were nothing.

Nhuri should've known. Millionaires run in the same circles. Of course, he had direct contact with the owner, Dana. She had followed her journey for years before she made it big, and it was so inspiring.

"Well, let your *friend* know I appreciate it," she said.

Shyriq held her gaze for a long moment before nodding. "I will. You deserve it."

Nhuri swallowed, suddenly feeling like they weren't talking about just the gifts anymore.

Shyriq leaned in just enough for his presence to feel heavier. "You know I want you, right?"

Nhuri's breath caught slightly, and her pulse kicked up a notch as her lips parted. "Shyriq . . ."

"Nah, none of that," he smirked. "I'm letting you know now. Just in case there's any confusion on your end. You may work for me, but I want something more with you."

Nhuri blinked, caught off guard by his directness. She didn't have any words.

"I like you," he continued, his tone even but firm. "And I want to see where this goes."

Her heartbeat thudded loudly in her ears.

She had felt the attraction between them from the start, but hearing him lay it out so plainly made it impossible to ignore.

Nhuri exhaled, trying to steady herself. "Shyriq, we work together."

He chuckled. "And?"

"And . . . This could get messy."

He nodded as if he understood her hesitation. And he did to a certain extent, but he was willing to take the risk if she was.

"Maybe." He shrugged. "Or maybe it turns out to be one of the best decisions you ever made."

Nhuri's lips parted, but before she could respond, he said, "Think about it."

She stared at him, realizing he had just completely flipped the dynamic on her. She tried to remain professional and listen to her big sister's words, but Shyriq made it difficult.

Checking the time on his watch, he stood up. "We got a meeting to get to."

Nhuri blinked, snapping out of her thoughts. "Right. Is there anything I need to know before we go?"

Shyriq rounded the desk, stopping at her side. Nhuri looked up at him, hating how the gentleness in his eyes made her heart flutter.

"Not necessarily. Just go with the flow. Input if you want. Let's roll."

Nhuri stood and headed for the door. His hand at the small of her back let her know that he didn't care that they were at work, but she did. Gently, she stepped to the side.

"You like me, but let's keep our hands to ourselves while working," she said.

Shyriq pulled his door closed. "Just at work? Got it."

When he smirked, Nhuri shook her head and headed down the hall toward the conference room. Chuckling, Shyriq fell in stride beside her, feeling much better than he had before she entered his office. Now, he needed to finalize the details of this launch party, and he'd be an even happier man.

SIXTEEN

NHURI SAT NEAR the middle of the sleek glass table, jotting down notes as the meeting progressed. Although the event was months away, and the launch of the new whiskey line didn't drop until the end of the year, planning ahead was always best. Plus, Shyriq wanted to blow the numbers out of the park with this limited-edition spice blend. She listened intently to the distribution manager discuss strategies when a smooth voice to her left grabbed her attention.

"That color looks good on you," Tyreek, the event coordinator, said, flashing her a charming smile. "I just had to let you know that."

Nhuri blinked, momentarily caught off guard by his compliment.

She was used to men complimenting her, but in a professional setting, during a meeting, wasn't the time. Clearing her throat, she offered him a polite smile.

"Thanks."

Shyriq had been flipping through a report but stilled for a second before lifting his head. His eyes traveled between the two, trying to see what they were discussing. He didn't say anything immediately, but the slight tightening of his jaws didn't go unnoticed. Nhuri tried not to make eye contact with him, and she could've passed out when Tyreek kept talking.

"Speaking of looking good," he said, clearly unfazed by the brief pause in conversation, "you should let me take you out to celebrate your first official week at GHC. I know a spot with the best seafood in the city."

Nhuri let out a soft, nervous laugh and shook her head. "That's sweet, but—"

"She'll be busy," Shyriq cut in, interrupting whatever she was about to say.

Nhuri looked horrified but turned on, and she couldn't place her feelings. Shyriq's voice was calm but firm, leaving no room for discussion on her schedule and whereabouts. He stacked his papers and gave Tyreek an unreadable expression. At least one Nhuri couldn't read, but man to man, Tyreek knew what it was.

"Nhuri doesn't need any distractions right now. We've got too much on the table, especially with this upcoming launch."

Tyreek arched a brow, and a slight smirk played in the corner of his lips. "Her personal life and work aren't separate?"

A tense silence filled the room. Nhuri wanted to sink into her chair as a few team members exchanged glances, sensing the power move each man was exuding. She'd been caught between two men who didn't even have to do all of this right now, but knowing the type of man Shyriq was, she knew he wouldn't stop until he got his point across.

Shyriq exhaled through his nose, pressing his tongue against the inside of his cheek before responding. "That's a question you'd have to ask her, but seeing as though we're in the middle of a meeting, I'd suggest not doing so."

His message was loud and clear. Nhuri tried to make him look her way, but Shyriq kept his eyes trained on Tyreek. The possessiveness in his tone, though masked under the guise of professionalism, had Nhuri squirming in her seat. The seat of her panties was damp, and she couldn't wait to call her girls. Sadly, Tyreek hadn't fully taken the hint.

Chuckling, he shook his head and said, "Got it. Ask her out when work ends."

Shyriq flexed his jaws and caught himself before he said something crazy. Tyreek was testing him, and he had no choice but to let it slide. At least for now. Business needed to be handled. Nhuri rubbed her glossed lips together, unsure of what to say or do. She wasn't oblivious to what just happened, but the last thing she wanted was to make a scene in the middle of a meeting.

Shyriq let the moment settle before redirecting his focus back to the matter at hand. "All right, let's get back on track. Tyreek, since you're so good at planning nights out, I assume you've finalized the guest list for the prelaunch event?"

Though his title was an event coordinator, Shyriq was being a sarcastic asshole with that comment. A few chuckles broke the tension, and Tyreek smirked, taking the jab in stride.

"Yeah, I did. VIP invites went out yesterday. We're expecting a solid turnout."

Shyriq nodded, flipping to the next page of the report. "Good. Let's make sure it stays that way."

Shyriq went around the room, letting everyone give their updates. The exclusive tasting event was high-end and invitation-only. Shyriq's clientele and the people he wanted in attendance played a pivotal role in the company's success, so it was only right that they got special privileges and early access. Nhuri was grateful there were no further interruptions, at least on her end, but she could still feel Shyriq's energy lingering.

Every now and then, she caught him watching her, though he never let his gaze linger for too long. It was subtle, but it was enough. She smirked when she thought he wasn't looking, and he cleared his throat, making her look up. Nhuri squinted at his hardened expression, and he smirked, making her smile.

"Valet service will be available all night, and we'll have a driving company for those who can't drive home on their own," Tyreek said.

"All right. And what about our Gold members? Are they receiving special perks like last year?" Shyriq questioned.

"Special perks, as in what?" the membership coordinator asked.

She specifically oversees subscriptions, renewals, and customer engagement.

"Something. They pay the most money every month and should receive something outside of what everyone else is getting," Shyriq said.

He waited for someone on the team to chime in. When they didn't, he started taking notes. Nhuri's brain was in overdrive. As a member of a few subscriptions, she enjoyed the incentives that came with paying just a bit more, especially if it was before the public had access to them.

"I'm not sure if it's been mentioned," she began, and all eyes landed on her, "but maybe have an exclusive lounge just for them?"

She noticed everyone's head nodding, agreeing with her suggestion. When her eyes landed on Shyriq, he was smiling.

"I love that idea. Exclusivity throughout the entire night. Tyreek, get with your team and get the ball rolling on that. Include Nhuri in the emails."

Her eyes widened. "Oh. He doesn't have to do that. I was just throwing it out there."

"And you can continue throwing ideas out there if they're beneficial. Cara will get today's minutes out. I'm looking forward to this event, team. I appreciate everyone's input and updates today."

Shyriq dismissed everyone, and when Nhuri walked out of the conference room behind him, she couldn't help but say something to him. She waited until they were close to the elevator.

"You didn't have to do that," she said quietly but firmly.

"Do what?" he asked, still walking.

"Shut Tyreek down like that. I could've handled him."

Shyriq called for the elevator, slipped his hands into his pockets, and faced her. "I know you could've, and it seemed like you were, but I'm not about to have him thinking he can push up on you."

Nhuri crossed her arms. "So, what? I'm off-limits to everyone now?"

His jaws flexed. "To him and every other man in this building? Yeah. Yes, you are."

Her breath hitched, and she smiled a little. His dominance never wavered, and Nhuri spotted the intensity of his words in his eyes and felt them in her chest. Shyriq was serious. Words were okay, but she needed to see him put some action behind them.

Nhuri exhaled, shaking her head. "You're gonna be a problem, aren't you?"

Shyriq smirked, stepping back so she could enter the elevator. "A good problem, but I think you like that."

Nhuri didn't say anything. She stood on one side of the elevator while he took up space on the other end. Before she could gather her thoughts, Shyriq spoke again.

"Do you have plans on Saturday?" he asked.

Nhuri glanced his way, surprised by his question. "Why?"

"Because I want to take you out," he said smoothly, his eyes locked on her. "That is, if you're cool with that. I was thinking something outside of work. No business. I'm not your boss, and you aren't my assistant. We leave work where it's at."

She hesitated for a moment. Before now, she might have second-guessed herself, but after seeing how serious he was, how his divorce was finalized, and how he was making his intentions clear, she let go of the fear holding her back.

"I mean, I guess a date wouldn't be bad considering I'm all yours," she said sarcastically, in a playful tone.

Shyriq grinned, pleased with her answer and the way she never really took things to heart. It was refreshing to know he could switch it up with her, and Nhuri wouldn't be offended. They stopped on their floor, and Nhuri exited first, turning to face him.

"I'm glad you know," Shyriq teased. "I'll text you all the details later today. That coo'?"

She nodded and hummed. "Mhm, it is."

Shyriq nodded and smirked, trying not to show his elation. "A'ight. Have a good rest of your day."

"You too, *boss*."

"Awww. Here you go," he chuckled.

Nhuri turned and walked off. Her heart was racing, but that didn't make her want to change her mind. It was just a date. She was going to have fun, but she also would guard her heart. The last thing she wanted was to get hurt unintentionally. But for now, she was willing to take the risk. There was no harm in that, and even if there were, she'd deal with the consequences later.

SEVENTEEN

RETAIL THERAPY WAS the best.

No one could convince Nhuri otherwise. She adjusted her shopping bags as she and Jazmyn strolled through the mall. The smell of fresh pretzels was left behind as they entered Nordstrom and inhaled designer perfumes mixing in the air. It was a gentle reminder for Nhuri to pick up a new scent. With her sign-on bonus, she felt she could splurge a little and not feel bad.

It'd been a while since they had a proper girls' day, and she didn't know how much she needed it until now. Nhuri planned to take full advantage of her early day off and catch her girl up. Thankfully, Jazmyn was also able to get off work early.

"Girl, I don't even know why you brought me in here," Jazmyn said, eyeing the shoe section with narrowed eyes. "You know I don't need to be spending no money."

Nhuri smirked, nudging her. "Nobody said you had to buy anything. I'll get you something, but window shopping ain't never hurt nobody."

Jazmyn sucked her teeth but followed her toward the clothes racks anyway. They flipped through racks, commenting on pieces they liked, the ones they'd never wear, and the ones that screamed money they didn't need to spend. Nhuri wanted to step up her wardrobe and get more statement pieces, so that's what she did.

"These jeans will look good on you," Nhuri said, holding up a pair of Levi's for Jazmyn to examine.

"Those are cute. Let me see," Jazmyn said, grabbing them.

Knowing she'd need to try them on before deciding, Jazmyn headed toward the fitting rooms. Nhuri wasn't too far behind her, with an armful of garments. She only planned on trying on a few things. Certain shirts were cute on the hanger, but Nhuri had to see if they still made the cut once she slid them on. They entered the fitting room and snagged rooms side by side.

"I think the jeans are on sale," Jazmyn commented.

"If they are, that's a steal. You know Levi's be taxing."

Jazmyn chuckled. "Hell yeah."

While Nhuri slid out of her shirt, she felt her phone vibrate inside her purse. She and Shyriq had been texting all morning after getting off the phone before he had to handle some business, so she wondered if it was him. Unlocking her phone, Nhuri's face screwed up when she realized it wasn't Shyriq who texted her; it was her ex-boyfriend, Dru.

"What the hell does he want?" Nhuri mumbled.

"What'd you say?" Jazmyn said, tugging the jeans over her hips.

Too engrossed in the text message, Nhuri ignored her. It'd been months since he reached out, and Nhuri wondered what the purpose was now. They didn't have anything to discuss, so she couldn't possibly understand what he had to say. Her eyes rolled before she could fully read the text.

What's going on, Nhuri? I know it's been a minute since you heard from me. I hope everything is all good with you. I'll be in your city next week and was hoping we could meet up and talk. Hit me back and let me know. I miss you.

Nhuri read the text a second time and got even more annoyed. *You miss me?* she thought with pure disgust, scrunching up her nose before exiting her text messages and locking her phone.

"Girl, what the hell are you doing?" Jazmyn asked. "I've been calling your name for who knows how long."

"My fault. Hold on. Here I come," Nhuri said, rushing to slide into one of the shirts.

She opened the door to Jazmyn, examining herself in the mirror. As she suspected, the jeans looked good on her, hugging her curves and making her booty sit up just right.

"You weren't lying," Jazmyn said, running her hand over them before making eye contact with Nhuri through the mirror. "What's wrong?"

She hadn't realized the expression on her face was one of pure annoyance. "Why did Dru just text me?"

Jazmyn pivoted so fast she could've given herself whiplash. "You're lying."

"I wish I was."

"What the hell does he want?"

Instead of reiterating what she read, Nhuri handed her the phone so she could read the text herself. It was just like a no-good man to reach out or pop up when she finally felt good about moving on. Whatever Dru wanted to discuss, he could talk to himself about it. *Where was this energy when I wanted him to talk and listen to me back then?* Nhuri thought as Jazmyn handed her the phone.

"Girl," Jaz dragged. "The audacity."

"Right."

"Does he expect you to just jump at his request?"

Nhuri shrugged. She wasn't sure, but knowing Dru, the answer was yes. He had this controlling behavior about him that Nhuri found unsettling. She didn't know when or why it began to happen in the last couple of years during their relationship, but she couldn't handle it. Any and everything she did seemed to tick him off and walking around on eggshells around someone who supposedly loved you wasn't how she wanted to live. It hurt to leave, but it would've hurt worse had she stayed.

"Probably, but I'm not," Nhuri said, returning to her dressing room. When she didn't feel Jazmyn behind her, she looked over her shoulder. "What? Why're you looking at me like that?"

"Because I know you. If you don't respond or give him an answer, you'll be thinking about it all day. I can already tell he ruined your mood."

Nhuri's nostrils flared. He had, but she was trying to shake it. Jazmyn wasn't lying, though. Knowing that his text was sitting there waiting for her to respond would irk her nerves all day, possibly all week.

"Yeah, but it's whatever. I can ignore him. It's not like I haven't before," Nhuri said, trying to sound convincing.

"You know . . . sometimes, no response *is* a response. He doesn't deserve to have you go out of your way to *hear him out*. His ass should've been more accommodating and a communicator back then. The ship has sailed, my boy," she said, stepping inside her room and then quickly popping her head out. "And get that shirt. It's cute."

Nhuri couldn't help but smile. It was just like Jazmyn to turn a bad moment into something good. While she tried on a few other items, Nhuri couldn't help but talk herself out of texting Dru back. A part of her was curious to know what he had to say, while another part didn't care. Her heart and mind were playing tug-of-war with each other, and she knew they shouldn't have been.

Plus, Dru should've been the furthest thing on her mind when she had a date to prepare for. She could tell Shyriq was excited through his text messages, and Nhuri loved his energy. Once he stopped being hot and cold, his true personality made Nhuri want to get to know him more. Jazmyn thought they were just coming out for a girls' day, but she hadn't told her about tomorrow.

After an hour of more shopping and spending more money than they intended, they went to the nail salon for their pedicure appointments. It was on the opposite side of town, and Saturday traffic was thick. The weather was nice, so that was expected. Once they made it inside, Nhuri settled into the plush massage chair and sighed deeply as her feet plunged into the warm, bubbly water.

"You had a long day already?" her nail tech Bia asked.

Nhuri chuckled. "Just came from shopping, so, yes. Kind of. You know how it is when you've been walking around the malls and stores."

Bia nodded. "I do. It's all good, though. I'ma get you right."

Nhuri smiled and glanced to her left as Jazmyn settled into her seat. "Whew. I needed this."

"Me too. After the week I had, all I want to do is relax."

"Don't tell me they're stressing you out already?" Jazmyn wondered, adjusting the massage settings to target her lower back. "It hasn't even been a full month."

Nhuri chuckled. "No, it's not that. I just had a lot on my plate mentally, but things are finally starting to feel good. I feel settled in."

Thanks to Shyriq's suggestion, Nhuri had been included in the setup and discussions about the VIP lounge for Nine Oak Gold members. The way she saw it, they deserved and had earned the privilege to have a grander experience. So, she didn't mind extending her ideas, but, boy, was she tired.

Jazmyn gave her a knowing look. "Mmm-hmmm. And does this 'settled' feeling have anything to do with a certain boss of yours?"

Nhuri rolled her eyes, but the heat creeping up her neck gave her away. "It's not like that."

Jazmyn leaned forward slightly, resting her elbow on the armrest. "Oh, but it *is* something. You can't hide that little smirk from me. Spill it."

Nhuri exhaled, staring at her toes as Bia removed her gel polish. "He asked me out."

Jazmyn's eyes widened. "What? When?"

"Earlier this week, after a meeting we had," Nhuri admitted, glancing at her. "It kinda caught me off guard. I mean, I knew there was something there, but I didn't think he'd just come out and say it."

Grinning, Jazmyn said, "Oh, there's *definitely* something there! So, what did you say?"

Nhuri hesitated for a second before shrugging. "I said yes."

"As you should've. I don't know why you wouldn't have."

"There were plenty of reasons. He checked one of his employees for flirting with me."

Jazmyn gasped, and the slight smirk Nhuri was sporting made her slap her arm. "Girl, what? Who was it?"

"The event coordinator. He asked to take me out in front of the entire room. It was hushed, but Shyriq heard him. Without saying too much, he basically told him to fall the hell back."

Jazmyn clapped and nodded. "I know *that's* right, Shyriq. Let these people know you're not about to play with them about your woman."

Nhuri snorted. "Oh, please. I'm not his woman yet."

"Yeah, but you have a date with him, so it could be more."

"Maybe, maybe not. I'm just seeing where it goes. But I'm not jumping headfirst into something."

Jazmyn squinted at her. "I understand you, I do. But how are you gonna keep your guard up when you already like him?"

Nhuri sighed. "I don't know, Jaz. I mean, he's intriguing. He's got this serious, no-nonsense vibe at work, but then he does things that throw me off. Like getting me a gift basket and a designer bag for finishing my first week. Is he love-bombing me?"

Jazmyn cackled. "Um, no. I wouldn't consider it that. I mean, why wouldn't a man want to show he's interested in a woman from the jump? Why not go all out in the beginning so there's no confusion about how he's coming behind you? Shyriq is trying to court you, friend. Let him. He's clearly serious about you."

Nhuri bit into her bottom lip and stared at the blue water surrounding her feet. "That's what I'm afraid of. It's been a while since I've let someone in, and I don't want to get caught up in something that could get messy. You know his divorce just finalized."

Jazmyn tilted her head. "I hear you. But listen, you ain't gotta map out the whole future today. Just go, enjoy yourself, and see how you feel. But don't overthink it."

Nhuri smirked. "You know I overthink everything."

Jazmyn laughed. "Exactly. So, this time, don't."

Nhuri let the thought settle as Bia began scrubbing her foot. Telling an overthinker not to overthink was like expecting a fish to drown. It would never happen. But maybe Jazmyn was right. For once, Nhuri just needed to let go and enjoy whatever this was without expectations.

EIGHTEEN

STEAM BILLOWED FROM the bathroom as Shyriq stepped out of the shower and wrapped a towel around his waist. Water dripped from his broad shoulders, rolling down the deep ridges of his back as he wiped a hand over his face and beard. He'd been anticipating this night since he asked Nhuri out. He wasn't surprised that she accepted but was surprised that she hadn't given him any pushback. For once, he felt like they were getting somewhere.

The finalization of his divorce may have played a significant role in her answer, but whatever the case, Shyriq planned to treat her to a nice evening. This was the first time in a while that he actually cared about impressing someone. Nhuri didn't seem materialistic, but that didn't matter. He wasn't going to treat her any less than the best.

Moving into his bedroom, Shyriq grabbed his phone from the nightstand just as it started buzzing. Rush's name flashed across the screen, and he smirked before answering and placing him on speaker. He already knew he was about to talk some shit. He felt it.

"What's good, lil bro?" Shyriq said, setting the phone down while reaching for the bottle of lotion on his dresser.

"Man, you tell me. You out here breaking hearts tonight or what?" Rush's voice came through the speaker, amusement laced in his tone.

Shyriq chuckled, rubbing the lotion over his arms and chest. "Nah, nothing like that."

"She must be special then, or are you just maturing?" Rush teased.

He chuckled. "Man, get off my phone."

"Nah. I'm just trying to see. Who is she?"

"Nhuri."

Rush whistled. "The assistant? The same one you said you were gonna keep it professional with?"

"Yeah, yeah," Shyriq muttered, grabbing a pair of black boxer briefs from his dresser. "Plans change."

Rush laughed. "You mean you saw what you liked and said, 'Fuck it.'"

Shyriq pulled the briefs up his toned legs, shaking his head. "Basically. She's different, though. Not just a pretty face. She got her shit together and is smart as hell. I respect that."

Rush hummed. "So, you like her."

Shyriq paused. That was the part that had been messing with him. It wasn't just attraction or intrigue. He liked being around her. Whenever she entered his office, or they had a conversation, everything shifted in her presence in a good way. That type of energy was hard to come by, so his answer came easy.

"Yeah, I do."

Rush clapped his hands in the background. "Damn, my brother out here catching feelings! What's next? Matching pajamas?"

"Shut the hell up," Shyriq laughed, stepping into his walk-in closet.

He ran his fingers over the neatly hung clothes, scanning for the perfect outfit. He settled on jeans, a tailored black button-up, and Prada sneakers. Where they were going didn't require him to dress it all the way up, but he still kept it casual and clean.

"You wearing cologne?" Rush asked, still amused.

Shyriq rolled his eyes. "When you gon' grow up?"

Rush laughed. "When I meet a woman who makes me. Until then, I'ma be a playa for life."

Shyriq shook his head. "That's sad. I'ma see if she got some friends," he stopped midsentence. "Actually, never mind. Ain't got time for you to be embarrassing me."

Rush laughed loudly. "Man, whatever. Where you taking her?"

"A little spot downtown. Real chill, a private chef, and good music. Nothing too much."

Rush whistled again. "Nothing too much? Look at you, pulling out all the stops. So, what's the endgame?"

Shyriq sighed, grabbing his watch from the nightstand and strapping it onto his wrist. "I don't know yet. But I'ma find out."

Rush was quiet for a second before saying, "I respect it. Just make sure you ain't moving too fast. Women like her . . . They don't play games. She'll cut your ass off quicker than you can blink or think."

Shyriq smirked. "Good. I don't play games either, so neither of us has anything to worry about."

"A'ight, big bro. Go do your thing. Just don't fuck it up."

Shyriq chuckled. "Yeah, yeah. I'll hit you up later."

Ending the call, Shyriq grabbed his cologne and sprayed a few dabs onto his wrist and neck. After brushing his waves, he took one last glance into the mirror and then headed out of the bedroom. Stepping inside the kitchen, he poured himself a glass of Nine Oak, letting the whiskey swirl in the glass before taking a slow sip. His nerves weren't bad, but there was an anticipation in his chest that he wasn't used to.

Nhuri wasn't just another woman. She wasn't an easy distraction or a way to pass the time. She challenged him, made him think, and had already started taking up space in his mind more than he wanted to admit. Shyriq didn't mind that. He just hoped she was ready for what came next. Some may have thought it was too soon for him to be dating right after a divorce, but he begged to differ.

He'd spent so much time prioritizing business and ensuring his life was airtight that he never really let himself indulge in anything outside of his failed marriage. It was sad to admit, but it was the past now. Shyriq wasn't the same man he'd been when his marriage crumbled, so he didn't want to give Nhuri any part of that. When his phone buzzed again, he was expecting it to be Rush, talking mess again, but it was a text from Nhuri.

Hey, I can't wait to see you in a little bit.

Shyriq smiled. It was short, sweet, and to the point. Grinning, he typed her a response.

I can't wait to see you either. I know you're looking gorgeous. I am.

Chuckling, Shyriq hoped she kept that same confident energy throughout the night. On the other side of town, Nhuri stood in front of her vanity, adjusting the delicate gold necklace. Butterflies swarmed her stomach when she saw Shyriq's text telling her the ride was heading her way. It was the good kind of nervousness that didn't make her want to cancel but made her want him to hurry up so she could be around him.

"Talking to someone new is so funny," she chuckled.

Nhuri had all these weird feelings happening at once, but she embraced them. Shyriq hadn't told her every place they were going tonight, but he did say dinner. So, Nhuri wore one of the outfits she picked up while shopping yesterday. The deep emerald dress hugged her curves in all the right places, stopping midthigh and showcasing just the right amount of boob action. Her black heels and clutch were the final touches.

She curled and pinned her hair up, leaving a few tendrils framing her face. Not wanting to do too much with her makeup, she went for sultry and subtle. It was just enough foundation and concealer to highlight her natural beauty.

When her phone vibrated and fell off the perfume bottle she had propped it against, Nhuri flinched at the sound, which caught her off guard. A FaceTime call came through, and the person calling made her smile. Swiping the screen, she answered, and Raniya's excited face filled the screen.

"TT!" Raniya shrieked, grinning wide. Her missing front tooth made Nhuri gasp.

"Oh my gosh, Niy! When did you lose your tooth?"

She grinned wider, putting her mouth closer to the screen, and Nhuri's heart swelled. The innocence of a six-year-old would never get old.

"Today! I have to put it under my pillow so I can get something from the tooth fairy."

"Yes! The tooth fairy comes at nighttime. That's so exciting, boo. You look adorable," Nhuri cooed.

"And you look pretty."

Nhuri blushed. "Thank you."

"My mommy said you going on a date!"

Nhuri laughed softly, finishing the last touches on her lip gloss. "Oh, she did, huh?" She flicked her gaze toward Natalia, who sat beside Raniya, smirking but saying nothing.

Raniya nodded enthusiastically. "Yep! She did, and I had to call you. Where are you going?"

Nhuri turned back to the mirror, checking her earrings. "Somewhere nice. It's a surprise, so I don't even know yet."

"Oooh! I hope he takes you somewhere with dessert! You *love* dessert," Raniya declared, bouncing on the couch.

Nhuri chuckled, warmth spreading through her chest. "I do. I'll send you some pictures wherever he takes me, okay?"

"Yay! Okay, have fun," Raniya said before hopping off the couch.

Natalia finally came into full view, and Nhuri couldn't help but pick up on how she was observing her. It wasn't in a judgmental way because that wasn't Natalia at all, nor was it disapproving. It was this quiet contemplation like she had a lot to say but didn't know where to place her words, afraid they'd land in the wrong spot. Natalia had always been protective of her, but tonight, her silence was different.

"Hello, sister. Are you going to say anything?" Nhuri asked, arching a brow.

Natalia exhaled a small breath, her eyes softening. "I'm just watching. You look happy, Nhuri. It's been a while."

Nhuri's heart squeezed at her sister's words. The past few years had been filled with so much hustle and sacrifice. She'd barely allowed herself to indulge in anything outside of work and responsibility. But now, she was allowing herself to breathe and see what life had to offer beyond her expectations.

She swallowed, blinking past the emotions rising in her chest. "I am happy," Nhuri admitted, her voice barely above a whisper. "This feels different, and I like it."

Natalia gave a knowing nod. "And you should. Change is scary but necessary. As long as it feels good to you, that's all I care about. Just be careful."

Nhuri rolled her eyes playfully but understood what Natalia meant. It wasn't a warning to scare her off but a reminder to protect her heart. Natalia didn't want her to lose herself in the fantasy of what could be without keeping her feet firmly on the ground.

Raniya popped back in the screen and pouted. "I wish I could help you pick your shoes."

Nhuri laughed. "I already have them picked out, princess. But you can help me next time."

"Okay. But TT, I hope he really likes you. If he doesn't, I'm gonna tell him he's crazy." Raniya said those words with all the confidence in the world, making Nhuri and Natalia proud.

They both laughed too.

"You better let him know you don't play about your TT," Nhuri chuckled.

"I don't!" Raniya said. "I love you."

"I love you too, baby," Nhuri replied with warmth, filling her chest and liquid pooling in her eyes.

Raniya blew her kisses before Natalia took the phone. "Don't start," she warned.

Nhuri fanned her face. "She's just getting so big and smart. Whew. Okay, okay. I'm good."

Natalia chuckled. "Enjoy your night, sis. You deserve it."

Nhuri nodded, a soft smile pulling at her lips. "I do, and thank you for pushing me to at least see what he's about. You know I'ma call and talk your ear off once I make it home."

"*If* you make it home," Natalia teased.

"Oh, please. I'm not sleeping with him after the first date."

Natalia leaned her head to the side. "I mean, how long has it been?"

"Bye! Get off my phone," Nhuri said, laughing.

"I'll talk to you later, girl. Love you."

"I love you more."

The call ended, and Nhuri plugged her phone into the charger. Taking a deep breath, she let the moment settle over her. She had to get out of her head. Glancing at her reflection one last time, she ran her fingers over her hair and stood up. Her nerves were still there, but her excitement was starting to overshadow them.

For the first time in a long time, she wasn't overanalyzing every possible outcome. She wasn't convincing herself that she had something to prove. Tonight, she would enjoy herself and see where the night took her. Hopefully, not to Shyriq's bed because it had indeed been a while since she got some, and having sex with her boss after one date wasn't ideal, at least in their situation.

NINETEEN

NHURI WASN'T SURE what Shyriq had up his sleeve for the evening, but from the moment she stepped into the sleek black SUV that arrived at her doorstep, she knew he was up to something special. When he texted telling her that he was on his way, she thought he'd be the one picking her up. Instead, a driver greeted her politely before opening the back door.

"Good evening, Ms. Coleman. My name is Rick, and I'm your driver for the evening. I'll be escorting you to Mr. Hendrix."

Nhuri smiled. "Nice to meet you, Rick. He didn't tell me a car service would pick me up."

"A man full of surprises. Shall we go?"

"Of course."

Rick helped her inside and shut the door. A single rose lying on the backseat made Nhuri smile. She lifted it to her nose while picking up the white envelope next to it and opening it.

I hope tonight continues to bring a smile to your pretty face. See you soon.

Nhuri blushed so hard she covered her face. "This man," she said, shaking her head. She couldn't wait to see what he had planned. Rick didn't reveal a thing when she asked where they were going, nor did he converse with her. That was fine with Nhuri.

Rick eased through traffic with the quiet hum of the radio playing slow jams. Nhuri took the city in and was amazed by some of the upgrades she'd missed out on witnessing over the last four years. She still had to explore so much and knew tonight was just the beginning. Shyriq was observant and thoughtful, in a way that caught her off guard at times. Whatever he had planned, she knew it would be nothing short of amazing.

Her brows lifted in curiosity when the SUV pulled up in front of an upscale boutique hotel. She didn't know what to expect, and that was secretly one thing she liked about Shyriq. He kept her on her toes.

Rick opened the door for her, and Nhuri stepped out. "Enjoy your evening."

"Thank you." Nhuri was prepared to enter the hotel and figure out where she needed to go, but Shyriq came through the doors, greeting her with a smile that almost made her stumble.

"Gorgeous, like I expected," he said, sweetly kissing her cheek. "These are for you."

The rose in Nhuri's hand matched the bouquet of lush petals in Shyriq's hand. Happily, she grabbed them, inhaling their floral scent.

"I love flowers. Thank you," she gushed.

"You're welcome. Tonight is all about you."

Nhuri blushed as he led her into the building. The concierge greeted them, leading them through the lobby to a private elevator. Nhuri's brow raised, and her stomach curled with anticipation when the doors glided open, but she just stepped inside. What she really wanted to do was ask a million questions.

Shyriq stood close by, examining her under the dim lights as best as he could. Her sweet perfume had him wrapping an arm around her waist and whispering in her ear.

"You smell divine and look absolutely beautiful."

The warmth of his breath made Nhuri shudder. She didn't bother to thank him; she couldn't speak. Of course, he smelled good, and his body heat was enticing her in ways Nhuri knew would get her in trouble tonight if she fed into temptation. Thankfully, the elevator dinged, notifying them that they had arrived at their destination.

When the doors opened, they were greeted by a breathtaking setup on the highest floor of the hotel. Floor-to-ceiling windows wrapped around the space, offering a panoramic view of the downtown city lights. Nhuri walked over to the window and took in the skyline. It stretched endlessly, with glowing buildings kissing the stars, it seemed. She took her phone out to capture the view, not realizing Shyriq was more enamored by her.

"Want me to take a picture of you?" he asked.

Nhuri pivoted, hitting him with a smile. "Sure. If you don't mind."

He reached for her phone. "I don't mind at all."

Nhuri struck a few poses, and Shyriq happily snapped them all. When she waved her hand for him to come over and take some with her, he didn't hesitate.

"You like capturing memories?" he asked, wrapping an arm around her waist as she held the phone in front of them.

"I do. This is our first real date, and it deserves a picture."

"Can't argue with you there."

They smiled, and when he leaned in to kiss her temple, Nhuri captured that one too. She told him he couldn't touch her while they were working, and Shyriq stuck to his word. Now, they were far from the main headquarters, so it was fair game. Respectfully, of course. He kept his hands right at her waist, fighting the urge to caress and grip her ass. It was poking out something vicious in her dress.

Nhuri's heels clicked as he walked her to a table in the middle of the room. It was covered with black linen with gold accents. Candlelight flickered, adding a warm, intimate glow to the mesmerizing ambiance. Nhuri released a soft gasp when her eyes landed on the open-concept kitchen where a woman in a crisp olive-green chef's jacket stood, ready to greet and serve them. The delicious aroma of something rich and buttery filled the air, instantly making Nhuri's mouth water.

"Shyriq . . ." she breathed, turning to face him. "You did all this?"

He pulled her chair out and nodded. "This is nothing."

Before she could respond, the chef turned to them and wiped her hands on a pristine towel. She had warm brown skin, with her hair pulled into a neat bun at her nape and a confident yet welcoming smile on her face.

"Good evening. My name is Torin. I'm your chef for the evening and I'll be preparing a special menu for you tonight. Shyriq told me you're a pasta lover."

Nhuri glanced at him. He asked her one day while they were grabbing lunch, and she didn't think anything about it.

"I am," Nhuri confirmed with a grin, knowing she was in for something amazing.

Torin gestured toward the table. "We'll start with a charcuterie board. It's filled with imported cheeses, thinly sliced prosciutto, marinated olives, and fresh figs. For the main course, I've prepared a truffle lobster fettuccine. Handmade pasta, creamy white wine sauce, chunks of tender lobster, and a hint of black truffle for depth."

Nhuri sighed dramatically, placing a hand over her heart. "You're speaking my love language right now."

Torin laughed. "I love to hear that. For the second course, we have a wild mushroom risotto, rich and velvety with a hint of Parmesan. Then, spinach ricotta ravioli in a brown butter sage sauce."

Nhuri's eyes widened. "Now you're showing out."

Torin smirked. "I'm just getting started. For dessert, if you aren't too full, we have a classic tiramisu."

Nhuri turned to Shyriq, shaking her head in disbelief. "This is crazy. How did you even pull this off?"

Shyriq waited for her to sit. "I pay attention," he said simply. "And I like seeing you happy."

Smiling, Nhuri took her seat. "Well, you've done that so far."

Pleased with her answer, Shyriq took a seat across from her. He reached for her wineglass and poured her a nice amount while Torin plated the charcuterie board. The first bite of aged Parmesan had Nhuri humming in approval.

"Good?" Shyriq asked.

She nodded. "Mhm. *So* good."

He passed her the wine, and she took a sip, letting the flavors marinate. Nhuri wasn't sure what Shyriq had up his sleeve, but she was glad it'd been revealed. She wasn't easily impressed, but she loved it when a man put in effort. It was the small details Shyriq had paid attention to since she met him that made this night even more special.

"I'm glad you said yes to coming out with me tonight," Shyriq said, pouring himself a glass of Cognac. It was only two fingers full because he planned on driving Nhuri home.

"Are you?" Nhuri teased, eating an olive.

Shyriq's gaze locked in on her lips, and he shook his head. "Yeah, I am. And I know you are too. You didn't have any plans."

Nhuri chuckled, amused and fake insulted. "Now, who says I didn't? Maybe I turned everyone down so my *boss* could wine and dine me."

"Maybe so. Either way, you still ended up with me."

"So cocky," she chuckled.

"Confident."

Nhuri couldn't deny that. Shyriq was sure of himself, but it suited him. She traced the rim of her wineglass and took in his handsome features. Shyriq was the kind of fine that made you do a double take, smile, and shake your head. It was unfair.

"Well, confidence looks good on you," she admitted, slowly sipping her wine.

Shyriq smirked, setting down his glass. "Yeah? I appreciate you saying that."

"You're welcome. But don't get used to it," she joked.

His smirk deepened. "Too late. You done spoiled me now."

She shook her head with a knowing smile, setting down her glass. "I should've known you'd take that and run with it."

Shyriq exhaled a quiet chuckle, resting his forearm on the table. "I don't run with anything that isn't real. And what's real is you sitting here, enjoying yourself, despite all that fronting you've been doing."

Nhuri arched a brow, feigning innocence. "Frontin'? Or just playing hard to get?"

He shrugged, watching her. "I'ma go with both, but it's all good. I'm not here to hurt you at all. Just wanna spend some time with you."

Nhuri's fingers brushed the stem of her glass, but she didn't lift it. Instead, she held his gaze, the weight of his words settling between them. A slow warmth crept up her spine, but she masked it with a teasing smile.

"As long as you continue making my time with you well spent, you'll get all the time you need."

Shyriq's head bobbed. "Noted."

They didn't have to wait long before food was brought out. Nhuri sampled the truffle-infused fettucine and fell in love. The flavors were so rich and authentic, and the lobster was beyond tender. She closed her eyes, savoring every bite.

"That good, huh?" Shyriq teased.

Her eyes peeled open. "Listen. You don't even understand."

She ate another bite and clumsily got some of the sauce on her exposed chest. Shyriq reached across the table without thinking and used his linen to swipe away the sauce. Nhuri's breath hitched as he casually sat back in his seat. The simple gesture sent a wave of heat through her while he looked as composed as ever.

She cleared her throat. "Thank you."

"You're welcome," he said and winked. "Want more wine?"

All Nhuri could do was nod. He poured her another glass, and the courses kept coming. She couldn't believe how each dish was more incredible than the last. By the time dessert arrived, Nhuri couldn't imagine there was more. She leaned back in her chair, shaking her head.

"I can't eat another bite. But I'm about to anyway."

Shyriq chuckled, watching her take a delicate forkful of tiramisu. He was happy to see her smiling. The rest he mentioned her getting when they first met seemed to have benefitted her. She was glowing more and had this new attitude about her that Shyriq loved. Still, he wanted to know what it was from her past that had her so guarded.

He wouldn't bring that up tonight and ruin the mood, but eventually, he'd get around to asking. As the night progressed and their conversation flowed, he reached into his pocket. Nhuri's brows pinched as he pulled out a small box and slid it across the table toward her.

She blinked. "What's this?"

"Open it and find out."

Nhuri lifted the lid, and her eyes twinkled as she took in the delicate gold bracelet. Hanging from it was a tiny pasta fork charm. Laughing, she unhooked it and ran it through her fingertips.

"You really got me a pasta fork charm?" she asked, grinning at him.

He shrugged, that signature smirk playing on his lips. "Had to make sure you always had a reminder of tonight."

Nhuri swallowed past the warmth blooming in her chest. This man . . . He was different. Thoughtful in a way that went beyond words. She reached across the table, intertwining their fingers.

"I don't need a charm to remember this," she murmured, holding his gaze. "You made tonight more memorable than you can imagine."

His thumb brushed over her knuckles. "Yeah? So I get another date tomorrow?"

She chuckled and squeezed his hand. "Only if you take me to The Spot. I miss those waffles already."

Chuckling, Shyriq nodded. "I got you, baby."

The endearment slid from his lips easily and surprisingly, didn't stun Nhuri. She actually wanted to hear him say it more. It sounded good. When dinner ended, Nhuri was sure to grab Torin's contact information. Learning that she was an award-winning chef with her own seasoning collection in stores worldwide, plus several other accomplishments, brought Nhuri so much joy. Seeing a Black woman win was equivalent to climbing into a bed with fresh linen right after a hot shower. It was one of the best feelings.

"You looking real comfortable over there," Shyriq teased, glancing her way.

Comfortable was an understatement. She was ready to slip off her heels and curl her feet up. Nhuri leaned back in the plush leather passenger seat of his SUV with a smile on her face. She was so content, and her stomach was so full that she didn't want the night to end. The evening had been better than she expected. And now, she was somewhat mad that she had resisted him all these weeks.

"That's because I am."

"And you're still smiling," Shyriq noted, his deep voice laced with amusement as he approached a red light. "This must be a record."

Nhuri scoffed but didn't bother hiding her grin. "Whatever, sir. This is my smile that says I'm beyond full and a little bit tipsy."

He smirked, drumming his fingers on the steering wheel. "I love that look. I'm glad you had a good time."

Before she could reply, her phone vibrated inside her clutch. Nhuri pulled it out, not thinking much of it. She glanced at the screen, expecting it to be one of her friends checking in, but seeing the multiple missed calls and frantic texts from Raniya sent a sharp pang of worry through her chest. When she tapped on the voicemail, she could've thrown up right there.

"TT. Something is wrong with Mommy. 911 is here. I had to call them. Please hurry."

Nhuri's breath hitched. "Oh my God."

"Is everything all right?" Shyriq asked.

Nhuri couldn't answer him. Her fingers trembled as she navigated to her call log and dialed Raniya's number. The phone barely rang before Raniya's trembling, panicked voice filled the SUV.

"Hello."

"Niy! It's your TT. What's going on?" Nhuri asked, on the verge of a panic attack.

"TT! They took Mommy! She . . . She wouldn't wake up right! And I—"

"Baby, slow down," Nhuri rushed out with her heart pounding. "Breathe, okay? Where are you now?"

"The hospital. I rode in the ambulance, but I'm scared," Raniya sniffled. "I'm by myself."

"Are you in a room?"

Nhuri hoped whoever brought her in had the decency to at least place her somewhere safe and not leave her alone in the waiting room.

"Yes. A nice lady put me in here and told me to wait."

Nhuri barely exhaled, but knowing her niece was safe loosened the tightness in her chest some.

"Okay. I'm on my way."

"You promise?"

Nhuri squeezed her eyes shut and choked on her next words as she struggled to get them out. "Yes. I promise."

"Okay," she sniffled again.

"I need you to be a big girl for TT and Mommy. Can you do that?"

Nhuri heard more sniffling, and the tears she was trying to contain slid down her face. This moment was her biggest fear, but she had to be strong for her niece.

"Y-Yes. I can be a big girl," Raniya answered.

"I know you can, baby. Just hold tight, and I'll be there in no time."

Nhuri ended the call with shaky hands and her mind all over the place. Her leg bounced profusely as she pulled up Raniya's location to see what hospital they were at. She could've asked her to take the phone to an adult, but she didn't want to put any more stress on her niece. And had an adult not had any answers for her, it would've made her nerves worse.

"What's going on?" Shyriq asked.

"Natalia—" Nhuri swallowed hard. "She was rushed to the hospital. That was my niece. She'd been calling and texting me, and I just saw it. I can't believe I didn't feel my phone. You have to get me to the hospital, please. My baby had to call the ambulance, and I . . . I wasn't there. Oh my God," Nhuri muttered, her heart breaking with each word.

Shyriq placed a hand on her thigh, trying to calm her down. His usual relaxed expression was etched with concern, and he wanted to do everything in his power to stop the tears from falling from her eyes. Gently, he grabbed her phone from her hand and checked the GPS.

"I got you. We're going to get to both of them," he said.

Without hesitation, Shyriq spun the wheel, making a sharp U-turn. Nhuri barely registered anything outside the speeding car. Anxiety knotted in her stomach, and her pulse hammered erratically as worst-case scenarios flooded her mind.

"She was fine earlier," she murmured, more to herself than to him. "We were on the phone, and she didn't say anything about not feeling good."

Shyriq glanced at her briefly before refocusing on the road. "Lupus doesn't give warnings, right?"

After visiting Natalia's house that evening, Shyriq forced Cara to tell him what was happening. He could've asked, but he figured if that were something Natalia or Nhuri wanted to share with him, they would've.

Nhuri inhaled shakily. "No." Her throat tightened. "She tries to hide it when it gets bad. But Raniya . . . She must've been so scared."

Nhuri shook her head. She couldn't imagine the fear in her niece's eyes or what her sister may have been feeling right now.

"She won't have to be," he reassured her. "And neither do you. Everything is going to be okay."

Something about the certainty in his voice anchored Nhuri, even as fear threatened to consume her. She hoped and prayed he was right.

TWENTY

SHYRIQ BROKE THE speed limit to get to the hospital. He pulled into the parking lot and snagged a spot near the front. Before he had fully parked the car, Nhuri was out and sprinting toward the entrance. Shyriq caught up to her as Nhuri rushed through the automatic doors. Her heart pounded against her ribs as she approached the receptionist's desk.

"Hi. Excuse me. My sister was brought in, and my niece said she was inside a room waiting for me," she rushed out.

Shyriq placed his palm against her back, rubbing it soothingly.

The nurse at the desk gave an empathetic smile. "Good evening. Please give me your sister's name."

"Natalia Coleman. My niece's name is Raniya Stewart."

She typed in some information, scanned the screen, and told Nhuri to give her one second. Nhuri exhaled and calmed a bit as Shyriq massaged her shoulders. Having him here made her realize how lonely she'd been in her relationship with Dru. He wasn't as comforting and only cared about himself at some point.

"Yes, the sister just arrived. Yes, we'll have her go right up. Yep, a few minutes. Okay, no problem. Thank you," the nurse said to whomever she was speaking with.

Nhuri was tuned in, waiting. "Which floor?"

"You'll need to go to the seventh floor, but I'll need some identification first."

"Of course," Nhuri said, frantically unfastening her clutch and searching for her license.

Shyriq did the same, and they handed them over. After placing their names in the system, the nurse returned their licenses. Since it was after hours, they had to be buzzed through a door. Once on the elevator, Nhuri couldn't help but bite the inside of her lips as her nerves got the best of her. Like before, Shyriq's hand soothingly brought her some peace.

The sterile disinfectant scent filled her nostrils as she scanned the waiting area. Spotting Raniya curled up in one of the stiff chairs with a blanket around her, Nhuri rushed over. The woman beside her stood from her seat.

"Niy," Nhuri called.

Raniya's head snapped up at the sound of her auntie's soft voice, even though panic raged inside her.

Her tear-streaked face crumpled with relief as they embraced. "TT!" She launched herself into Nhuri's arms and gripped her tightly.

Nhuri held her just as fiercely, pressing a kiss to her forehead. "I'm here, okay? You did so good calling 911."

Raniya sniffled. "Mommy wouldn't wake up right. She was sweating and breathing funny, and I didn't know what to do." She shrugged, but she had done the absolute best thing.

Nhuri swallowed the lump in her throat and smoothed a hand down Raniya's back. "You did the right thing, baby girl. She's in the best place now."

They hugged again, and Nhuri couldn't help but notice her racing heart. She rocked them side to side with her eyes closed before she peeled them open at the sound of someone clearing their throat. Nhuri glanced at the woman who'd been sitting down.

"Hi. My name is Misty. I'm the social worker on shift tonight. Please let me know if you need anything."

Nhuri was trying to think of why she would need her, but then it dawned on her that Raniya may have needed counseling or just someone to talk to about what happened tonight. Nhuri was all for people caring for their mental health, regardless of age. Trauma had no age limit.

"Okay. Thank you. Have the doctors said anything or given any updates about what is happening?" Nhuri asked.

"I'm not sure, but I can send one of the nurses on duty out here," Misty said.

"Yes. We'd appreciate that," Nhuri replied.

Misty nodded and disappeared down the hallway. Exhaling, Nhuri took a seat and pulled Raniya onto her lap. She'd always have a spot there no matter how big she got. Nhuri soothingly rubbed her back and pressed her lips against her temple. She was centering her and didn't even know it.

"TT, they wouldn't let me go with Mommy."

Nhuri squeezed her eyes shut, not knowing what to say. Words failed her, but thankfully, the man beside her had some. Shyriq, who had remained silent thus far at Nhuri's side, crouched in front of Raniya. His voice was gentle, making Raniya glue her eyes to him.

"That's because they're taking care of her. She's in good hands."

Raniya squinted as her hold on Nhuri loosened. "I know you."

Shyriq smirked. "You saw me at your Mommy's house a while back. You were peeking from behind the wall."

"I was!" she beamed, remembering that day. "You brought my TT here?"

Shyriq nodded. "Yes, I did."

Raniya peered back at Nhuri, leaned in, and whispered in her ear. "Did he get you dessert?"

For the first time in what felt like forever, Nhuri smiled. "Yes," she whispered back.

Raniya wasn't that great of a whisperer, so Shyriq heard her question and couldn't help but smile. Nhuri figured she could introduce them now that Raniya seemed to approve of his presence and thoughtfulness.

"Niy, this is Shyriq."

Raniya gave a small wave. "Hi."

"Nice to meet you, Raniya. You're really brave for taking care of your mama."

Raniya sniffled but seemed to relax a little at his words. Before more could be said, a nurse approached them through the doors. "Natalia Coleman's family?"

Nhuri placed Raniya on her feet and stood immediately. "We're her family. Is she okay?"

"She's stable," the nurse assured them. "It looks like she had a flare-up due to her lupus. It triggered severe inflammation, making it difficult for her to breathe and causing her extreme fatigue. We have her on fluids and medication, but she's still very weak."

Nhuri exhaled shakily and nodded. It wasn't the worst, but it wasn't the best, either. "Can we see her?"

"Of course. She's been asking for you."

Nhuri was happy to hear that. Natalia knew in her heart that her sister was near, and she was correct.

Nhuri squeezed Raniya's hand. "You ready?"

Raniya nodded hesitantly and gripped her hand tighter. Nhuri looked toward Shyriq, who placed a hand on her back.

"Go ahead. I'll wait out here," he said.

"You sure?"

He nodded. "Yeah. I'm not going anywhere."

Nhuri glanced at him, and her lips parted, but no words came out. She appreciated his reassurance and presence more than he knew.

"Thank you," she murmured before following the nurse down the hall.

Nhuri stepped into the hospital room with Raniya clinging to her side. Her heart thudded in her chest as she took in the sight of Natalia lying motionless against stark white sheets. The coldness of the room caused a chill to slither up her back. The beeping monitors were the only sound in the quiet place.

Natalia's normally warm brown complexion looked dull under the fluorescent lighting, and her face was drawn with exhaustion. The IV in her arm fed her fluids, and it was a clear reminder of just how fragile her body was at that moment.

Raniya stood on her tippy toes, peering at the bed. "She doesn't look okay, TT," she whispered.

Nhuri swallowed hard, pushing down her own panic to be strong for her niece. She bent down, pressing a gentle kiss to Raniya's forehead. "She's going to be okay, baby. She just needs rest."

Nhuri's words felt weak and empty, but they were all she had to give. Natalia's eyelids fluttered open, and her unfocused gaze landed on Raniya. A tired, barely-there smile covered her face.

"Hey," she rasped with a hoarse voice.

Raniya's eyes lit up. "Mommy," she whimpered, letting go of Nhuri's hand. Carefully, she crawled onto the bed, wrapping her small body around her mother's. "I was so scared."

Natalia weakly lifted her hand and cradled Raniya's head before rubbing her back in slow, soothing circles. "I know, baby. But I'm okay. I'm here."

Nhuri stepped closer, her fingers curling into her palms as she fought the stinging in her eyes. "You scared the hell out of us," she said, her voice breaking.

Natalia exhaled. She smiled weakly but was genuinely apologetic. "I wasn't trying to."

Nhuri's throat tightened. She reached out, wrapping her fingers around Natalia's cold hand. "Niy had to call 911. You were—" Her breath hitched as the visual of Raniya crying flashed through her mind. "She thought you were gone."

Natalia's eyes widened slightly, and she turned her attention to Raniya, still curled on her lap. "Baby, I'm so, so sorry. Mommy didn't mean to scare you like that."

Raniya sniffled. "It's okay. You taught me what to do, and I did it. I called TT too. I just wanted you to wake up."

They heard the bravery in her voice, but her body still shuddered at the thought of her not waking up. Natalia gathered all the strength she had to pull her daughter closer.

"And I'm *so* proud of you. You were so brave," she whispered, kissing the top of her head. "Thank you for saving me."

Raniya shook her head against her mother's arm. "I don't wanna do that again."

Nhuri had to turn away for a moment, inhaling sharply to steady herself. Seeing her sister like this, so vulnerable and weak, was breaking her in ways she hadn't been prepared for. She knew that the worst could happen one day, and so far, this was it.

A light knock at the door made her turn, and Shyriq stood there. His broad frame filled the space, and it looked as if he were hesitating to step inside.

"That was TT's date," Raniya tried whispering.

They all smirked, and he entered, figuring that was his invite inside. He didn't feel right not coming in to check on them.

"How are you feeling?" he asked, stepping beside Nhuri.

Natalia exhaled. "Exhausted, but I'm alive, and that's what matters the most."

Shyriq nodded while Nhuri blinked back the emotion clogging her throat.

Natalia's gaze shifted to her sister, and her tired eyes flickered with regret. "I ruined your date?"

Nhuri's head jerked back slightly. "What? No! You didn't ruin anything. It was perfect."

Shyriq's heart swelled with pride beside her. Even in her despair, she made him feel like the luckiest man.

Natalia sighed dramatically, even in her weakened state. "And here I was hoping y'all were about to pick out wedding invitations."

Nhuri narrowed her eyes at her, shaking her head. "Please, don't start."

Natalia smirked but winced slightly, shifting to get more comfortable. After a moment, her eyes danced with mischief. Despite her apparent exhaustion, she had to take advantage of this moment.

"You know," she started, "he asked about you before."

Nhuri's brows shot up. "What?"

Shyriq's posture stiffened beside her, but Natalia just grinned, clearly enjoying herself. "Months ago. I think it was right after you got fired. He was trying to be all smooth, asking if you were single but disguising it like he was just checking on me."

Nhuri turned slowly to look at Shyriq. He didn't waver under her scrutiny and kept eye contact.

"You were asking about me?"

He exhaled through his nose. "Yeah. I was . . . curious."

Natalia snorted. "That's what we're calling it?"

Nhuri shook her head, a slight smirk tugging at her lips despite everything. "So, let me get this straight. You were interested in me but hired me anyway?"

"I knew you needed a job. That was more important."

For a moment, something passed between them. Shyriq was always subtle but intense with his gaze. Nhuri felt her stomach flip, but she quickly looked away, focusing back on Natalia. "Well, there goes your big romantic moment," she joked, trying to lighten the sudden shift in the room.

Natalia sighed dramatically again. "Well, I guess my duty is almost done. Next, it'll be wedding bells and me telling the story of how y'all met."

Nhuri chuckled, shaking her head. "If you don't hush and get some rest."

Natalia's smile softened. "I'm glad you had someone with you, though."

Nhuri's eyes flickered toward Shyriq before she could stop herself. She wrapped an arm around his waist, leaning into his chest. He squeezed her frame, silently letting her know he was glad he was there too.

"I am too," she admitted quietly.

"I think visiting hours are almost over," Natalia said.

Nhuri's posture straightened. "We're not leaving."

"I'll be okay, sis. It's just overnight, and Malik is coming up here."

Nhuri's throat tightened. "You don't want us to stay?"

Her feelings were a bit hurt, and Natalia knew it. Her expression softened.

"It's not that. You need some rest, and so do I."

"But what . . ." Nhuri took a deep breath. "But what if something else happens? I can't lose you."

Natalia's eyes watered. "You won't. I promise."

Nhuri wanted to believe her. She really did.

Raniya popped her head up, wiping her eyes. "You get to come home?"

Natalia brushed a curl from her daughter's face. "Not tonight, baby. But soon."

Raniya frowned but nodded. Nhuri mimicked her facial expression, and Natalia shook her head.

"Go home with Niya. You'll feel better in the morning, and I'll be sure to check in," Natalia said.

Nhuri sighed. "Fine." She looked over her shoulder at Shyriq. "You don't mind taking us home, do you?"

He shook his head. "Not at all. You just let me know when, and I got y'all."

Raniya clung to her mother for another moment before Nhuri gently pulled her away. "Come on, baby girl."

Natalia gave them both a tired smile. "I love y'all so much."

"We love you too," Nhuri whispered, kissing her cheek.

"I'll see you in the morning, Mommy," Raniya said, holding her auntie's hand.

Natalia smiled. "Yes, you will, baby. Be good."

"I will."

"Rest up," Shyriq told her. "I'll make sure they get home safely and back up here tomorrow. You need anything?"

Natalia shook her head. "I don't but thank you."

Her exclamation held more weight than she let out. Natalia wasn't just thanking him for asking if she needed him. She thanked him for being there for her sister and daughter but more so for Nhuri. She would forever cherish his support during one of the scariest moments of her life.

"It's nothing, but you're welcome," Shyriq said before heading out the door.

As they stepped into the hallway, Malik was walking up. They embraced, and he hugged Nhuri and Raniya tightly. She could feel his heart beating quickly, and her reassuring smile settled him some.

"She's waiting on you," Nhuri said.

"A'ight. Let me get in here. How you doing, man?" he asked Shyriq, sticking his hand out. "Malik."

He shook his hand. "I'm Shyriq. Good to meet you. I'ma get them home, but they'll be back in the morning."

Malik nodded. "A'ight. Niya, make sure you charge your iPad so we can call you."

"Okay."

"Sis, I got her. If anything changes, you'll be the first to know," Malik reassured her.

Nodding her head, Nhuri glanced at her sister's door, and then they approached the elevator. The automatic doors slid open once they reached the lower level, and Shyriq told them to wait while he grabbed his truck. Nhuri stood on the curb, holding Raniya's tiny hand in hers. Though the breeze was nice, Nhuri couldn't enjoy it.

Exhaustion was creeping up on her now that the initial rush of fear had subsided. She and Raniya yawned simultaneously as Shyriq pulled up to the curb. She helped Raniya in the backseat and buckled her in as she rubbed her eyes. Nhuri knew she'd be asleep before they made it to her home. Nhuri settled into the passenger seat and was quiet for a few minutes. Her thoughts were everywhere, and her mind was racing, but it seemed to calm when Shyriq reached for her hand. Like at the restaurant, he intertwined their fingers, soothingly rubbing her knuckles.

"How you feeling? Talk to me," he said.

He was concerned, and Nhuri felt every bit of it through his tone and affectionate gesture. The weight on her shoulders made her hesitate, but she talked anyway.

"Overwhelmed. It's a lot to process," she admitted.

He nodded. "It is, but that's why you have people in your corner who can help you sort everything out."

She glanced at him, and he turned to look her way. Shyriq didn't say anything else, but his eyes told her everything she needed to know. It was the type of reassurance she'd need to rest tonight. Nhuri didn't think sleep would come easy. For once, the silence in the car wasn't uncomfortable. It was thick with emotions that neither was ready to put into words. Tonight had changed the trajectory of their relationship, and they knew it.

Nhuri leaned her head against the window, exhaling deeply. "I didn't expect the night to go like this," she admitted, finally breaking the silence.

Shyriq glanced at her before returning his focus to the road. "Yeah," he murmured. "Not exactly first-date material."

Nhuri let out a soft, tired laugh. "Not at all." She turned her head to look at him. "But I'm grateful you were there."

He tapped his fingers against the steering wheel before speaking. "You don't have to thank me. Family is everything. I get it."

She studied him, taking in the way his usual guarded expression softened just slightly. "Yeah?"

He nodded, his jaws ticking as he switched lanes. "Yeah. I know what it's like to see somebody you love struggling and feel helpless. That shit doesn't sit right."

Her heart clenched at his words. There was something deeper there, something he wasn't saying. But she didn't push. Instead, she reached over and lightly touched his arm, the warmth of his skin seeping through his jacket. "Still . . . I appreciate you."

His grip on the steering wheel tightened just a little before he exhaled and gave her a small smirk. "Yeah, well . . . Don't think this gets you out of breakfast."

Nhuri's lips curled. "Oh, so we're still on for that?"

"That's if you still want it," he said, glancing at her with a raised brow. "I promised you a second date, and I'm a man of my word. Even if that means I have to order food for you and baby girl back there."

Nhuri's heart fluttered. "I guess I can't argue with that."

Hour by hour, Shyriq was proving her wrong. The guard she'd had up was slowly crumbling, and Nhuri had no intentions of picking up the pieces. Minutes later, he pulled up to her home. The street was quiet, and she was so happy she'd chosen to live somewhere peaceful.

Nhuri turned to check on Raniya and smiled softly when she saw her completely knocked out. Her mouth was open, showing her missing tooth. She had an eventful day, and Nhuri knew she needed that sleep.

"I got her," Shyriq said, already unbuckling his seat belt.

Nhuri hesitated. "You don't have to—"

He shot her a look. "Nhuri. Relax, okay, baby? You don't have to do everything and be everything to everyone. Let me take some pressure off of you. I got her."

Her eyes watered as she nodded. "Okay."

"You want me to carry you inside too? You've had those heels on for a long time."

His concern for her feet was sweet, and she chuckled. "No, you don't have to."

Shyriq nodded and stepped out of the truck. He'd carry her if she wanted him to, no questions asked. He rounded the vehicle and gently unbuckled Raniya. She stirred slightly but didn't wake as he carefully lifted her into his arms, cradling her against his broad chest. The sight of Raniya wrapping her arms around him and Shyriq carefully carrying her to the door after opening hers did something to her heart that she wasn't familiar with. But it felt good.

Nhuri unlocked the door and stepped inside, flipping a small lamp on in the living room. Shyriq stood idly by while she locked the door before Nhuri told him to follow her. He followed her down the hall to her bedroom. Nhuri pulled the covers back on her bed, and Shyriq carefully lowered Raniya. Then Nhuri removed her shoes and tucked the blankets around her before kissing her forehead.

Staring down at her for a moment, Nhuri prayed she had a peaceful night of sleep. They stepped out of the bedroom, leaving the door slightly cracked, and entered the living room. Shyriq stuffed his hands into his pockets but removed them when Nhuri stepped his way. She fell into his chest for a hug. She didn't know she needed it, but she was glad he gave it. Shyriq held her close, trying to hug the pain and fear out of her frame.

Nhuri broke the embrace first, stepping back to look him in the face. "I needed that."

"You feel better?"

She nodded. "Yes. A little bit. You give great hugs. Goodness."

Shyriq smirked. "Thank you."

"Yes. You can say thank you. It was a compliment," Nhuri teased.

"I appreciate that. I'm glad you're feeling better. Everything is going to work out. Just from seeing her tonight and knowing how hard she works, Natalia is resilient. Put a lil faith in your sister 'cause I know she believes in you."

Nhuri nodded. "She most definitely does. And thank you for noticing that. She does any and everything she puts her mind to and I admire her so much for that."

"It's a good trait to have to be fearless."

"Most definitely," she said, shaking her head with a smile slightly lifting her cheeks.

"What?" Shyriq questioned.

"Seeing this side of you . . . I don't know. I guess I wasn't expecting it."

"What side?" he asked, humored and intrigued to see how she felt about him.

Nhuri shrugged. "The soft one. The caring, gentle side."

He liked how she didn't hold her tongue. "Yeah, well, there's more to me than what meets the eye."

"I see that now. I mean, I kind of witnessed it and heard about it through the grapevine, but experiencing it is something different."

"So you like me?" he asked, smirking.

Nhuri smiled. "That'd make your day if I said yes, huh?"

He laughed lowly. "It would, but I don't need you to confirm anything. That smile on your face lets me know everything I need to know."

She blushed, hiding her face behind her hand. "Mhm. Whatever."

His smirk deepened, but instead of answering, he simply headed toward the front door. Nhuri followed behind him. As he stepped onto the porch, he turned to face her. Nhuri shut the door and pulled her bottom lip into her mouth. The action caused Shyriq to stare at her lips and pretty face. She tucked a piece of hair behind her ear, feeling his pull on her with his eyes alone.

"Thank you again for tonight. For everything. I know it was a lot, and you weren't expecting to have to—"

Her breath hitched as Shyriq reached for her. His fingers gently traced the inside of her wrist. "What did I tell you? Stop thanking me. Let me just be here."

Nhuri's pulse quickened at his words, and before she could tell him okay, Shyriq's head dipped, and his lips brushed against hers. The kiss was so soft and deliberately sweet that it stole the air from Nhuri's lungs. He didn't linger too long but didn't pull away as if he didn't want her to feel him. To feel whatever it was she needed to feel from him and for him.

When he pulled back, his eyes lingered on hers for a beat longer before he smirked. "Get some rest. I'll see you in the morning."

Nhuri licked her lips. "O-Okay," she murmured. "Good night."

"Good night."

He walked to his truck and didn't pull off until she was inside the house. Nhuri peeked out of the window with a hand over her heart, which was beating faster than she had cared to admit. Tonight had been a lot, but the time spent with him had been everything. It felt like something real. Something to look forward to, and she almost couldn't wait until tomorrow morning, when minutes prior she had been dreading it.

TWENTY-ONE

NHURI MANEUVERED HER cart through the aisles of the local grocery store with her phone to her ear. She only needed to run in for a few things and was glad it wasn't packed for a Friday evening.

"Girl, when I tell you this week drained me, I mean it," Nhuri sighed, stopping in front of the wine section. Her eyes scanned the selection, debating between a rich red and crisp white. She wasn't sure what she was in the mood for, but one of the two was coming home with her.

"I'm already knowing it did," Jazmyn said.

"Between work and picking up Raniya while Natalia recovers, I'm tempted to get both of these bottles."

Jazmyn chuckled. "That's exactly why you need to pull up on me this weekend. It's supposed to be real nice outside tomorrow too."

Nhuri smirked, grabbing a bottle of tequila and placing it in her cart before reaching for the red wine. "I'm not trying to be around a bunch of people. Let's just chill tonight, and I'll think about going out tomorrow. Maybe," Nhuri warned.

With Shyriq having to make an impromptu trip out of town, Nhuri felt like her workload had tripled. When he called to check on her, she didn't let him know that she was a bit overwhelmed, but she could've. The Exclusive Wine-Tasting event was approaching, and final details needed to be handled so there would be no complaining. Nhuri got the job done.

It wouldn't have seemed like a lot had she not also been on auntie duty. Nhuri had Monday off, but Raniya still went to school. Per the doctor's orders, Natalia was to rest as much as possible, so Nhuri picked up where she couldn't. She wasn't complaining and never would, but she wanted this weekend for herself. A little decompressing and self-care was a priority over the next few days.

"Now *that's* what I like to hear," Jazmyn said approvingly. "So ... How's your *boss* doing?"

Nhuri rolled her eyes, biting back a smile as she pushed her cart forward. "You mean Shyriq?"

"Yes, him."

"He's fine."

"*Just* fine?" Jazmyn dragged out with her tone full of curiosity.

Nhuri sighed, lowering her voice as she turned the corner into the snack aisle. "Jaz, I don't even know what to call this. One minute we're on some professional shit, then the next, he's carrying my niece into the house like he's been in our lives forever. And don't even get me started on the kiss."

Jazmyn gasped dramatically. "Wait, wait. A *kiss*? You kissed this man and didn't tell me? I thought we were closer than that. You're so fake."

Nhuri shook her head, grabbing a bag of chips off the shelf. "It wasn't a whole thing, Jaz. It was sweet. Real gentle like ..." She hesitated, chewing on her bottom lip. "Like he meant for me to remember it and want more."

"Girl," Jazmyn exhaled. "That's dangerous."

"Tell me about it."

Nhuri grabbed another bag of chips, still lost in her thoughts. She wanted to kiss him longer, and had the circumstances been different, they would've taken things much further. She was still thinking about his soft lips when she suddenly heard a voice from behind her. It was so familiar her chest tightened.

"Damn, so you just wasn't gon' text me back?"

Her entire body froze at the sight of Dru. Dressed in dark jeans and a fitted Nike crewneck, he looked the same yet somehow different. His beard was a little fuller, and he looked like he'd been in the gym. His eyes still held that same intense energy that once used to catch Nhuri up.

Nhuri exhaled sharply. "Dru."

He smirked, leaning on his cart. "That's all I get? Not even a 'hey' or 'how you been?'"

She crossed her arms, gripping her phone tighter. "I didn't think I owed you that."

Jazmyn's voice crackled through the speaker. "Wait, who is that? Who are you talking to?"

Nhuri blinked, remembering she was still on the phone. "Jaz, I'ma call you back."

"Nhuri—"

She ended the call before Jazmyn could protest and slid her phone into her back pocket.

Dru chuckled. "Damn. That bad?"

She sucked her teeth. "Dru, what do you want?"

He tilted his head slightly, studying her. "Can we go somewhere and talk? I'll be in town for a couple of days."

Nhuri frowned so hard. "What do we have to talk about?"

"A lot, considering you just up and left," he said.

Nhuri let out a dry laugh. "I didn't just 'up and leave.' You and I both know why I left, so let's not play games."

Sighing, Dru moved his cart out of the way for someone to get by. "A'ight. I do, but can you at least hear me out? You never responded to my text."

"For a reason," she scoffed. "I left you and what we had in the past."

"And I never liked how things ended between us," he said smoothly. "Just hear me out. Can you give me that while we're in person?"

Her stomach flipped at his words, and she hated that he still had that effect on her. Nhuri felt her phone vibrating in her pocket but ignored it. She knew it was no one but Jazmyn calling or texting her.

"You can't just pop back up and expect things to be cool between us," she muttered.

"I don't expect anything, but damn . . . Is there really that much bad blood between us?" Dru questioned, honestly curious.

It was, at least on her end. Once again, like nothing had changed, Dru was deflecting. Or maybe he was being delusional. Nhuri wasn't sure.

She swallowed, gripping the cart tighter. "There is, but you seemed to have forgotten."

"Did I?" he challenged, stepping closer.

Nhuri stiffened but held her ground. "Yes."

His jaws flexed, and for a moment, he looked like he wanted to argue. But instead, he exhaled, glancing down before meeting her eyes again. "Look, I know I messed up. And I know I can't just walk back in like nothing happened. But I'm here for the weekend, and I'd really like to talk. For real this time."

Nhuri hesitated. Every logical part of her told her to say no and to keep it moving. She could simply tell him no, head to checkout, and go home with her things. But a part of her did want to hear him out. *Maybe he has changed, and I'm just overlooking it,* she thought.

Nhuri wasn't sure if it was her curiosity or wanting the closure she never got, but she gave him an answer that she knew had made his entire day.

She sighed, shaking her head slightly. "Fine. We can talk."

Dru raised an eyebrow, almost like he was surprised she agreed. "Yeah?"

"Yeah."

He smirked. "Bet. Tonight?"

Nhuri sucked her teeth. "Um, why tonight?"

"Because I don't need you changing your mind."

She rolled her eyes. That was exactly what she would have done had she gotten home and talked herself out of wanting to hear anything he had to say.

Dru chuckled. "Exactly. I know you."

"No. You know the *old* me. Don't forget that," she said seriously.

The smirk on his face fell, and before he messed up things, Dru nodded.

"A'ight. I'm at the hotel around the corner from here. We can talk in the lobby or the restaurant. Is that cool?"

Nhuri nodded. She hoped his intentions weren't to get her up to his room because that wasn't happening. Talking in public meant she had free will to leave at any moment.

"Yeah. Let me pay for my things, and I'll be right out."

Dru nodded, lingering for a second longer before finally stepping back. "A'ight. I'm in a grey Kia."

As he walked away, Nhuri released a deep breath. She wasn't sure why she agreed to meet him, but something told her this conversation was long overdue.

Nhuri pulled into the hotel parking lot and parked. Dru hadn't lied about being around the corner. It took them three minutes to reach their destination, and Nhuri fussed at herself during the entire drive. She should've been going home and relaxing. Dru waited for her at the entrance, and they stepped inside.

"The lobby, or you wanna grab a table at the restaurant?" Dru asked.

"A table."

He nodded and walked ahead, confident that she'd follow him. Nhuri couldn't help it, but she thought about Shyriq and how he'd never let her walk behind him. He always made sure she was either by his side or in front of him. Nhuri rolled her eyes at the vast difference in mannerisms between the two. The hostess walked them to a booth in the middle, and Nhuri slid inside.

"Someone will be right with you," she said.

Nhuri nodded politely. She wouldn't be ordering any food, but a glass of water would do. Seconds later, that's exactly what she ordered when their waitress appeared.

"You sure you don't want any food?" Dru asked.

"I didn't come here to eat, so no."

The seriousness in her tone made him sit up straighter. Dru looked at the waitress.

"We're good for now. 'Preciate it."

"No problem."

She returned seconds later, placing the ice water and a straw before Nhuri, who thanked her before she walked off. Besides the jazz tunes playing over the speakers and the low chatter of guests, silence surrounded them. Dru had initiated this sit-down, so he had better start the conversation.

The dim lighting cast a warm glow over their booth, but there was nothing warm about the tension between them. It felt as cold as ever. Dru sat across from her with one arm propped on the table, watching her with that same unreadable expression that used to drive Nhuri crazy. She had no idea why she agreed to this, and her annoyance grew by the second. Her good heart and open mind somewhat wanted this conversation to help make their past make sense.

Or maybe she just wanted to let go finally.

Dru leaned back, scratching his beard. "So, you gonna keep staring at that water, or are we actually gonna talk?"

Nhuri scoffed, looking up at him. "Oh, now you want to talk? That's new."

Dru exhaled, shaking his head. "Here we go."

"No, for real," she pressed. "You barely had anything to say back then. You walked around like you didn't care, like nothing I said ever mattered. So, what's changed now, Dru?"

He rubbed his chin, and his gaze flickered with something she couldn't quite place. "I didn't come here to argue, Nhuri."

She let out a bitter laugh, sitting back. "I can't tell, but what's new? So, what did you have me come here for? Let's have a real conversation for once."

Dru's jaws clenched, and for the first time, his expression cracked. "A'ight, you're doing too much."

"Am I?" Nhuri's eyes narrowed. "What's doing *too much* is how you made me feel crazy for wanting more from you. Like I was asking for too much."

Dru exhaled sharply, shaking his head. "You act like I ain't give you nothing, Nhuri."

"Did you?" she challenged, leaning forward. "Because from where I'm sitting, I remember a man who stopped trying. A man who acted like I was just *there*. Like our relationship was just something to pass the time."

Dru's eyes darkened. "That's bullshit."

"Is it?" she shot back. "Tell me, Dru . . . When was the last time you made me feel wanted? When was the last time you acted like you gave a damn about us?"

He stayed silent, and his lips pressed into a thin line.

Nhuri nodded slowly. "Exactly."

Dru dragged a hand over his beard, exhaling roughly. "Man . . . You always did this. Always turned shit into something bigger than it needed to be."

Nhuri blinked, heat rising to her face. "*Something bigger than it needed to be?*" Her voice dropped, shaking slightly with restrained anger. "So, me walking away from you, from *us*, was just me being *dramatic?*"

Dru shifted, looking uncomfortable. "That's not what I meant."

"No, Dru, that's *exactly* what you meant," she snapped. "You think I wanted to leave? That I just woke up one day and decided I was done? I *loved* you. I gave you everything I had, and all you did was act like you couldn't be bothered."

Dru's nostrils flared. "Man, I had a lot on my plate back then, Nhuri. Work, family shit. You knew that."

"Oh, I *knew*," she said, her voice thick with sarcasm. "I knew that everything else came first. I knew that no matter how much I tried, I would never be enough to make you *want* to put in the effort. I knew I was in a relationship with a man who cared more about control than compromise."

Dru's expression hardened. "Control? *That's* what you think it was?"

Nhuri tilted her head. "Am I wrong?"

Dru clenched his jaws, looking away.

"That's what I thought," she murmured.

Silence stretched between them, thick and heavy.

Finally, Dru exhaled, his fingers drumming against the table. "I wasn't perfect, Nhuri. I know that." He hesitated, then met her gaze. "But you didn't have to leave the way you did. You at least owed me a conversation or something. But you got up out of there with no warning and then ignored me. That shit hurt."

Welcome to the club, she thought. Nhuri's heart clenched, but she refused to let sympathy take over. "I tried, Dru. I tried so many times to make things work, but you never listened. The way you acted so nonchalantly about my feelings, not caring if I stayed or left, made it much easier for me to choose for you. It made it easier to choose me."

Dru exhaled and shook his head, running a hand down his face. "I cared. I didn't know how to show it, but I did. And I know me saying that now won't change shit, but I need you to know that."

Nhuri remained quiet, but his next words made her tune all the way in.

"I was selfish in our relationship because I felt I wasn't doing enough for you. Couldn't do enough for you. So, I stopped. I made you feel like you were in the wrong because I was lacking, and that was fucked up."

Nhuri's chest tightened. For months, she'd wanted to hear him say *anything* to prove she wasn't just tripping and had left for nothing. All those restless nights, crying because she saw the change and how whatever she did to make him feel secure in their relationship didn't matter because he didn't feel man enough to even keep it real with himself.

Now, sitting across from him, Nhuri realized something. Whatever he said, the things he needed to get off his chest, didn't mean or change a damn thing. Dru wanted to talk to her to clear his conscience . . . like always.

Nhuri took a sip of her water. "And instead of you expressing your feelings, you treated me badly," she said and chuckled with a scoff in disbelief.

"Not on purpose. That's what I'm trying to get you to understand," Dru said, sounding regretful.

"There is no understanding between us. I want you to know that how you treated me was unfair. No, let me finish," she said, stopping him from talking over her.

Dru clenched his jaws but let her continue. Nhuri leaned closer.

"You were wrong, and you checked out of our relationship long before I saw the signs. Maybe it was your immaturity or lack of accountability, but what happened between us was on you. *You* are the reason I left. I was never the bad person, maybe just not the person for you, and I'm okay with admitting that now. Hopefully, you can do the same."

She stared at Dru with a mix of frustration and exhaustion but complete peace. He needed to hear every word she said because he wouldn't let her get a word in before now. Nhuri felt like she was finally letting go of something that had been weighing her down for far too long.

This situation had knowingly and unknowingly held her back from her full potential to love again and be the woman she was always meant to be. It felt good to stand up for herself. Just as she reached for her purse, a familiar face came into her line of vision.

"Ayo, ain't this something? I was just talking about you."

Nhuri's eyes squinted before they widened some. Shyriq's brother, Rush, stood tall and confident with a smirk. The iced-out chain around his neck gleamed in the low lighting, making Nhuri wonder what he did for a living. His attire of joggers and a crisp white tee with some Jordans on his feet was vastly different from Shyriq's style.

"Rush?" Nhuri blinked, surprised. "Hey. What are you doing here?"

Rush grinned, sliding his hands into his pockets. "Man, just grabbing some food. I was about to head out, but then I saw you sitting over here looking all serious. Thought I'd come say what's up." He pinned his eyes on Dru, sizing him up before focusing back on her. "Everything good?"

Before Nhuri could answer, Dru scoffed and leaned back in his seat. Irritation was written all over his face.

"Oh, I get it now," Dru said. His voice was laced with bitterness.

Nhuri frowned. "Get what?"

"This is why you left, huh?" Dru gestured toward Rush. "Because you had some new dude lined up the whole time?"

Nhuri's mouth fell open in shock. "Are you *serious* right now?"

Dru's jaws clenched. "Nah, it makes sense. You dipped out so easily you didn't even look back. You just needed an excuse to go be with whoever was waiting in the wings."

Rush let out a low chuckle, shaking his head. "Yo, homeboy, you got me fucked up." He glanced at Nhuri and scowled. "Who is this clown?"

Nhuri sighed heavily, pinching the bridge of her nose. "He's nobody."

Dru, clearly agitated, snapped. "Nobody? Yeah, okay. How long was it before you moved on, Nhuri? A week? A month?" His eyes burned into hers, and his temper flared the way it used to when he didn't get his way. "All that talk about me not giving a damn, but the whole time you were just waiting to be on some foul, ho shit."

Nhuri slammed her hand down on the table, spilling some of her water. "You got me messed up," she hissed, pointing a finger at him. "*Don't* disrespect me."

"Nah. You got yourself messed up. Sitting up here like you're just the best woman in the world. Fuck out of here," Dru spat.

Rush stepped forward, ready to snatch him out of his seat. "Aye, you better lower your tone and watch who you talkin' to. Shit can get real ugly in here."

Dru huffed. "Man, whatever. This ain't got nothing to do with you."

"It had something to do with me the moment you raised your voice at a woman who clearly ain't fooling with your lame ass anymore."

Nhuri shook her head, disgusted. "You know what? I should've never agreed to this. I thought we could have a mature conversation, but clearly, you're still the same bitter, insecure, controlling man I left."

Dru's nostrils flared as he exhaled. "You just mad 'cause I caught you in your bullshit."

Nhuri stood abruptly, grabbing her purse. "No, I'm mad because I wasted my time thinking you had actually grown the hell up." She pulled out her phone and turned to walk away. "Don't bother texting or calling me, Dru."

Dru chuckled sarcastically. "Go ahead and block me. That's real mature of you, Nhuri."

She ignored him and walked out of the restaurant. Rush walked quickly behind her. He was amused by everything he was witnessing right now.

"Aye, Nhuri. You good for real?"

Nhuri turned to Rush, her face tight with irritation. "I'm fine."

"A'ight, but if you need backup next time, let me know."

Nhuri knew he was trying to be funny and lighten the mood, but she was too heated to feed into it. Shaking her head, she left the hotel without saying another word.

Climbing into the driver's seat, she took a deep breath, inhaling deeply before letting it all out. Going to her contacts, she blocked Dru's number and everyone associated with him. She thought talking to him would provide the closure she needed, and that wasn't the truth at all. She felt more stressed than before entering the grocery store, and she blamed no one but herself.

"So glad I have some liquor waiting on me," Nhuri mumbled, pulling out of the parking lot.

TWENTY-TWO

THE AROMA OF collard greens, baked chicken, dressing, macaroni and cheese, plus an apple pie for dessert lingered in the air. Full as a tick, Shyriq leaned back in his chair and folded his arms across his chest. He watched Rush savagely eat the last of his plate like he hadn't just eaten two full servings of their mama's cooking. With the way his hangover had been on his ass all day, this was just what he needed to refuel. A nap was coming shortly.

Sunday dinners at their parents' house had been a thing for as long as Shyriq could remember, and despite how busy life or their schedules got, neither brother dared to skip out too often. Joyce Hendrix wasn't playing that. Usually, the table would be filled with conversation about their week, but today, Shyriq hadn't chimed in much.

It'd been hectic with the unexpected trip he had to take, but besides work, his mind kept drifting, and he knew exactly why. Nhuri hadn't texted or called him since last night. He'd fallen into a comfortable routine of talking to her once they were settled in for the night, but that hadn't happened.

She wasn't the type to be glued to her phone, and he respected that, but this was different. Nhuri was responsive. If not immediately, then at least within a reasonable time. But his call had gone unanswered, and his message had been sitting on delivered since earlier that evening.

Something was up.

Rush wiped his mouth with a napkin before leaning back and rubbing his stomach. "Man, Mama . . . You put your foot in that food today."

Shyriq grunted in agreement, still lost in his thoughts.

Rush glanced his way. "You good, bro?"

He nodded. "I'm straight."

Joyce narrowed her eyes, looking between her sons. She'd picked up on the tension the moment they entered the house but hadn't said anything about it yet. She peered at Shyriq with curiosity.

"What's going on with you?"

Shyriq shook his head, trying to play it off. "Nothing. Just work. You know how it is."

Joyce gave him a look that said, *"Boy, please."* "You think I raised y'all and don't know when you're holding something in? Try again."

Rush chuckled, studying him for a beat. "So, you just gon' sit there and act like you ain't stressin' over shorty?"

Shyriq exhaled through his nose. "Who said I was stressing? You tripping."

"Who is shorty?" Joyce asked, making them and their father, Kenny, chuckle.

"His assistant," Rush answered.

Joyce's brows dipped. "She's messing up already? Your father told me you had to get a new one since Michelle went on maternity leave."

Rush barked out a loud laugh, and Shyriq shook his head.

"No. It's not that," Shyriq replied.

"Well, someone better tell me something because it feels like I'm being left out of the joke," Joyce said, glancing at Kenny.

He stuffed some dressing into his mouth and chewed. "I'm not in it, baby."

Shyriq's nostrils flared. It was one thing to be dating Nhuri, but to be caught up in his feelings the way he was had him a bit spooked. To his knowledge, she hadn't done anything for him to be tripping on her like this, but his feelings were involved, so it didn't matter.

"Mmm-hmm," Joyce hummed. "Of course, you aren't. Rush, tell me what's going on. I know, you know."

Rush was about to shrug, and then he remembered what he meant to tell Shyriq yesterday. He'd been at the hotel meeting a few of his homeboys who were in town for a birthday party and forgot all about his run-in with Nhuri and Dru.

"I'm not saying he's in his feelings about her, but I would be too if I caught her in public arguing with some dude."

That seemed to get Shyriq's attention. He sat up slightly, keeping his expression neutral though he felt everything but. "Arguing with who?"

"Some lame," Rush scoffed, disgusted that he couldn't hem Dru up on his brother's behalf. "You know I met up with Monte nem' over the weekend. I'm in the hotel's restaurant about to grab a quick bite to eat before we start drinking, and I see Nhuri."

Rush drank some of his Sprite before continuing.

"I don't know who dude was that she was arguing with, but it was serious. I ain't catch what was being discussed, but they were going at it. Her hands were moving, and her neck was twisting like she was ready to slap him. Whatever he said had her in her feelings."

Shyriq clenched and unclenched his jaws. "Yeah?"

It was all he could say. He hadn't thought about the man Nhuri used to deal with, and she never really talked about him. Dru was mentioned subtly in conversation, without his name being brought up, but Shyriq didn't doubt that he was the guy she was arguing with.

Besides the time when he looked her up on Facebook, Shyriq hadn't gone digging for information anymore. He figured that with him opening up about his past and how close they had gotten over the months, she would do the same. But now Shyriq knew why she hadn't. Knowing she had been at a hotel ignoring his calls but sitting with her ex didn't sit right with him. Shyriq exhaled through his nose. He didn't like the thought of Nhuri being upset, especially not over some old shit that should've been left where it was.

"Yep," Rush nodded. "I forgot to tell you."

"He say somethin' foul?" Shyriq wondered.

"Yeah, but you know I checked that shit," Rush said, and Joyce threw her napkin at him.

He raised his hands in defense as she pointed at him with a warning in her eyes. "You better stop cursing at my table."

Rush chuckled. "It slipped, Mama. My bad. But, yeah, bro. The dude is a lame. It sounded like he was trying to guilt-trip her. Was on some accusing her of leaving him 'cause she wanted to mess around. I don't think that was why, though."

Shyriq's hand curled into a fist.

Rush chuckled under his breath. "Yeah . . . I figured you wouldn't like that."

Shyriq sat back, trying to push down the irritation bubbling in his chest. He had no right to be mad; Nhuri wasn't his. Not completely, anyway. They weren't in a relationship, but damn, if hearing about her sitting across from some bitter-ass ex wasn't pissing him off. At first, he'd let her unresponsiveness slide, figuring she'd had a long day, but all bets were off now.

Rush shook his head. "She ain't even see me at first. I walked over when I heard his tone gettin' real disrespectful. Told her I'd catch her later, but you should've seen how dude looked at me."

Shyriq's gaze darkened. "What you mean?"

"Like he was tryna figure out if I was one of her new men or somethin'. Mad insecure." Rush laughed. "I ain't say nothin', but I could tell it struck a nerve. She looked fed up with him, though. As soon as she walked out, she pulled her phone out. I don't know if she hit you up after that or what, but she left."

Shyriq pulled his phone out, but there was still no response from Nhuri. His thumb hovered over her contact briefly before he locked the screen. What he wanted to say had to wait. He was trying to play it cool but was failing miserably.

"I'm just sayin', big bro . . . You might wanna check in with your woman."

"She's not my woman."

Rush let out a short laugh. "Yeah, a'ight."

Shyriq stayed quiet, but the conversation had shifted something in him. Maybe it was time he made sure she knew where he stood before somebody else tried to step in. Joyce was feeling the same way. She wasn't hip to the nature of their relationship, but she knew her son. When he liked someone, he was all in until they gave him a reason not to be—so, hearing him not claim Nhuri as his woman was all the proof she needed.

Joyce folded her arms and studied her oldest son. "She's not your woman, yet you're sitting here about to blow a gasket because she was arguing with another man?"

Shyriq pulled at his chin hairs. "She can do whatever she wants."

Laughing, Joyce shook her head. "Okay. You don't like that, huh?"

"It's not about me liking or not liking it."

"Mmm-hmm," Joyce said, unconvinced.

Rush snickered. "Yeah, a'ight. You should've seen dude's face. Looked like he was ready to spin the block."

Shyriq rolled his shoulders and pushed back his plate. He wasn't about to give his brother the satisfaction of seeing him pressed over a situation he had no claim over. "Like I said, she can do whatever she wants."

Rush gave him a knowing look. "Yeah? Then why you so tight right now?"

Shyriq exhaled sharply through his nose. "I'm *not* tight."

Joyce just shook her head, smiling. When Kenny interrupted, giving him a piece of his mind, she couldn't have been happier. Hopefully, Shyriq listened to him.

"Son, let me tell you something. If you want that woman, you better make sure she knows it. Otherwise, don't be surprised when she ends up with somebody else."

His father's words hit him harder than he expected for many reasons. One is because of his divorce. Shyriq knew he was right. He also knew he wasn't about to chase behind a woman who still had one foot in the past. But damn if the thought of Nhuri sitting across from her ex, giving him any part of her energy, didn't make his chest tight.

"And don't sit there like everyone doesn't have a past. You just ended a marriage, and I'm sure she had her reservations about you, but that didn't stop her from going out with you," Kenny said.

Joyce sucked her teeth. "So, all of y'all have just been keeping me in the dark? I see how it is. This apple pie is just for me."

Rush looked bewildered. "Mama, stop playing. I have nothing to do with your son's love affairs."

"Oh, now he's *my son* and not *your brother*?" Joyce teased.

While they stood from the table bickering over the pie, Shyriq stayed seated. He was contemplating his next move. He was all for communicating and letting it be known how he felt, but he saw no point doing so if Nhuri wasn't willing to do the same. Plus, he has some questions. Of all the places they could've met, why was she at a hotel? Shyriq didn't know, but he wanted answers, and he hoped she gave them up willingly without him having to ask.

TWENTY-THREE

NHURI RUSHED THROUGH the office, waving quickly at Ashley before frantically pressing the elevator button. She was back late from lunch by fourteen minutes and was slightly panicking. Not because she couldn't run over some, but because she was already twenty minutes late this morning.

Her entire day had been thrown off by having to take Raniya to day care because Natalia had spent the wee hours of the morning throwing up. And then, traffic had been backed up. She'd barely had time to throw on something decent before rushing out the door, and everything had been a mess, including her outfit, since.

Once she reached her floor, she hurried inside her office and placed her things down before heading to Shyriq's. She knocked on the closed door and waited for him to tell her to come in. Nhuri eased the door open when he said nothing and poked her head inside.

"Um, hey," she said lightly, trying to test his temperature.

He'd been in a shitty mood all morning, and she got it. It was just one of those days for them both. The second she stepped inside, Nhuri could immediately feel the tension in the air. Cautiously, she took a seat in front of his desk. Shyriq had his eyes glued to his screen and didn't bother to look her way until Nhuri sucked her teeth.

"You have something to say?" he asked with irritation written all over his face. He'd had the same expression all morning.

"I know I'm late, but what's with your weird mood today? Is everything okay?"

Her sincerity almost made him forget why he was pissed. "Why wouldn't everything be okay?"

Nhuri was confused by his question. "Um . . . I'm not sure. That's why I asked."

"You should be asking yourself that."

His clipped tone made Nhuri draw her head back. "*Excuse me?*"

She could already tell he was in one of those moods where he was meticulous, nitpicky, and snappish, but this was different. It felt like he was personally attacking her.

"First, you show up late without my chai tea, and then you mosey in here after taking a longer lunch like everything is cool. Is that how I operate?"

In the chaos of her morning, she'd completely forgotten to grab Shyriq's drink from Sip. She couldn't even think straight this morning, so, of course, stopping to grab their usual wasn't on her mind.

She tried to keep her tone steady and not give him the same energy he was giving her. "I had a rough morning, Shyriq."

"So did I," he said, placing his arms on his desk. "But I still managed to be on time. Life is going to get rough. It doesn't mean you get to do what you want."

Nhuri forced herself to stay calm as she stared at him in disbelief. "Are you serious right now?"

He scoffed, rubbing a hand down his beard. "Do I *look* like I'm joking?"

She let out a humorless laugh, shaking her head. "You've been nitpicking all morning, but me being late and not having your chai tea is what you're upset about?"

He shot her a look. "It's not just about the drink, Nhuri. It's about reliability."

Something about that word made her chest tighten.

"Oh, so now I'm *unreliable?*"

Shyriq's jaws flexed. "I didn't say that."

"You didn't have to," she shot back. "Because that's exactly what you're implying."

Now, an even thicker tension filled the room, and it suffocated them both. Nhuri's breathing was shallow as anger burned hot in her chest. He had the audacity to be talking to her crazy like she didn't bust her ass every day, putting in extra hours and making sure his life ran smoothly. But none of that mattered because she was late and forgot his damn tea? Nhuri was beyond pissed.

Not just as his assistant but as a woman she thought he cared about.

"You don't get to talk to me like this," she said, her voice shaking slightly. "I have been nothing but good to you and to this job. And the one time I slip up, you're acting like I'm some kind of disappointment?"

Shyriq exhaled, rubbing the bridge of his nose like he was trying to keep himself in check. "Nhuri, that's not—"

"No," she cut him off. "You've been in a mood all morning, and I've been letting it slide, but not anymore. You're snapping at me over some bullshit, and I don't deserve that."

Hearing her curse at him made Shyriq realize he had crossed the line, but his pride wouldn't let him say it. So, he deflected and told her the real reason he was in his feelings and tripping.

"Did you have fun this weekend?" he asked.

Nhuri frowned. "What? Why are you asking me that?"

"Because I know how it is when you run into an old fling. Meeting up at hotels and all that. You must've had a grand ol' time to be rushing in here late and making excuses."

Nhuri's throat ached from unshed tears. She was so angry that her leg bounced, and her skin flushed. He had no right to speak to her like that, and she let him know it.

"You're being really disrespectful, and I'ma need you to dial it back some," she said, putting aside all professionalism.

"Nah, what's disrespectful is you publicly arguing with your ex. What, you want that old thing back?"

Nhuri's lip trembled. "That's low. You don't know what we were talking about, and your brother is weak for running his mouth."

"Well, someone had to tell me. You weren't," Shyriq stated.

"And I'm glad I didn't. Look how you're acting. I see why your wife cheated on you."

Her words hit Shyriq in the face as if she'd slapped the black off him. His head reared back, and he coughed to ease the tightness in his chest.

"*That's* how you feel?"

Nhuri's nostrils flared. Her feelings were beyond hurt, and now she knew why Natalia had warned her. Men like Shyriq didn't deserve her love.

"Yep, and for the record, what I do and who I converse with isn't any of your damn business, *boss*. From now on, if it isn't work-related, do me and yourself a favor and leave me the hell alone."

She stood from her seat and walked to the door. Opening it, she looked back. "And have Ashley grab your chai tea from now on since you need them so badly, and I'm unreliable. Cranky-ass grown man," she mumbled loud enough for him to hear and pulled his door shut.

Nhuri barely made it to her office before the emotions crashed over her. Her heart was pounding so hard that she could hardly breathe. The second she shut the door behind her, her hands trembled as she pressed her back against it. Tears burned the back of her eyes, but she swallowed hard, refusing to let them fall. She wasn't going to cry over Shyriq or the shitty morning she had.

But it wasn't just about this morning.

It was the weight of everything. Natalia's health scare, stepping up for Raniya, the stress of a new position she hadn't even asked for, and now Shyriq, snapping at her like she hadn't been holding it all together.

She roughly wiped at her face and took a deep breath, but it was no use. The tears came anyway. Her office felt too small and too suffocating. Nhuri pushed herself off the door and walked over to her desk. She gripped the edges as her body shook.

She was tired.

Tired of feeling like no matter what she did, it wasn't enough—not for Dru, not for Natalia's healing, not for this job, and not for Shyriq. She had been breaking her back to prove herself to be strong for everyone, and yet, here she was, being talked down to over something as stupid as a latte.

She squeezed her eyes shut as tears coated her cheeks. *Why does this hurt so much?* she thought. Nhuri wasn't sure if it was because she respected him and had grown feelings for him. Or was it because she actually liked her job, the feeling of being needed and being seen? Whatever it was, it held no candle to how small she felt right now.

Sniffling, she inhaled deeply through her nose and exhaled slowly. She wasn't about to sit here and break down over a man who was too damn stubborn to admit he was wrong. He didn't deserve that power over her. No one did. If Shyriq hadn't understood that before now, Nhuri would make sure he felt it from here on out.

Shyriq had royally messed up and had no one to blame but himself.

It was the evening of the Nine Oak Exclusive Tasting, and he was going through it. True to her word, Nhuri had kept her distance and remained strictly professional. Not just today but for the last two weeks. She'd been short with him, only answering and responding to emails, phone calls, and questions related to work.

He couldn't blame her and was glad she hadn't quit because that would've really made tonight drag on. Shyriq was impressed, though. Despite his annoyance and behavior with Tyreek for pushing up on Nhuri, he hadn't half-stepped with the decorations or the guest list.

The private venue screamed sophistication and luxury. The restored historic loft space had exposed brick walls, sleek black steel beams, and floor-to-ceiling windows with a view of the city, while chandeliers hung from the ceiling.

At the entrance, a custom-built oak barrel engraved with the Nine Oak logo grabbed the guests' attention as soon as they entered. There were two backdrops to snap photos and three photographers walking around capturing the moment. Shyriq went all out and spared no expense when Nhuri suggested they get a floral arrangement of deep red roses, eucalyptus, and black calla lilies for the wooden barrel centerpieces. They paired perfectly with the gold-rimmed glassware. Every detail embodied the Nine Oak's spirit, including the sleek leather-bound menus with the evening's whiskey tastings and food selections.

Shyriq hadn't made his way to the Gold members' exclusive lounge, but the velvet burgundy drapery that separated them from the crowd was an eye-turner. Nhuri knew what she was doing. She wanted to ensure that tonight was an unforgettable, top-tier event that upped the notch on Nine Oak as a brand synonymous with class, quality, and craftsmanship. Instead of being able to praise her for her skills, Shyriq had to admire and congratulate her from afar.

Nhuri was right at the center of it, moving effortlessly through the room. Shyriq clocked her the second she walked in, and so did every man with roaming eyes. The sight of her in a fitted black silk dress that stopped just below her knees, hugging every inch of her thick frame, was hard to ignore. Her jet-black hair was silk-pressed and parted down the middle, stopping below her bra strap.

Shyriq kept his eyes on her as her heels clicked against the marble floor. Nhuri was moving with confidence as if it were her second skin. She was in her element and engaging with the guests as if she'd known them her entire life. She was doing all of that while ignoring the hell out of him.

For things to flow seamlessly, she had to keep her distance. Shyriq looked too damn good and tempting in his tailored black suit that fitted his stocky frame to perfection. She tried not to get caught up in how his muscles flexed whenever he shook someone's hand or embraced someone for a hug.

Nhuri would purposefully step out of his line of vision because she knew he was watching her. Shyriq tried not to let it get to him, but it was impossible. The way she refused to even glance in his direction was maddening. The way her energy never wavered, even though he knew she still had to carry some weight from their argument, messed with him. He knew he'd been on some bullshit and had taken his frustrations out on her.

But now he was seeing just how much he'd underestimated her. Nhuri wasn't some fragile thing who folded under pressure. She'd been pressured her entire life. Tonight was no different. She collected herself, stepped into this event, and showed him *exactly* why she was built for more than just being his assistant.

"She's incredible," a voice said beside him, pulling Shyriq from his thoughts.

He turned to meet the knowing gaze of Anthony, one of his associates. The older man swirled his whiskey, nodding toward Nhuri, who was conversing with a group of investors.

Better her than me, Shyriq thought.

"She's sharp, professional, and charming as hell," Anthony smirked. "You have a gem working for you, Hendrix."

Forcing a smile, Shyriq exhaled through his nose. "Yeah, I know."

And that was the problem. He knew exactly how much of an asset Nhuri was. How much he depended on her and needed her period. Yet, he'd let his pride trip him up.

"She's my assistant," he offered, not wanting him to get any ideas about getting her to work for him.

Anthony's brow raised. "Really? She seems much too advanced to just be at your side. A woman like that? You either elevate her or lose her."

He didn't know just how correct he was. Shyriq didn't respond. He focused back on where Nhuri was now standing with Natalia, Malik, and some man. He placed the glass of spiced whiskey to his mouth and sipped slowly with squinted eyes as Nhuri shook the unknown man's hand. Her smile was too bright, and the man's eyes lit up like he'd just hit on all his bets on FanDuel.

Shyriq's jaws clenched.

The man was clearly interested, leaning in just a little too close and smiling big for no reason. Shyriq couldn't hide his disgust when Malik patted the guy on the shoulder as he said something that made Nhuri laugh.

"What this nigga doing, playing matchmaker?" Shyriq grumbled, grateful that Anthony had walked off. He was the man of the hour, but he needed everyone to leave him be for a few minutes while he checked the scene.

Shyriq knew that laugh. It wasn't forced or just her trying to be polite. It was genuine, and hearing it flow from her lips and not because of him had Shyriq tight. His fingers tightened around his whiskey glass, and he clenched his jaws . . . again.

He was supposed to be mingling, talking business, and celebrating a new venture, yet all he could do was watch as another man engaged Nhuri in the type of conversation that should've been his to have.

"Pops told you to get your woman. Now look at you. Over here about to throw the fuck up," Rush said, walking up to him.

Shyriq scoffed. "I ain't in the mood, Rush."

"Man, I don't care. This is a special occasion, and instead of enjoying the fruits of your labor with her, you're over here in the corner pouting because you can't man up. Get it together, bro."

Rush patted Shyriq on the back and walked off. His little brother's advice, which made sense, let Shyriq know he was definitely tripping and in the wrong. Rush never made sense. He knew it already, but somehow, being called out made Shyriq pull it together.

He didn't like seeing another man looking at Nhuri as if she were the only thing in the room worth paying attention to. Nor did he like that she was letting it happen while pretending he didn't even exist.

And maybe he deserved that.

Shit, he *knew* he did. But that didn't make it any easier to stomach. When the man leaned down to whisper in Nhuri's ear, Shyriq had seen enough. He put his glass on the marble table, and his feet moved before his brain caught up. He wasn't trying to cause a scene and wasn't about to let this turn into some spectacle. But what he *wasn't* about to do was stand on the sidelines and watch this play out like he wasn't even in the damn building.

The crowd shifted, making room for him to walk through. A few people tried to grab his attention, but Shyriq was locked in on Nhuri. Natalia noticed him first, and she smiled before seeing the grim look on his face. Nhuri hadn't gotten her up to speed on their falling out, and for a reason. Hearing "I told you so" from her sister would make her feel worse than she already did.

Nhuri had her back to him, still engaged in conversation and utterly oblivious to the fact that he was walking up on them until Natalia acknowledged his presence.

"Hey, Shyriq. This was such a great turnout," Natalia said, smiling but trying to read his expression.

Nhuri didn't turn quickly at the sound of his name. She took her time, letting it be known his presence didn't move her.

"Hey, Natalia. Thank you." His tone was dry and unwelcoming.

Before he could address Nhuri, the guy who'd been holding her attention spoke up.

"Shyriq Hendrix." His voice carried excitement as he extended his hand, completely unaware of the energy shift. "Man, I'm a huge fan of your work. Your whiskey is some of the best I've ever had."

Shyriq barely spared him a glance. He looked down at him and his hand, considering his much shorter height, and didn't bother shaking his hand. Shyriq didn't even acknowledge the praise.

"Who you here with?" Shyriq asked.

The man looked confused for a second. "Oh, uh. I'm here with my cousin as a plus one."

"Next year, tell them I said not to bring you."

Shyriq's words made Natalia choke on her drink and sputter laughter. Malik looked stunned, while Nhuri still had her cool, calm, and collected expression. In fact, she smirked while Shyriq stood there looking like he wanted to knock the guy's head off.

"Nhuri, let me talk to you for a second."

She cocked her head to the side and blinked slowly. Her lips pressed together, and for a moment, Shyriq thought she was about to shut him down, and she had every right to.

"In private, please," he added tensely.

She hesitated before turning back to the guy, giving him a tight smile. She felt bad for him but wasn't about to pacify his feelings. But she didn't want to be ruder than Shyriq had already been. "Excuse me for a second."

Shyriq didn't wait for her to second-guess it, nor did he wait for the dude to get another word out. His hand was on the low of her back, escorting her out of the main ballroom. Nhuri took her time and even stopped to talk to a few of the guests. Shyriq stood by like this was her event, and he let her do her thing.

Finally, they reached a private location, and Shyriq pushed open one of the side doors leading out of the ballroom before entering another door. The hallway was quieter, and the heavy bass from the jazz music in the main room was muffled. He took a breath, trying to level himself before turning to face Nhuri as she walked through the doorway, letting it close behind her. She crossed her arms and waited.

His jaws tightened. "You gonna keep giving me the silent treatment and cold shoulder all night?"

Nhuri arched a brow, her lips pressing together as she tilted her head. "Is that what you called me in here for?"

"Just answer the question."

"That isn't an apology."

Shyriq exhaled, rubbing a hand down his face before meeting her eyes again. "Nhuri—"

"No, let me stop you right there," she interrupted calmly but firmly. "You may run this company, but you *don't* run me."

His brows drew together. "I never said I did."

"You didn't have to." She shifted her weight from one high-heeled leg to the other. "You think because you're frustrated that you get to take it out on me? Because you were in a mood that morning, you had the right to nitpick and snap at me like I don't mean shit to you?" She shook her head. "That's *not* how this works, Shyriq."

He sucked in a breath, shoving his hands into his pockets. "I know I was out of line, and I'm truly sorry about that. You *do* mean something to me, and instead of communicating, I lashed out."

Nhuri huffed a short, humorless laugh. "And yet, here you are, acting like *I'm* the one who needs to fix this?"

His gaze dropped to the floor briefly before he looked back at her. "I didn't mean to take it out on you."

"But you did." Her expression softened, but there was still a guardedness in her eyes. "And you never even acknowledged it. You just expected me to brush it off and keep it moving like nothing happened."

Shyriq sighed, stepping closer. "You think I *wanted* to come at you like that? That I wanted to see you walk away from me?" His voice dipped lower. "'Cause I didn't, Nhuri. Not then and not now."

She held his gaze for a moment, trying to read between the lines of what he was really saying.

"You hurt me," she admitted, her voice quieter but just as steady. "I know your life may get stressful with everything you have going on, but that doesn't give you a right to disrespect me. I'll let a lot of things slide, but that isn't one of them. And I won't keep making space for somebody who doesn't respect mine. If you wanted to know about my ex and why I was at the hotel that day, you should've just asked like a grown man instead of playing little boy games. *That's* why he's my ex, and I can guarantee we're never getting back together."

Shyriq exhaled through his nose, nodding slowly. "You're right. I should've come to you and talked it out before jumping to conclusions. Again, I'm sorry. I mean that."

"Mm-hmm. I hear you."

"So, how can I make things right?"

Nhuri stepped to him and smiled. "You grow the hell up and enjoy this tasting like I'm about to do," she said before patting his chest and walking out the door.

Shyriq stood there stunned with his dick so hard and a smile while shaking his head. Nhuri wasn't letting him off that easily, and he couldn't do anything but respect it.

TWENTY-FOUR

THE TASTING HAD finally come to an end, and the guests hadn't stopped giving their praises since entering the venue. The guests slipped out in pairs and small groups, while some lingered around holding conversations with more plans for the evening. Nhuri was glad to call it a night as she and Natalia hugged goodbye.

"Listen, all that hard work you were doing really paid off," Natalia praised, making Nhuri blush.

She was slightly tipsy but still coherent and could walk. "Thank you, sis. That means so much coming from you."

"And I mean it. Are you good to drive, or are you staying here with Shyriq?"

Nhuri forced a smile. "Um, I actually booked a room."

She was so grateful the venue was in the same place she was about to lay her head.

"A room for yourself?" Natalia's brows dipped.

Nhuri nodded and before she could pry any further, Malik appeared, placing a hand at the small of her back. "You ready to head home?" he asked.

"Yes. Just seeing what Nhuri has planned."

"A'ight. I'ma have valet pull the vehicle up. Meet me outside," he said, kissing her cheek. "Sis," he said teasingly, "we gotta talk."

Nhuri shook her head and smiled. "Have a good night, Malik."

His laughter echoed as he walked out the door. Natalia got right back to the subject at hand.

"Why did you get your own room? I thought things with y'all were progressing?"

"They were, and then he pissed me off. So ..." Nhuri shrugged.

Natalia sighed dramatically. "Oh, goodness. Well, okay. That makes sense about why there was so much tension tonight. He was about to knock Rodney's head off for talking to you."

"Rodney?" Nhuri questioned, highly confused. "Who is that?"

"Girl, the man whose face he came and snatched you out of."

Nhuri chuckled. "Oh. I guess I forgot his name."

"Or didn't care to remember it," Natalia laughed. "You are something else."

"But you love me."

"I do, and I'm so happy we got to share tonight together. Whatever you do, please be safe."

Her words had an underlying warning. Natalia wanted her to protect her heart.

"I will. Text me when you make it in, and I'll do the same."

Natalia told her okay, and they hugged once more before she went to wait for Malik. Nhuri waited until she saw him tuck her safely into the car before she headed toward the elevators. The cleaning crew had already begun breaking everything down, and since Shyriq hadn't let it be known she was needed, Nhuri was making her exit.

The whiskey had settled into her bloodstream, warming her from the inside out, making her limbs loose but her thoughts sharp. She needed to get upstairs, take a long shower, and sleep off this ridiculous night.

But fate had other plans.

As she stepped further into the hotel lobby, she spotted Shyriq. His suit jacket was unbuttoned, his tie loosened, and his posture was still commanding even in the dim glow of the chandeliers. Nhuri's body reacted before her mind could stop it. Heat curled in her belly, and not just from the alcohol but from the memory of the way he had looked at her earlier, how he had followed her out of that ballroom with purpose. He felt it too . . . She knew he did.

Shyriq turned his head slightly and licked his lips as he eyed her frame. A slow, knowing smirk tugged at the corners of his mouth. His scent hit her first, and Nhuri rolled her eyes.

"I didn't know you were staying here tonight," he said with his voice lower than usual.

Nhuri nodded. "Mmm-hmm. Figured it was best."

"Is that right?"

His question was asked teasingly, and Nhuri wasn't about to fall for it. She couldn't let him see how much he affected her when he'd already been the cause of her soaked thong without touching her.

The elevator doors slid open, and he allowed her to step on first. The moment the doors shut, the sudden stillness amplified the budding tension between them. Nhuri stood stiffly across from Shyriq after pressing the button for her floor. She crossed her arms to hide her erect nipples, but it did nothing to lessen her arousal.

Shyriq leaned against the opposite wall with his broad shoulders relaxed. Nhuri felt the heat of his presence, even from a few feet away. He smelled like whiskey, wood, and leather. A dangerous and intoxicating aroma that clung to the air and muddled her thoughts. She tried to ignore the way her pulse quickened with each breath and the way her body seemed to betray her, but how could she? Shyriq was every bit the magnetic force she tried to stay away from.

"You still mad at me?" he asked. His voice was deep yet gentle.

Nhuri exhaled sharply. "That's not an apology."

A slow, deep chuckle rolled from his chest, sending shivers down her spine.

"You gonna keep saying that, or you want me to show you how sorry I am?"

Her breath caught. The space between them suddenly felt too small. Nhuri's glossy eyes made contact with his as Shyriq approached her. Before he reached her, he swiped a card and pressed a button on the wall that made the elevator stop.

"Shyriq," Nhuri whispered, with her heart racing.

He stepped closer, invading her space. His hands found her hips, trailing them softly before wrapping his arms around her waist.

"Shyriq, what?" he asked, kissing down her neck.

Nhuri's eyes fluttered, and she moaned softly. "I don't know why you're acting like this," she said.

He moved to the other side of her neck and kissed there. Nhuri's body shuddered.

"Acting like what? Like I want you?"

His voice was calm, but she could hear the heat simmering just below it.

"I'm just trying to get you to understand how sorry I am."

"You told me," she breathed out as he kissed the top of her exposed breasts.

Seeing how far he could take it, Shyriq bit her nipple through the silk fabric and earned a moan so sweet he had to give the other breast the same attention. Nhuri's head swirled as he made her body heat up. He kissed down her stomach, lifting the hem of her dress, and placed one leg over his shoulder.

"I said, I wanted to show you. Can I do that?" he asked.

Nhuri didn't feel herself nod, but she felt his lips, which was clearly all that mattered. Her breath caught in her throat as he moved the seat of her panties to the side and swiped his tongue along her pussy. Nhuri knew she was wet, but hearing him slurp up her essence had her so turned on. Shyriq held her leg up and suckled her clit into his mouth as if he were dehydrated.

"Oh," Nhuri gasped, clutching the railing.

His tongue flickered harder, and she saw stars. He ate her pussy with earnest, leaving no doubt in her mind that he was, indeed, sorry. Shyriq was literally on his knees, begging, licking, slurping, and eating his way out of the doghouse. Nhuri scooted back when it began to feel too good.

"Stop running from this," he growled, smacking her bare ass cheek.

Nhuri could've melted. Instead, she followed his instructions and let him have his way. Rolling her hips, she let him bring her to a climax that brought tears to her eyes.

"Oh my gosh," she groaned, squeezing his shoulder. "Yeeees. Right there, right *there*."

Shyriq didn't move or stop licking her until her legs trembled, and then he placed the sweetest kiss on her puffy lips before standing to his feet. He held her tightly with his face inches away from hers. His breath was hot against her lips, and his eyes were dark with almost feral restraint.

"Do you feel how sorry I am?" he asked.

Lazily, Nhuri nodded.

"Good."

Shyriq kissed her lips, sliding his tongue into her mouth. It was needy and fierce and would've caught Nhuri completely off guard, but she was prepared this time. She wanted to taste herself on his lips. The way he kissed and held her made Nhuri's entire body respond in ways she couldn't control. His free hand cupped the back of her neck, pulling her closer as though he needed to feel every inch of her pressed against him.

Nhuri's breath caught, her mind scrambling for clarity for some kind of reason. But there was no space for reason in the way he kissed her. In the way his hands moved over her body, gripping her ass until she was flush against his erection. Shyriq was blessed. The type of blessing that Nhuri would be praising the Lord for. When she went to wrap her legs around his waist, she caught herself and softly pushed him back.

Raw, unfiltered lust danced in Shyriq's eyes. "What's the matter?"

She swallowed hard. "Nothing. I just . . . Maybe we should slow down."

Confused but understanding, Shyriq nodded. He stepped back and licked his lips before running a hand over his beard that she soaked with her juices. Swiping the card against the panel again, the elevator came to life, and he pressed her floor number.

Nhuri adjusted her dress and removed her thong while the elevator ascended, all while keeping eye contact with him. She wanted him in the worst way and had officially forgiven him. When the elevator stopped and the doors slid open, Shyriq cleared his throat.

"Have a good night," he said, 100 percent sure she would after climaxing the way she just did.

On shaky legs, Nhuri stepped forward but not off of the elevator. Instead, she pressed a button for the doors to close, then pushed the button for the penthouse suite where Shyriq was staying and entered the code so they could access it. After all, she was the one who booked the room, so she knew it.

"Nhuri," Shyriq called her name in warning once they made it to the penthouse.

She stepped off and ignored him. Shaking his head, Shyriq followed her. He gave her a second to take in the breathtaking views of the suite while he washed his hands before calling her name again.

"Nhuri," he said more forcefully this time.

She swiveled in her heels to face him. "What? What is it? Do you not want me here? You keep calling my name as if I did something wrong when you're the one who just ate my pussy like you're starving. Now, I can't—"

Shyriq's strides to her were quick and intentional. He kissed whatever words she was about to say from her lips and smacked her on the ass.

"Mmmm," Nhuri moaned against his lips, and he pulled back.

"If you would've listened to me and come here, you'd know that I *do* want you here. Not just tonight. But I want you in my life. You've done nothing wrong, but everything right. You made tonight even more special, and I'm grateful. So, thank you. That's why I was calling your name, and you're upset for no reason."

Nhuri simpered at his confession. It was unexpected, but it was everything she wanted to hear.

"I'm not upset. I'm horny. I want you in my life too, but right now, I need to feel you inside of me," Nhuri said with pure lust. "Let's make tonight even more special."

Shyriq licked his lips and swooped her up. "Say no more, baby. You don't have to beg . . . yet."

Nhuri giggled as he took them to a part of the suite she'd have to tour in the morning. Right now, she didn't care what it looked like. All she knew was that they were in a bedroom, and Shyriq gently laid her on the bed. The lights from the skyline lit the room up, giving her just enough lighting to see him strip from his shirt and unbuckle his pants, letting them fall to the ground. His bulge was prominent and saluted Nhuri.

Biting her lip, she scooted to the edge of the bed so he could help her remove her dress. Shyriq unzipped it slowly, not leaving any part of her buttery soft skin untouched by his hands or lips. Shyriq took in her frame when their clothes were discarded and shook his head.

"You're beautiful," he said, tugging one of her nipples into his mouth.

They felt much better bare, and he savored their taste before dipping his head lower for a second time between her legs. Nhuri was loud this go-round, and that made Shyriq go even harder. Nhuri pinched and squeezed at her nipples as he ate her out. When he slid his middle and ring finger inside of her, her back arched.

"Shyyyy," she moaned his name so beautifully.

"Mmm-hmm," he hummed, applying pressure to her walls and sucking on her bud. "You taste so damn good, baby. Let me hear you."

She gave him exactly what he wanted. Ever so talented, Shyriq multitasked with his fingers and mouth, bringing her to the second orgasm of the night. This one had her clawing at his back and scooting up the bed, but Shyriq didn't let her run too far. She'd been doing that enough since he met her.

"Nah," he grumbled, hooking her thighs in his arms. "Bring your ass here. I'm not finished."

"But I can't," she whined.

Shyriq licked her slowly. "You can't what?"

"I can't take it anymore. Come make love to me."

Her whimpers turned him on, and Shyriq had no choice but to oblige. Locating a condom in his wallet, he slid it onto his erect dick and kissed her lips. Hovering above her, Shyriq took in her pretty face and pleading eyes.

"Once I slide in you, you're mine."

"And you're mine," she declared. "I don't share, and I used to beat up bitches back in the day, so don't play with me."

Shyriq laughed heartily, tapping his bulbous tip against her clit. "I ain't gon' ever play with or about you. I mean that."

Her legs circled his waist, and Shyriq shuddered as her wetness engulfed him. He slid in slowly with fluttering lids and grunted once he was fully inside of her.

"Gotdamn, Nhuri," he groaned, pulling out and sliding back inside.

Nhuri gasped. "Oh my gosh."

"I know. I know," he said, long stroking her.

Nhuri took every inch, keeping eye contact and fucking him back when he went deeper. Pressing her legs against the mattress at the bend of her knees, Shyriq delivered strokes that had them both moaning. He kept the pace as they kissed nastily until she clawed at his back.

"Yes! Harder. Fuck me, Shy," Nhuri moaned in his ear.

Shyriq pounded into her, giving her strokes that she'd forever remember. Her walls tightened around him, and he dropped his head into the crook of her neck. He thought that not looking at her would stop his nut from surfacing, but feeling her warm, soft body pressed against him and smelling her sweet scent only brought him closer to the edge. Yet, he kept giving her what she needed.

"This what you been keeping me away from? Do you know how good you feel?" he asked, groaning in her ear.

Nhuri's eyes rolled at the sound and feel of him. She couldn't talk. That was okay with Shyriq because he was about to make her scream. His strokes intensified when he felt her climax again.

"Yes, yes, yes," Nhuri cried.

She came hard, wetting him and some of the bed. Clinging onto him tightly, her body trembled as it went through the motions, and only then did Shyriq allow himself to release. He wasn't a selfish lover by far, and he had the rest of the night to prove just how selfless and loving he was. Nhuri didn't know it, but her title in his life had officially been promoted. And unbeknownst to Shyriq, she wouldn't be his assistant for much longer. Maybe it wasn't meant to be.

TWENTY-FIVE

SHYRIQ HAD EVERY intention of having a good week, and it was going good . . . well, until Cara called his office phone. He leaned back in his office chair, rubbing his temples as he listened to her on the other end of the phone. It was late in the day, and he was swamped with deadlines for the upcoming holiday season. The last thing he needed was more stress.

"I hate to drop this on you at the last minute, Shy," Cara said with a tone filled with genuine concern.

"What is it?" he asked.

"So, you know Natalia had a health scare earlier this month?"

He nodded, though she couldn't see him. "Yeah. What's going on?"

Nhuri hadn't told him anything, so he hoped everything was all good.

"Natalia called me earlier. Per doctor's orders, she has to take a leave of absence," Cara said.

Shyriq sat up, gripping the armrest of his chair. "Today? Is everything all right?"

He was about to head down the hall and check on Nhuri or see why she hadn't approached him.

"She's managing," Cara assured him, though the worry in her voice was evident. "But you know how lupus is. Her flare-ups are getting worse, and she said she needs to focus on her health and Raniya."

Shyriq exhaled sharply. He couldn't even be mad. Natalia had been a rock in his business for years, pulling her weight and then some. She deserved the time to rest, but damn, the timing couldn't have been worse.

"We're about to enter the busiest season, Cara," he muttered, staring at the half-empty glass of whiskey on his desk. "I can't afford to lose her right now."

"I know," she said sympathetically. "That's why I'm calling with a solution."

Shyriq's jaws tensed. He didn't like surprises, and something about Cara's tone told him she was about to hit him with one. "I'm listening."

"Nhuri."

He smiled at the mention of her name. Waking up to her this morning in his bed was how he wanted to wake up for as long as she'd let him.

"What about her?"

Cara sighed as if she knew she'd have to sell him on the idea. "Natalia told me before that when she was too sick to handle things, Nhuri would step in and take care of everything. Reports, strategies, presentations. I've seen work come across my desk with Natalia's name on it, but I *know* Nhuri did it."

Shyriq frowned. He wanted to act surprised by that revelation, but he wasn't. Nhuri was intelligent and had made his workload a hell of a lot easier since she came on board. The way she'd been taking over meetings and getting this new campaign together was brilliant.

"Natalia never mentioned that, but I believe it."

"She wouldn't," Cara said knowingly. "Nhuri probably wouldn't have minded, but that's their thing. She does some of the work behind the scenes when Natalia can't, so she's already invested. Then you made her your assistant, so . . ."

Shyriq chuckled. "So, what, Cara? Just promote her?"

"Like you don't already want to?"

He smirked. What he wanted to do was move her to a different department so he wouldn't be tempted to kiss, touch, and slide his dick in her all day. Shyriq would call or stop by her office just to see what she was doing, somehow constantly interrupting her workflow. It was cute. After their night together, things between them had become crystal clear. They were dating and would only be seeing each other.

"I'm not saying that. I can see her moving into that position, but I don't want to just spring this on her."

Shyriq was being considerate, considering all the changes she had undergone over the months. He didn't doubt her capability at all and had all the faith in her, but first, he needed to see where her head was at. He didn't have a staff of messy employees, but he noticed the stares he and Nhuri got whenever a hug between them lingered too long or he was caught staring at her during a meeting. As private as she wanted to keep them at work, Shyriq didn't care who knew about them.

He was the boss, but he respected her.

Moving from an assistant position to the executive research marketing manager in less than three months would surely have folks questioning her skills and whether she was qualified . . . or if she received the promotion because she was fucking the boss. But that was the thing; Shyriq didn't care what any of them thought. Yes, she was fucking the boss and laying it on him quite nicely, but that had nothing to do with what Nhuri brought to the table workwise.

"You don't have to. Just see what she says and get back to me. I'm sure you'll hear from Natalia, but if you don't, you're hearing it from me. Which is just a courtesy call because you aren't her boss," Cara said, laughing.

"Right," Shyriq chuckled. "Just her sister's."

"Speaking of Nhuri . . ."

"Nope. We're not going there. We're good, and that's all you need to know."

Cara laughed into the receiver. "Well, I'm glad. I love her, and it's good to see you not being so damn . . . I don't know. Stuck in your ways."

Shyriq shook his head. "Thanks, Cara. Nice of you to approve and tell me about myself. I'll let you know what I decide once we talk."

She chuckled. "No problem, and okay. Talk to you later," she said before hanging up.

Shyriq wasn't expecting an email from Natalia so soon, but like her sister, she was professional and handled business respectfully. She attached the letter from her doctor and let him know she and Cara would discuss her return dates. It was straight to the point, with no mention of Nhuri. Natalia wasn't asking for time off; she was taking it regardless of whether they approved it. Shyriq couldn't do anything but respect it, and now, he had to see how Nhuri felt about everything.

He reached for the phone, dialing her office number. A few seconds later, Nhuri's voice filled the line, sounding smooth and professional as if she didn't know it was him.

"This is Nhuri Coleman. How can I help you?"

Shyriq couldn't help but grin at her tone, knowing she was probably neck-deep in work, just like him. "You're a busy woman, huh?" he teased, leaning back and making himself comfortable.

Nhuri let out a soft sigh, and the sound of papers rustled in the background. "You could say that. How can I help you, sir?"

His smile grew as he lowered his voice. "Just checking in. Did you enjoy your late lunch?"

It was well past four o'clock, and neither had stepped foot outside of their office since midmorning. So, Shyriq ordered her favorite from The Spot and had it delivered.

"I did, thank you. What are you over there doing?" she asked.

"Thinking about you and the way you felt this morning."

Nhuri's face heated, and she squeezed her thighs together tightly. "Shy, stop," she whined, only making him want to press her buttons again.

"Why? You asked me what I was doing, and I told you."

"But we're on company time *and* company phones."

"It's a good thing I own the company then, huh?"

Chuckling, Nhuri shook her head. "You're too much. But seriously, what do you need? You know, when you call, I get distracted."

"You're right. I do need something. Can you come to my office when you get a chance? It'll only take a minute."

There was a slight pause at the other end of the line. He could almost hear her considering his request, trying to figure out his true motives.

"And it can't be discussed over the phone?" she asked curiously.

Shyriq chuckled. "No, baby. It can't. Just come here real quick."

"Fine," she said and sighed. "I'll be there in a second."

He grinned. "Thank you."

Before she could respond, he hung up, setting the phone down with a soft click. He leaned back in his chair again, staring out the window, trying to calm the flurry of anticipation building inside him. Shyriq had never been the one to get nervous when it came to anything business related, but this wasn't just business. It was personal, and he had to handle the situation with care.

Nhuri knocked on his door three minutes later and entered. "You requested my presence?" she asked, grinning.

Shyriq stood from his chair, rounded his desk, and embraced her. Feeling safe in his arms, Nhuri exhaled and let him hold her. She'd been swamped with work, and it felt good just to unwind, even if for only a few seconds.

"You good?" he asked, holding her at arm's length.

Shyriq examined her as if he hadn't seen her in days when it'd only been a few hours. Nhuri loved it. Today, she wore a black blouse tucked into a pencil skirt, her hair falling in perfect waves that framed her face. Shyriq couldn't help but peck her lips.

"Yes, I'm good. Are you?" she asked.

Shyriq nodded and sat on the edge of his desk. He pulled her into his spread legs, holding her around the waist.

"How are your sister and niece?"

Nhuri's brow dipped. "They're fine. Why'd you ask that?"

"I was just wondering."

"Oh. Okay," she mumbled, her mind trying to piece together what he might possibly say next.

Like always, Shyriq was unpredictable.

"Where can you see yourself with this company in a few years?" he asked.

"Um," Nhuri chuckled. "I'm not sure, but I wouldn't mind being more hands-on with the branding aspect. I loved working with Tyreek—"

"I bet," he groaned, cutting her off.

Nhuri slapped his arm and giggled. "Don't be that way. Had you claimed me early on and made me your woman, he wouldn't have had the chance to flirt with me."

Shyriq squeezed her ass cheek. "You're right. Continue."

"So, yeah. I loved working with him and everyone involved in the tasting. Why? Where can you see me at in a few years?"

"Exactly where you want to be. Honestly, I see it much sooner."

Her eyes lit up. "Really? You're getting a new assistant?"

"Possibly. That's why I called you in here," he said and sighed. "I want to offer you the executive research marketing position."

"My sister's position?" Nhuri asked.

Shyriq nodded. "Yes."

"What? Why?" she questioned, tugging his arms from around her. "You fired her?"

"No, baby. I would never do that. She requested time off. A leave of absence," he explained.

Nhuri stiffened. "What? Why would she do that?"

"Wait. You didn't know?"

"Of course, I didn't know."

Confused, Nhuri slowly paced his office, trying to wrap her mind around what he just told her. Natalia hadn't mentioned anything about needing time off, so this blindsided her. Shyriq could tell she was caught off guard by the news, and for a moment, he regretted not being more prepared for this conversation. But there was no turning back now.

"I didn't know you guys hadn't discussed it. Cara just called and told me. It's per her doctor's request," Shyriq offered, hoping that eased some of her nerves.

Nhuri's expression faltered momentarily, and she got somewhat out of her feelings. "Oh. Well, if it's an order, then okay. I guess I'm just a bit hurt that she hasn't said anything to me."

"Maybe she was waiting for the right time."

Nhuri liked how optimistic he was, so she went off his energy and returned to the other matter at hand.

"So, you want me to take over her position?" she asked.

"Yes. Cara suggested that, given your work over the last few months, you've stepped into Natalia's role, at least temporarily. She said you've been picking up the slack during her absences, and it just makes sense."

He wouldn't mention why or how she was doing Natalia's job because it didn't matter now. Nhuri was silent for a long beat, processing what he had just said. He could see the contemplation swirling through her mind.

"And you trust me with this?"

Shyriq nodded. "Yes."

Nhuri looked at him for a moment, clearly processing the finality in his voice. Her lips parted slightly as if she were trying to find the right thing to say. But instead of speaking, she shook her head slowly, and her gaze moved to the floor for a brief second.

"Why me?" she finally asked, wanting to know. "You could've chosen anyone else for the position."

Shyriq stepped closer, pulling her back into his space. "Why *not* you? You've earned it. Not only did you step in when your sister needed you the most, but you've also been an asset to me and this company from day one. Plus, you're smart as hell, resourceful, and I trust you."

Nhuri's eyes flicked up to his, meeting his gaze with an intensity that made his heart skip a beat. "And you trust me with this . . . even after everything?"

Shyriq swallowed hard, the weight of his words settling between them. "*Especially* after everything."

Sighing, Nhuri played with the gold Cuban link bracelet on his wrist. "I don't know what to say. I mean, I want to say yes, but it's a big responsibility."

"That you're more than capable of handling. If it makes you feel any better, I didn't know either. I just found out minutes before I called you. We're in the same boat. I understand if you're not ready to decide right now."

Nhuri's eyes softened, but the frustration was still there. "I just wish Natalia had told me herself."

"I get that. How about y'all talk about it, and you let me know by the end of the week what you decide? Cool?" he asked, rubbing her back and shoulders.

Nhuri nodded. "Okay. And who's going to take my position? I'll have to train them."

He smirked. "Look at you, all concerned. You didn't even want the position at first, and now you wanna train somebody."

Laughing, Nhuri tilted her head back, exposing her neck. Shyriq didn't waste any time kissing it, leaving a heated trail up to her ear. She shut her eyes and relished this moment before responding.

"That's the past. But answer my question," she said, letting her head fall so she could look into his eyes.

"I don't know yet, but you can train them. You can also do me a favor as well," he suggested.

Nhuri blinked slowly. "And what might that be?"

"Come to dinner with me so you can meet a few of my friends."

"Today?" she asked in a panic.

Shyriq chuckled. "No. I've sprung enough on you today. This weekend. I think it's time that everyone met."

Instead of overthinking like she usually would, Nhuri nodded. "Okay. I'd love to meet them."

"I'll let you know the details. You met Cane but not the others."

"They better not act weird toward me like I'm a rebound."

Shyriq laughed heartily. "Never that, baby. I wouldn't ever let them disrespect you or me like that. Shit, I wish I would've met you first."

Nhuri smiled, thinking the same thing.

The workday couldn't come to an end quickly enough. While Nhuri had every intention of going straight home, running a bubble bath, and relaxing for the rest of the evening, she had to make a pit stop at Natalia's house first. She hadn't even had time to fully process the offer before her frustration sent her straight to her sister's doorstep.

After parking in the driveway, she used her key to enter and found Natalia in the kitchen making a salad.

"Well, hello to you too," Natalia said, popping a cucumber into her mouth.

She was dressed in a pair of leggings and an oversized sweater, with her hair in a messy bun. Nhuri had to admit that she looked comfortable and at peace—a drastic difference from how she had looked weeks earlier.

"Oh, don't hit me with that," Nhuri fussed, flopping onto the bar stool. "When were you going to tell me you were taking a leave of absence?"

"I take it Shyriq told you."

"Of course, he did." Nhuri turned to face her, confusion and hurt written all over her face. "Why didn't *you* tell me?"

Natalia rubbed her temples and walked over to the sink to rinse her hands. "I didn't tell you because I knew how you'd react," she admitted, sliding a glass toward Nhuri before leaning against the counter. "I needed to do this for *me* without feeling guilty about it."

Nhuri frowned, twisting the cap on the bottle of wine slid her way. "You really think I would've made you feel guilty?"

"No, not intentionally," Natalia said, shaking her head. "But I know you, Nhuri. You would've tried to talk me out of it or convinced me to push through like I always do. And honestly? I don't have it in me anymore. I needed a break. Financially, I could take one. Mentally? I *needed* to take one."

Nhuri exhaled, and some of the tension left her shoulders. She hadn't even considered how much Natalia had been dealing with. Between work, her health, and being a single mother, she had every reason to step back. She got it.

"I just wish you'd told me," Nhuri said, softer this time. "You know I would've supported you."

Natalia gave her a small smile. "I know. But I also know you. You're a fixer like me. You would've tried to take on my stress along with your own, and I couldn't let you do that."

Nhuri bit her lip, realizing she was right.

Natalia took another sip of her water before setting down the glass. "And honestly? With Raniya spending every other summer month with Raheem, I want to enjoy my time with her while she's here. She's growing so fast, and I don't want to miss out on these moments because I'm drowning in work."

Nhuri's heart softened at that. She'd always admired the way Natalia put her daughter first.

"I get it," Nhuri finally said, nodding. "I just . . ." She let out a dry laugh. "I just wasn't expecting it. And then, on top of that, Shyriq and Cara are offering me your job like it's no big deal."

Natalia chuckled. "Well . . . It makes sense. You've been handling a lot of my workload anyway. They see what you bring to the table."

Nhuri scoffed. "That's not the point."

"I know," Natalia said with a smirk. "Still, it's nice to be recognized, right?"

Nhuri rolled her eyes but couldn't help the small smile tugging at her lips. "It is."

Natalia reached over and squeezed her hand. "I'm sorry I didn't tell you. But I hope you can understand why."

Nhuri squeezed her hand back. "I do."

"Good. And know that I am so damn proud of the woman you've become. I know it wasn't easy, but you pushed through. Everything happening in your life and for you isn't a coincidence. You deserve it all."

Nhuri's eyes watered. "Thank you, sis. Your resilience and strength will always make me go harder and fight for what I want."

"And I wouldn't want it any other way. Now, come in here, and let's gossip about what's going on at work. I heard Tyreek and Ashley are messing around," Natalia said.

Grabbing her glass of wine, Nhuri followed her sister into the living room. She was grateful that they could discuss things openly. Fear had never held either of them back, and it wouldn't now. Nhuri couldn't wait to see what this new journey took her on.

EPILOGUE

MONTHS LATER

SHYRIQ SAT AT his desk, reviewing the latest reports on the distillery, when a knock sounded at his door. Before he could respond, the door pushed open, and Natalia and Michelle stepped inside like they owned the place.

"Well, look who it is," he teased, leaning back in his chair with a smirk. "Did I invite y'all in?"

Still glowing from delivering a healthy baby girl, Michelle waved a dismissive hand as she eased into one of the chairs in front of his desk. "We're family, so technically, yeah."

Natalia laughed, settling into the seat beside her. "Exactly. Besides, this is an important visit."

Intrigued by their impromptu pop-up, Shyriq gave them his full attention. "Oh yeah? What's up?"

Michelle exhaled deeply, placing a hand on her stomach. "I wanted to officially inform you that I won't return after maternity leave."

He wasn't surprised. Not after hearing through the grapevine that Michelle's husband had made sure she didn't *have* to work. Still, he appreciated her telling him in person.

"I figured as much," he admitted, nodding. "You sure about it?"

She smiled. "Positive. Charles and I talked it over, and honestly? I'm looking forward to staying home with the baby. But I wanted to thank you personally for everything. You've been a great boss, and I loved working here."

Shyriq chuckled. "You just loved bossin' me around."

Michelle grinned. "That too."

Natalia cleared her throat, drawing his attention. "I also wanted to say something," she started. "About Nhuri."

At just the mention of her name, Shyriq straightened a little, curious about where this was going.

Natalia met his gaze. "I just want to say thank you."

Shyriq frowned. "For what?"

"For loving my sister the way she deserves," Natalia said softly. "For seeing her, even when she tried to hide. For pulling her out of her shell and helping her see her full potential."

Shyriq was caught off guard by the sincerity in her voice. He had never been the type to take credit for someone else's growth, but hearing Natalia say that? It hit somewhere deep.

"I didn't do all that," he muttered, rubbing the back of his neck.

Natalia smirked. "You did more than you think."

Michelle nodded in agreement. "You really did, Shy. I've known you for a long time, and I've never seen you like this about anyone. Whatever y'all have going on? Hold onto it."

Shyriq swallowed. He was unsure how to respond, so he simply nodded.

Natalia glanced at the time and stood. "That was all I wanted, and I wanted to bother you," she chuckled. "Nhuri's about to hold her first meeting as the marketing director, and I can't miss it."

"I'll be right behind y'all," he said.

Shyriq stayed seated for a few more minutes, letting Natalia's words settle in his brain. Nhuri entered his life when he least expected her to, but he was grateful she had. It'd been nothing but good since then, and though they had a few rocky, unsure moments, they were all worth it.

Standing from his desk, Shyriq grabbed the bouquet of roses waiting behind it and headed out to see his baby live in action. Nhuri stood at the head of the conference table, speaking confidently to the team of marketers and strategists.

This was her moment.

Taking a deep breath, she began.

"I want to start by thanking all of you for your hard work and dedication," she said, her voice steady despite the nerves swirling in her stomach. "As we head into the holiday season and the launch of our new wine collection, Divine, our marketing strategies must be stronger than ever. This isn't just about pushing products. It's about telling a story, a Great Hendrix story."

She continued breaking down her vision for their upcoming campaigns, incorporating innovative ideas to elevate the brand. As she spoke, she felt herself settle into the role, and all traces of lingering doubt disappeared.

"We don't just want people seeing the product; we want them to buy it. There's a list of influencers, regular everyday women and men, and small business owners I want you all to reach out to. PR boxes, brand trips, billboards, release day wine tastings, and more are on the agenda for Divine. I'm a wine connoisseur, so if I'd buy it based on the marketing alone, I'm sure other people will too."

At some point, the door opened, and from the corner of her eye, she spotted Shyriq, Natalia, and Michelle slipping in quietly. She gave them a soft smile and finished strong. By the time she wrapped up, the room was filled with nods of approval and murmurs of agreement.

"That was impressive," one of the senior strategists admitted.

Another added, "You've got a strong vision, and I like where you're taking this."

Nhuri exhaled, smiling. "Thank you. Let's make this holiday season and launch our best one yet."

As the team gathered their things, Shyriq made his way over, holding out the bouquet of roses.

"For the *new* boss," he said proudly, handing them to her.

Nhuri beamed and kissed him. "Thank you so much. Did I look nervous up there?"

"Nah. You looked like the pro you are. You did amazing, baby. I'm proud of you."

Warmth spread through her chest as she inhaled the flowers. "I'm proud of me too."

"You should be. Aren't you glad you met me during Cane's engagement that night?"

"Hmmm," Nhuri hummed playfully. "Maybe. That depends."

"Whatever it depends on, just know *I'm* glad I met you," he declared, pulling her into a hug. "I think I may even be falling in love with you, Nhuri."

She looked stunned and blushed. "Awwww. Are you?"

Pride and ego nowhere in sight, he nodded. "I am. I don't expect you to feel the same, but just know you're not alone in this. I got you."

She pecked his lips again. "And I got you."

For what it was worth, Nhuri was glad she moved back home and met Shyriq. Surrendering her heart, leaving her past behind, stepping into the woman she was always meant to be, and flourishing in life wasn't anything to take lightly. What they shared was inevitable . . . the kind of love that was unexpected but always meant to be.